# THE COMPLETE CASES
# OF NEEDLE MIKE, VOLUME 1

WILLIAM E. BARRETT

# THE COMPLETE CASES OF

# NEEDLE MIKE

## VOLUME 1

## WILLIAM E. BARRETT

### ILLUSTRATIONS BY
## JOHN FLEMING GOULD

## BOSTON • 2018

# TABLE OF CONTENTS

# THE TATTOOED CORPSE

BLAZONED ON HIS CHEST THEY WERE, THAT CRAZY SET OF NUMERALS—1860—1029—3— AND NO ONE GUESSED THEIR MEANING, KNEW WHY MAGEE HAD TURNED HIMSELF INTO A WALKING ADDING MACHINE. WHAT GHASTLY SECRET LAY BEHIND THAT CIPHER-SERIES? HOW COULD THEIR SUM ADD UP TO ANYTHING BUT DEATH?

# CHAPTER ONE
# NEEDLE ARTIST

**K**EN McNALLY had been born with a silver spoon in his mouth and he had spent his youth and young manhood in trying to spit it out. He had never fully succeeded, but he had found partial escape. For a part of each month, while his family imagined that he was visiting with friends on a yacht or at some country place, Ken McNally swapped the silver spoon for a set of tattooing needles and his name for that of Needle Mike. While McNally went the dull social round for the other half of the month, the associates of Needle Mike imagined that he was off on a periodical drunk.

Life was that simple.

McNally was busy now on the job of swapping identities in the musty office that he maintained as a "change" room in lower St. Louis. The job was far from simple, but his fingers moved deftly with the skill of long practice.

A few touches transformed the tiny measle scars on his cheek into blue-black powder burns; his sleek black hair became tousled and touched with gray; a mild irritant reddened his eye-lids and gave a bleary look to his eyes. His fingers flashed to a compartment in the make-up box and came out with a specially made dental bridge. A snap fastened the clips to two sound teeth while the oversize gold crown pressed down over a gleaming gold tooth in

They stole the body at the point of their guns.

front. The gas light in the room fluttered and flared as McNally leaned closer to the mirror in the dressing-case top. He dipped a cloth in stain and rubbed it lightly over his face and neck. His red tan changed to a yellowish hue.

The transformation of his face was nearly complete. It needed only the drawing of a light scar that ran to the edge of his lip; then a chunk of wax under the lips where the scar touched. McNally stood up. The carefully groomed

aristocrat had vanished and Needle Mike was standing by the black leather case; a shabby individual in stained gray trousers, rumpled blue shirt, tan brogans and cap. Reaching into the case, McNally brought out an ovular device of cork and rubber that was of his own invention; a device that fitted close against his leg and defied detection through the trouser, but that kept that leg stiff. Needle Mike would never betray himself by forgetting to walk with a limp; he couldn't walk any other way.

"Good enough. Now for the whiskey breath."

McNally took a bottle of a particularly vicious blend from the case and rinsed his mouth with it. His face puckered wryly. The taste was villainous, but a man couldn't get such an odor with a rinse of anything else. With a flip, the bottle went back in the case, the case went under the boards and a shabby desk went over the whole. McNally turned out the light and lurched down the hall. It was one of those buildings where people came and went and nobody asked or answered questions.

Slowly and unsteadily, McNally made his way along South Broadway. Men looked out of sunless places and grinned. The Needler was a town character on the fringe of the half-world where one has to be "wrong" or "a character" to get by. Two doors from his grimy-windowed tattooing parlor, McNally stopped for another drink. He growled and grumbled and spilled half his drink, but the furtive-looking crowd in the smoky, low-ceiled room was only amused. At a few tables, old-timers wised up the lamisters from other towns.

"Just back from a bat. Guy gets barrelhouse every month and won't touch it any other time. When he touches it, he goes to the floor with it—but he lays off when he's workin' the needles. He won't paint no skin pictures now for twenty-four hours."

McNally reeled out. It was all part of the picture. The underworld is suspicious of anyone who does not have habits that can be tagged. The identity of Needle Mike was built to specifications.

**THE TATTOOING** parlor had a window almost flush with the sidewalk. There was a narrow door to the window's left. On the other side was a locksmithing and repair shop that Needle Mike also operated in spare moments.

He fumbled with his key and got the tattooing-shop door open. The shabby, littered room came to life when he winked on the overhead bulb. McNally looked around at the unsanitary, unclean, odoriferous quarters with a feeling almost of affection. His soul had craved adventure and he had found it here. He threw up the cracked green shade and let his feeble yellow light mingle with the other furtive lights of the neighborhood. He turned to his needle cabinet and had taken only a couple of hobbling steps when there was a protesting squeak from the hinge on his front door. He wheeled.

The man who stood there was thin and shabby, hungry-looking, dirty and unkempt; not a depression victim or a hobo, obviously, but merely another chronic loser in the game that doesn't pay. His eyes told the story plus that shrinking, hunted manner that is the hallmark of the beaten crook.

"You Needle Mike?" His voice was like a cracked whistle.

McNally drew his eyebrows down in a frown. "Wha'd'ye want?"

The shabby man fumbled in his pants pocket. "Will you chisel a couple o' numbers on me chest for a couple o' bucks?"

McNally waved his hand. "Go 'way," he growled. "T'morrow night. Me, I never do no work right after I come back—"

The prospective customer took a backward step before the growl. He passed the back of his hand across his forehead. "I'll never remember 'em," he muttered. "Never remember 'em." Suddenly he stepped forward and all but dropped to one knee.

"Cap'n," he said, "you gotta chisel them numbers on for me. Tomorrow won't do. They gotta be put on tonight. You're the only guy in Saint Looie that can do it. You gotta, Cap'n."

"I don't gotta do nothin', mug, and don't you forget it." McNally had been feeling a stir of interest, but he kept Needle Mike hard. The shabby man was looking behind him now; his voice had dropped and there was a wheeze in it like a peanut-stand siren; but there was a horrible urgency in it, too.

"Cap, I didn't mean it like you took it. I meant that I got to have them numbers on. I gotta. I'm goin' away for a long time and I gotta remember somethin'."

"What does a mug like you have to remember so hard that it's got to be needled into him?"

The other made a despairing gesture. "I can't tell you. It don't mean nothin' to nobody but me."

"O.K., but I don't never work anyhow till I've had my rest." McNally turned his back and hobbled over to the instrument case. For a moment, the shabby one stood irresolute; then he was across the room, pleading again.

"Show me how and I'll do it myself, Cap'n. Or if two bucks ain't enough, you kin trust me. Everybody on the East Side knows me. They'll tell you I'm all right. Snuffle Magee is my name. I'm all right, Cap'n... just a few numbers. Take you just a minute."

McNally turned slowly. There was an intense curiosity burning in him. His agile mind had been able to furnish no answer to the problem which Magee presented. He could think of no reason in the world why such a charac-ter should have to have numbers written permanently on his skin, nor why the job was so urgent as to send the man into a sweat of fear and make a sniveling pleader out of him.

"Write the numbers on a piece o' paper if you got to remember 'em," he growled.

Magee shook his head. "Please, Cap'n. That won't do. I gotta have 'em permanent."

McNally continued to stare at him. He wanted to know what those numbers were like which were so important and there was only one way in which he was likely to find out. He didn't like that one way. The half-world in which he lived was too observant and any break in a man's habits was enough to cause speculation. Needle Mike did not take jobs within twenty-four hours after a drunk and the fact was established. Why destroy a carefully nurtured tradition for a slinking slum bum like this?

**HE ASKED** the question, but at the same time he answered it. He had come to this fringe of the shadows for adventure, for the taste of drama in the raw. Tonight, Snuffle Magee represented just that. The business of the life-and-death numbers was inexplicable and the inexplicable thing was nearly always dramatic. McNally picked up the electric tattooing machine and let it whir. He selected several gleaming needles and put a couple of spares in the cuff of his trousers. His face was grim.

"You're a Gawd-blasted pest," he said heavily, "and I ain't had my rest, but I'm sick o' your yammering. Gimme your arm!"

Snuffle Magee had paled at sight of the pistol-like machine. He shook his head now. "Not my arm, Cap'n. On my chest—"

"Nix. That's twice as hard."

McNally felt his interest quicken. Magee shook his head. "Fellers lose their arms sometimes, and most anybody can see what I got on my arm in the place where I'm goin'. There ain't everybody goin' to be seein' my chest."

McNally hesitated just long enough to make the other uneasy; then he growled and picked up another needle. "O.K. Take your shirt off and gimme the list."

"I'll tell 'em to you." Magee was peeling out of an exceedingly dirty shirt.

"Tell me nothin'. I gotta copy the list."

The little man was adamant. He was a creature of no spine, but there was some great urgency on him that gave him a certain stubbornness. "I'll tell 'em to you."

McNally growled. There was no moving this chap while he remained in the character of Needle Mike. Needle Mike could growl and swear, but Needle Mike had to perform eventually. With an almost savage roughness that was also Needle Mike's characteristic, McNally shaved the scraggy hair off the man's chest, swabbed him and lifted the machine.

There was a small crowd gathering outside the window as crowds always gathered during an "operation." Magee was in a cold sweat of fear, his little eyes darting toward the sidewalk.

"Cap'n," he said hoarsely, "you gotta pull down that shade."

"I never pull down the shade. It advertises me." McNally poised the needle again.

Magee made a nervous, snuffling sound. "Cap'n, it's important."

McNally grunted, looked at him sharply and then pulled down the shade in the faces of the disappointed crowd. There was precedent for this. He had done it before when he had fussy customers; still, it added another touch to the mystery of the numbers.

"You want a lot for two bucks," he growled. "What's the numbers?"

Slowly, one digit at a time, while he suffered under the needle, Snuffle Magee fed the numbers out. As they went along, McNally's furrow of bewilderment deepened. They didn't make sense. As they spaced out on the man's quivering chest, the numbers stood—

1860

1029

3

The slightly cockeyed hunch, that the all important numbers might be a safe combination, vanished. Such a set was not the key to a strong box. The 3 eliminated the possibility, too, of their being pawn-ticket numbers. The whole series, in fact, was low for that. He laid the machine aside, baffled.

Snuffle Magee gave a gasp of relief and struggled up groggily. He fished two damp and grimy bills from his pants pocket and laid them on the table.

"You got no idea, Cap'n," he said huskily, "what a big lift you gimme. Maybe some day if you're still around when I come back I'll make that two bucks look like a tip."

**FOR TEN** minutes after Snuffle Magee left, McNally sat and stared at the wall. He could not match the numbers that he had written on the man's flesh with anything within his scope of knowledge. The *1860* had looked like a date but the others did not link up with it and even if they did, it would be hard to reconcile Magee's terror and his sense of urgency with anything linked to an ancient date like 1860. Magee's roots would not go deep. His hopes and his fears would be hours old rather than years; yet he all but prayed for the permanent inscription on his flesh that would brand him with the numbers forever.

Why would a scummy, down-at-heel slum bum part with his last two bucks to preserve the numbers of anything? And of what significance could these particular numbers be? Code? McNally doubted that very much. Magee had been too afraid of forgetting—and the key of a code could be remembered easily.

"Up or down, sidewise or held to the light, it still doesn't make sense."

McNally stood up and stretched. It had been eight o'clock, or a little after, when Magee left. It was nearly half past now; too long entirely to worry about a slum bum and a riddle to which he would probably never have the answer. He crossed to the shade, raised it and puttered with his instruments. He would have to keep his place open until eleven even if he turned away all the business which came in; as he would. That, too, was tradition and there was even a neighborhood joke about it. They said that he kept open just for the satisfaction of turning the business away when he had a hangover.

He spent an hour fussing with his instruments, smoking a thick cigar and glowering at the passers-by, then he went into the little locksmithing shop that was his sideline.

It was a grimy place with less than half the window space that the tattooing parlor occupied. Odds and ends cluttered it and he began to straighten it up. The first day back was always like this—deadly dull. The underworld is never rushed. By tomorrow, his neighbors would have all but forgotten that he had been away and he could move naturally in his role of Needle Mike. Tonight he just showed himself on the scene.

He had decided to leave the locksmith shop and was crossing to the door which connected the two places of business when he heard voices. There was a quality in them that made him come to a dead stop and glide noiselessly sidewise to an empty supply cabinet that he had rigged especially for possible occasions. He had been trapped once before by hostile gangsters in his other hideout and it had not been a pleasant experience.

This cabinet was built flush against the connecting partition between the two shops, and it was equipped with an invisible set of hinges on the side opposite the regular hinges; also with a dummy Yale lock. It would look locked and act locked if anyone tried to open it from the outside once he was in it, but he had chinks and peepholes which enabled him to see into either room.

There were three men in his parlor and he recognized all of them. Loop Grenado, who had been many disreputable things and who still looked less like a wolf than he should, was standing in the middle of the room with his hands in the pockets of a Norfolk jacket. A narrow-featured, thin-mouthed young man, he might have been a gigolo; he decidedly wasn't. There was death in the two guns that he carried and he had a following. Jack Maxwell was nosing into the back room. He did the bull-rushing for Grenado and he was built for the job. He had been a middleweight pug and he had the battered features of the born punch-catcher. Boastful, swaggering, dumb; he was still a tough man in a brawl. Rex Weimer stood by the door. He was fat, paunchy, wet-handed and small-eyed. He drove cars.

Maxwell swung away from the door leading to the back room. "Nobody in there, chief. I figger we're wasting time. That Needle Mike's a souse pot. He probably fell down some place and couldn't get up."

"Yeah, chief. We ought to go. Quicker we get that guy the better. Maybe the cops ain't seen it yet."

Grenado was standing quietly. His face didn't change expression but his eyes glittered. "Try the next room, Jack. Snappy."

**MAXWELL SHRUGGED** and turned to the door of the locksmith shop, a flashlight in his hand. There was a nerve-cracking tension in the room. The three men were keyed tight. Weimer was cursing plaintively.

"Geez, chief. We saw him come outta here, didn't we? What more do you need? This needle puncher ain't goin' to help if you find him. He's a souse and—"

"I'm running this, Rex." Grenado spoke out of the corner of his mouth. "Getting this bird, Mike, might save some more second guesses. We've been dumb enough for one night."

Jack Maxwell came swaggering back out of the locksmith shop. "No click," he said. "The dump's clean. Like I said before, this souse pot probably fell over some place."

Grenado balanced up on his toes; then he snapped his fingers. "All right," he said. "Let's go."

He turned on his heel and almost crashed into the slower moving Rex Weimer who bulked in the doorway. All three men were cursing as they piled out on Broadway. McNally eased out of the close quarters of the cabinet and stood breathing a little heavily in the darkness.

"Those three mugs are tied into those numbers some way, too," he said softly. "They had to mean Magee because nobody else left here. But what's the scenario?"

He wiped his hands against the rough trousers. It was no nerve tonic to know that human jackals like Grenado and his henchmen had been looking for him. They were specialists in one-way rides and if they suspected him of knowing something that might be used against them, they'd eliminate him without a qualm; the fact that he did not understand what he knew would make no difference.

For an interval, McNally waited in the darkness; then he stepped into the tattooing parlor and sat down. Grenado's mission was vague at best. It was a good bet that he would be back, but there was no alternative for McNally except to run away and keep dodging. Eventually, if he kept in the character of Needle Mike, Grenado would catch up with him. It was inevitable, so he might as well step out and wait for it as run away from it.

He rolled a cigarette, sat down under the light near his work desk and waited.

## CHAPTER TWO
## BODY SNATCH

**I**T WAS almost eleven o'clock. The crowd had thinned out along the stem and those who passed were either shuffling along furtively or in too much of a hurry to stop. One pair of heels, however, clicked the pavement hard and McNally straightened. He knew that step. Near the entrance of the parlor, the clicks slowed, stopped. McNally looked up.

Detective Sergeant Pete Corbin was standing in the doorway, his hat a little cockeyed and one eyebrow raised to balance his face with the hat. "Wrong again, ain't yuh, Mike?"

His voice was heavy, positive. McNally looked at him. "The cops should chirp about people being wrong. What's the matter. Liquor's legal, ain't it?"

"Liquor's all right; always was." Corbin's set expression didn't relax. "That ain't what I'm talking about and you know it."

"A guy that tried to learn anything from your answers wouldn't ever know anything. Say something once."

Corbin held to his stare. He was short and squat and he sported a big bay window, but he managed to make his bulk loom impressive. He had a cold eye.

"How come," he said slowly, "that you tattoo a guy and right afterwards he gets bumped?"

McNally couldn't have kept the surprise out of his face if he'd tried. He didn't try. Needle Mike wasn't supposed to have a poker face. "Bumped?" he said hoarsely. "Where? Why?"

Corbin continued to stare him down, his eyebrow cock-eyed. "The 'where'," he said, "was a country road a couple o' hours back. Mebbe you know somethin' about the 'why,' huh?"

A couple of hours back. McNally digested that thought, frowning. Less than half an hour ago, three hoods had left his place and they were talking about getting someone who could be none other than Snuffle Magee. If Magee had been found a couple of hours earlier on a country road, they were very late—and it meant that someone must have grabbed Magee with a car right after he left the tattooing parlor and killed him soon after.

Corbin lolled against the door. "You're innocent like a baby, huh?"

"Sure. I don't guarantee a guy's life when I needle him. I just give him a picture he can live with all his life."

"Yeah. Or a set o' numbers."

The eyes of the two men locked and held. McNally shrugged. "If they want numbers, they get 'em. So what?"

Corbin hitched the belt up over his bay window. "So," he said gruffly, "you trot down to the morgue with me and look 'im over."

There was a hard finality to his voice and people who lived on that particular stretch of South Broadway didn't argue when a cop called the shots that way. McNally shrugged and stood up. As he put his stuff away and fumbled with his keys, his brain raced.

It was a bad spot. He had tried to keep out of the clutches of the law and here, through sheer hard luck, he was thrown right into a mess. And the worst was yet to come. Once let them take him to the hall for a sweating and he was through. The disguise that would stand up along the grimy stem would break down in the pitiless glare of a police examining pen. He shrugged. Some way could be managed. There had to be an out.

Corbin was not talking. Friendly enough in his rough way on routine rounds, the plainclothesman froze up when he was out on business. He belonged to the old school which believes that a suspect talks more when a cop talks less. The walk to the morgue was a solemn affair. Corbin was old-fashioned enough, too, to walk a prisoner instead of riding him. Some men couldn't stand the strain of walking long blocks quietly. They talked.

McNally didn't. Keeping to his character of Needle Mike, he growled and swore occasionally and muttered about his bum leg; but there was no comfort in that for a curious cop.

They crossed Twelfth Boulevard at last. Several cars with green lights showing were drawn up by the morgue entrance and, as though he sniffed excitement, Corbin quickened his step. They swung through the white-fronted entrance where a uniformed cop stood guard. The man started to say something when he saw Corbin, but changed his mind.

**INSIDE THERE** was confusion; a half dozen men in uniform or plainclothes moving about, shooting questions. McNally hung back almost forgotten. Corbin shouldered up to the superintendent's little desk. The door to the ice-house where bodies await autopsy was open. McDavitt, the morgue superintendent, was running his hands through his thin hair.

"They took your man right out of here, Corbin," he said. "Just walked right in with masks on their faces and took him away."

"Who took who away?" Corbin's face was very red.

A thin, sad-looking man who was chewing a long match supplied the answer. "Three hoods," he said tonelessly. "There wasn't nobody in here but McDavitt and Sweeny and the two shines. Sweeny had his coat off and he was drinkin' beer. The hoods cracked down with the drop before Sweeny could lay the can down. Then they walked off with Magee's body and—"

"They dumped Becker off the slab and kicked his body around." McDavitt's voice was bitter. He didn't like to see corpses manhandled.

McNally, standing on the fringe of the group, felt a vague excitement go through him. "You mean Herb Becker?" he said.

Corbin and the funereal man swung around to him, their eyes glinting hard, suspicious. Corbin's hat slid further down on his forehead. "Wha'd'yuh know about Herb Becker?"

McNally shrugged. "I see him around the spots. He came in my place once and watched me needle a sea-serpent on a punk."

"Yeah? Well, that's nice," Corbin's voice slurred out. "You needle up this Magee cookie and he gets the bump and just a few hours before that another pal o'yours gets rubbed out down on Fourth Street. Awful funny, ain't it?"

McNally was mentally kicking himself for the slip from the role of Needle Mike which had prompted the question. "Ought to have a cork jigger on my tongue, too," he decided mentally. Aloud, he said: "Naw. It ain't funny. I just live where the population ain't permanent. Somebody's always forgettin' to duck."

Corbin's keen eyes probed him for a moment, then the man's whole attitude changed. He discarded his program of attack and shifted to diplomacy. "O.K., Mike," he said. "Maybe we've been rough, and you with a hangover, too. Maybe you didn't know about Becker. You'd been a fool to've asked that question if you did. Maybe you didn't put Snuffle Magee on the spot neither. I'll take a chance on you." He paused, lighted a cigar and talked through the smoke. "Just what," he said slowly, "did those numbers mean that you put on Magee's hide?"

McNally shrugged. "I dunno. I just gave him what he wanted. He said he was going on a trip and he wanted to remember something."

Corbin prided himself that he knew when a man was holding back. He decided suddenly that he would get nothing by riding the tattooer. McNally saw the decision in the shifting of the man's body before he spoke. Corbin waved.

"He went on his trip all right," he said, "but he ain't remembering a damn thing. O.K. Get outta here, Mike, and better stick to your dump. I may want you."

He turned his back but McNally wasn't fooled. He saw the man who caught Corbin's signal. He was going to have a tail.

**IT WAS** midnight. McNally hobbled along Clark Street to Twelfth and turned toward Market. There was a newsboy yelling, "Extra," with the bulldog edition of the *Globe* and McNally bought a copy. Conscious of the police shadow, he sat down leisurely on the low stone barrier that ran around the old court house. The lights of Twelfth Boulevard were brighter than the yellow bulb of his shop. He read. The morgue robbery, of course, had been too late for the bulldog. So had the murder of Snuffle Magee. Magee rated a last-minute flash in heavy type. Herb Becker had headlines.

GANGSTER SHOT TO DEATH DOWNTOWN

The swift-running account told of a chase through downtown streets in which a big gray sedan had tried to close in on a low blue coupé, a chase in which a police car and motorcycle joined in. Where the tangle of narrow streets head for the levee, the chase had ended. The police pursuit, temporarily thrown off, had not quite made it—to be in on the death. The police had heard a rapid exchange of shots and had turned a corner to see the blue coupé against the curb with no sign of its driver. The gray car had been slowed down, but it picked up speed and roared down to the waterfront with the men in it firing at the police. Under the elevated tracks of the Pennsylvania Railroad, the men had abandoned their car and escaped. Returning to the blue coupé, the police found the crumpled body of Herb Becker face down in an alley just off Fourth Street. There was a trail of blood behind him which indicated that he had crawled after he was shot. The police were trying to link the shooting to the recent Shuler kidnaping case.

That was all. McNally's eyes narrowed. He could not connect Magee and his numbers with this case yet—but the connection probably existed. Magee was not the type of man to ride a death car or to be in the confidence of the high-powered snatchers who had taken Ben Shuler for a hundred grand. His eyes shifted to the leaded type of the flash.

Edward T. Magee, Blast St. Louis underworld character, was found last night at a late hour on the Big Bend Road just over the county line with his head crushed in. Magee, who has served terms in prison, was wanted by the East St. Louis police in connection with a rooming-house burglary in which, it is alleged, he was recognized by one of the victims. Police are investigating a possible connection with the shooting earlier in the evening of Herb Becker, local police character.

McNally rolled a cigarette. His shadow was sitting far back along the barrier. McNally hoped that he was getting impatient. He didn't like being shadowed and he saw no reason why he should make the trailer comfortable. He puffed hard on the cigarette and as the smoke curled upward, he struggled with the scattered pieces of the jigsaw puzzle that had started with three numbers.

Only one piece had clicked into place and that piece was minor. He had been puzzled when he heard that Magee had been dead for hours. The three visitors had spoken of going after him. He knew now that they were probably speaking about Magee's body and not Magee. Right after their fruitless visit to the tattooing parlor, they had obviously raided the morgue.

But if they were the same three who had killed Magee, why did they have to steal his body later? Were they the same men who had killed Becker? It looked like it since they had shown their contempt for Becker's body, dumping it off the slab. There was a single thread. Those three men checked right through from Magee to Becker to the morgue. They had wanted something desperately when they chanced the raid on the morgue within a few steps of police headquarters. What was it? And how did the numbers tie in?

McNALLY FINISHED the smoke, tossed it away and came to his feet. He hobbled slowly toward the Twelfth Boulevard crossing and was conscious of the fact that the shadow had come to his feet, too. Then a big car that had just swung out of Pine Street speeded up and raced down on him. He had only time to look up when there was a screech of brakes and the skid of rubber. The big car lurched and came at him broadside. He ducked back and a man swung from the tonneau, a black automatic in his fist.

"Keep the lip buttoned and get in!" The man's body was crouched so that the bulk of him hid the gun. He might have been an acquaintance dropping off to greet an old friend. McNally recognized him without difficulty despite the pulled-down hat brim. It was Jack Maxwell.

"Hell! Why the hostility?" McNally grunted, made a gesture of protest. Maxwell's jaw stuck out; he growled out of the corner of his mouth: "In, mug!"

"Hey! Just a minute—"

The police shadow had just tumbled to the fact that there was something wrong. He took a step forward, his hand in his side pocket. That one step was all.

There was a flash of flame from the seat beside the driver and the man seemed to break in the middle. As he slumped forward, Jack Maxwell brought his gun up fast and clipped McNally in the side of the head. Reeling unsteadily,

McNally found himself half pushed and half lifted into the back of the car. The motor roared and as the car leaped away, there came a single shot from close to the ground behind them.

The driver snarled viciously: "Dammit! You only half-croaked that cop—"

The man beside him leaned back. "What you're doing, Rex," he said, "is driving this hack, see?"

McNally shook his head, forced his dizzy senses to remember that he was Needle Mike. "What is this?" he growled.

Maxwell lit a cigarette. The gun was still in his hand. "This, sweetheart," he said softly, "is a snatch."

## CHAPTER THREE

## THE THING ON THE BED

**IT WAS** a long ride, a monotonously long ride, but although the car made many twists and turns, the three men were obviously not making any attempt to deceive McNally. They ignored him. Their chief concern seemed to be whether they were being tailed. At length, after heading westward, very close to the city limits, they swooped back, hit South Grand Boulevard and left it far south to swing into South Broadway just above Jefferson Barracks. They were pretty far out of the gang beats now and they swung carelessly and at moderate speed into a side street. The house into which McNally was ushered was old, nondescript and built of red brick. It would arouse no suspicions and there were no close neighbors.

Downstairs the house was quiet and dark. The three men left it so. In a big room upstairs they got down to business. Loop Grenado sat behind a big table, his eyes on McNally. Jack Maxwell dropped his big body into a chair and tilted it back on its hind legs. He rode it thus with his legs spread wide, like a prizefighter waiting the bell; seemingly indifferent and relaxed, actually tense. Rex Weimer flowed all over a wide easy chair, his paunch spilling into his lap and his narrow eyes half hidden in folds of fat. There was a petulant expression on his face, his small mouth drawn close. Loop Grenado's face was expressionless, but his wet-looking eyes were cruel.

"Mike," he said, "what did those numbers mean that you chiseled on that slob, Magee?"

McNally blinked. "You and the cops both," he said. "I wouldn't know. That was his business."

Grenado's eyes narrowed to mere slits. McNally felt the other two men edge forward. "So the cops were interested?"

McNally had been standing. He found a chair, pulled it up and sat down. "You mugs ain't polite," he said.

"What did you tell the cops?"

"Just what I told you. I don't go sticking my nose in my customers' business."

Rex Weimer bounded to his feet like something made of rubber. His fat fist started from somewhere around his waist and connected with the side of McNally's jaw. McNally went over and took the chair with him. Weimer's foot glanced off his ribs and Grenado was on his feet.

"That'll be all of that," he said. His voice was soft but there was a deadly quality in it.

Weimer poised his foot again, but didn't kick. He turned slowly, belligerently—but his voice wasn't hard. It had a whine to it. "You can't get nowhere with these tramps by babying 'em," he said plaintively. "This guy is clowning—"

McNally came slowly to his feet. Hampered by the artificially lame leg, he rocked badly. He shook his head. There had been weight behind that fist of Weimer's but it had lacked shock-power. He measured the man and decided that he'd like to have Weimer alone. He'd spot him the fifty pounds advantage in weight that he packed. Grenado was still standing. He had made no hostile move but his eyes were too much for Weimer.

"When I want any extra acts, I'll order them," he said. "Stay out of this until you're called in. If there wasn't so damn much of this would-be hard stuff, we wouldn't be in this jam."

Weimer's mouth was as petulant as a woman's but his eyes were dirty pools of hatred and envy. He rocked on his feet, his body poised like a fighter's, his voice shrill. "You can't hang that bump on me. I only—"

"Close that trap, Jack." Grenado snapped his fingers. With a smooth, gliding motion, Jack Maxwell came out of his chair. There was no motion to him; he flowed. Weimer turned halfway around and Maxwell's fist took him flush on the button. He went down with a crash.

Grenado's eyes shifted to McNally; looked at and through him. "You remember what those numbers were?"

McNally wiped his lips; then scratched his head. "Lemme see. There was a date. Eighteen-something, as I recollect. Then there was another number and a small number. One figger."

"Yeah? Well try again. That wasn't a date." Grenado was tense, weighing McNally, judging him. McNally knew his life was in the balance and the cards were stacked. He didn't like the carelessness of these men, the way that they talked and the fact that they had made no attempt to hide their identities. He threw up his hands.

"I wouldn't know then. I never had no list to copy. This mug wouldn't trust me with one. I just put them down as he called them."

**HE STOOD** there with his shoulders hunched and he looked like a bewildered old sot. Weimer was getting to his feet, muttering. Maxwell was balancing on his chair again and smoking quietly. Grenado leaned forward, his lips twisted.

"You figured to split with Magee, you rat!" he snarled. "He didn't have nowhere to put it fast and he was taking a rap. Those numbers are some sort of code you rigged up." He rose and walked around the table. "You'll spit out the answers damn quick, too. You've stalled long enough."

Something had snapped inside of the leader. His eyes were glowing, his mouth twitching. Weimer stopped grumbling and settled back in his chair with a grunt that sounded satisfied somehow. Maxwell ceased to rock his chair. Grenado walked around the desk. McNally drew back as Needle Mike would be expected to do.

"You're wrong," he said. "I never knew this mug. I—"

Grenado snapped his fist up and there was shock in it even if it didn't travel far. McNally, just rising from his chair, was knocked back into it. He shook his head, started to rise and took another on the jaw.

**THE NEXT** two minutes were a blur of punishment. Grenado hit and kept hitting. He shot questions between punches but he didn't wait for answers. It was as though he had been thwarted so much in one evening that he couldn't take any more. He was expressing his feelings on McNally, and McNally, hampered by the bum leg and the reputation of Needle Mike, couldn't be too good. He had to take it or give himself away. Finally Jack Maxwell got up.

"The guy's goin' to cave on you, Loop. He's getting over a bat. Two corpses is twice as worthless as one."

Grenado pulled up panting. For a moment he stood irresolute and then he walked around the desk, pulling down his cuffs. He looked over at Weimer and Weimer was sneering at him. Grenado spat. McNally was shaking his head, trying to clear it of the ringing noise. He looked up at Grenado through a haze. Grenado rocked slowly back and forth from his toes to his heels.

"You'll maybe get sense out of those numbers if you look at them long enough," he said grimly. "Take him back, Jack."

Jack Maxwell looked startled, then a grin split his battered face. He got slowly to his feet. "O.K., Mike," he said. "You heard the chief. Let's go."

McNally was ready to go anywhere. He was tired and he wanted a chance to think. With Maxwell walking behind him, he went down the hall and turned into a big double room. Maxwell shoved him into the inner room of the two, a windowless, black room that was little more than a cubbyhole. As he slammed the door and turned the key, he laughed. McNally strained his eyes in the blackness and could see nothing. He felt for a wall switch and could find none. He had used the last of his matches for his smoke at the court house. There was a bed. He could tell because he bumped his knees against it. He could barely make out its outlines when he stood over it, but he reasoned that there would probably be a light in the room and that, since there was no wall switch, the lamp would in all probability be of the droplight variety.

He groped in the air above the foot of the bed and cut wide circles with his hands until he felt contact with something that gave. He let the lamp swing, caught it and felt for the switch. As he clicked it, the light came on blinding him. He blinked and then looked down. His breath caught in his throat.

The half-clad corpse of Snuffle Magee was sprawled on the bed, face to the ceiling. On its chest, the mocking numbers stood out blotchily—

1860

1029

3

**McNALLY STOOD** a long time looking down at the stiffened corpse of the little crook from East St. Louis. Seen thus, with his body sprawled on a mussed bed with the pitiful skinniness of it exposed, he seemed even more insignificant than he had when he was pleading with Needle Mike. Death had given him nothing of dignity. His mouth was half open, the stubble on his face shone gray against the chalkiness of the dead flesh.

The numbers marked the man's life and his death. His life had been a succession of numbers as he passed from pen to pen for petty crimes that had netted him nothing and finally brought him to this, death without peace or dignity. The very device on his chest was the brand of futility. He had tried somehow to cheat his destiny with those cryptic numbers and he had lost; lost bitterly.

"If I only knew the stakes in the game he was playing!"

McNally hobbled around the little room. The dead man held the key to something and, though it challenged McNally, he could not see how it would do him any good if he held it. He couldn't buy his life from this gang with knowledge. The possession of knowledge was a death warrant rather than a life-insurance policy.

He was alert now though and, with the necessity of playing a part lifted, he could be himself. The presence of the corpse was disturbing but not too much so. He didn't look at it. His eyes measured every detail of the room. It was small, hot, airless, uncomfortable. There was a plain dresser, one straight chair, the bed and a waste basket. The waste basket was empty but the room was unkempt, unswept, shabby. The only ventilation was through the narrow transom over the door.

The details fixed in his mind, McNally checked over again for any little incidentals that he might have missed. He looked under the bed, then under the dresser. There was a wad of paper back near the wall and he all but missed it due to the heavy shadow. He went down on his knees, reached far in under the dresser and pulled it out. Still crouching, he smoothed it on his knee. It was a clipping from the *Globe*. The headlines leaped at him.

## BENJAMIN J. SHULER KIDNAPED

Benjamin J. Shuler, prominent St. Louis real-estate man, was kidnaped early today by four men who drove up in front of his home as he was leaving for the office and forced him to accompany....

The clipping was over a week old and McNally had read the news item when it was news. Now, however, it hit him harder than if the news were fresh. The fact of the wadded clipping being here was, of itself, significant of course, but one small word in those first few lines stood out as though it were in bold-face type. In that word he sensed a starting point for unravelling the riddle that challenged him.

"For an old soak with an hangover, you move around!"

The cold challenge from behind him spun McNally around. Loop Grenado was standing in the doorway, his feet braced far apart, his eyes narrow with suspicion. McNally lurched to his feet.

"A feller can't stay looking at a corpse," he said thickly. "He'd go nuts."

"You're going to look at him!" Grenado's tone was clipped, curt. He jerked his head. "Tie him up, Jack!"

Jack Maxwell came in grinning slyly. There was not much brain matter disturbing the inside of the ex-bruiser's skull and he took his laughs at simple things. McNally remembered that he was Needle Mike. He cringed back.

"You guys are picking on me bad enough," he said, his voice a half-scared growl. "I don't do a damn thing but pick up a couple o' bucks needlin' a few numbers and I get pushed around by all the cops and mugs in the world. I...."

Jack Maxwell pushed him under the chin and sent him sprawling across the bed. He threw his hands out to save himself and came in chilling contact with the corpse. As he jerked away, Jack Maxwell laughed immoderately and shoved him back again. Maxwell was on top of him then before he could scramble up and the man knew his job when it came to tying knots. He twisted McNally's arms up behind his back, lashed them at the wrist, then whipped a turn of the rope around Magee's cold body and finally drew taught the thick cord through an ankle loop that pulled McNally's left leg waist high, and left the stiff right leg straight out and unfettered, save for a single tight loop at the knee.

"You're goin' to have lots o' time to think about them numbers," he said cheerfully. "You ain't never goin' to forget 'em or this either."

Quickly, Maxwell stooped and fumbled with the lace of McNally's left shoe. Before McNally could guess what he was about he had whipped off the shoe and the worn sock under it. Crossing to a cupboard built into one wall the ex-fighter rummaged for a minute and returned with the stub of a plumber's candle he had found. Lighting it he drew his gun from a shoulder holster and covering McNally he slowly brought the flickering tongue of the candle flame against the sole of the tattoo artist's bare foot.

At the touch of the licking flame against his flesh McNally cringed back, a wave of sickness sweeping over him. He caught the look of brutal gratification that crossed Weimer's face as the fat man licked his lips and grinned.

"Don't this help stir up your memory about them numbers?" Maxwell asked. He moved the candle tip up and across McNally's foot. The pain was frightful and McNally writhed back.

"Hold still, damn you! And take it!" Maxwell commanded. "Or else—" he gestured meaningly with the gun.

"Geez! Didn't I tell you—"

The pain was more than even McNally in his own character could have stood much longer, after the punishment he had undergone at the bruiser's hands before. In his role of Needle Mike it was anything but unexpected to the trio when he slumped back against the cold form of Magee apparently out cold.

As he lay there, he heard as in a dream, the sneering voice of Weimer.

"That's a lot of bother," he said shrilly. "A load o' lead in the guts would be a lot safer and—"

And then Grenado's tones cutting him off.

"O.K. I'm leaving you to guard him. Give it to him if you want to. Give him some more of what Jack did. Come along, Jack."

McNally opened an eye wide enough to see Weimer's jaw drop. The fat man made a gurgling noise, then he found his voice. "What's the idea? I'm going along where you fellows go. I'm—"

"You're staying, Rex. I'm too damn' sick of your advice to listen to any more of it." Grenado crossed the other room and was lost in the hall. Jack Maxwell swung his wide shoulders and rolled after his chief. He was grinning broadly.

"Don't forget you got permission to shoot that guy in the guts," he chuckled. "Ain't that a help?"

Rex Weimer made a whimpering sound that might have been baffled rage and banged out of the room after the other two. He slammed the door after him and left McNally lashed to the gruesome thing on the bed.

McNally grunted. "One thing I got out of that," he said to himself, "is that this Rex is no killer. If he were, they wouldn't kid him about it. He's the kind that takes it out in kicking helpless guys around. Maybe I can use that."

McNALLY WAS straining his muscles against the bonds, but it didn't take him long to find out that there was no give to the handiwork of Jack Maxwell. The more he struggled the closer the rope seemed to draw him to his ghastly companion. The stiffness of his right leg was a handicap, and the pain from the burns on his left. He found it almost impossible to change his position, and with one leg straight out and the other one bent to the waist, he could get no spring to his body and no twist. He lay quietly for a moment and considered the jam he was in. The closeness of the corpse was more than just disturbing now. It gave forth a strange unpleasant odor and there was a definite chill to it that penetrated clear through McNally's clothes to his skin. He could see the numbers on the man's chest from where he lay—

1860

1029

3

He remembered all too well the fear of the man, his cringing from the needle and.... Suddenly, McNally stiffened. As his memory reconstructed the scene, he got another detail. He had set two needles in the machine and, as was his habit, he had stuck a spare into his pants cuff. There was no particular sense to the gesture, but he had noticed that the crowd and the customers found it a colorful touch. They usually commented on it and they waited for the needle to emerge from the cuff and come into play. They never did; it was just a piece of stage business. Now....

He strained and twisted until his shoulders almost popped from their sockets, the leaden lump of the corpse hampering his every effort. But finally his fingers were free and by torturous fractions of an inch, he worked them to a point where they were in reach of the pants cuff. At last he felt the point of a needle and worked back. His muscles cracked.

Slowly, with the sweat rolling in rivulets down his face, he forced the needle back through the fabric. As he felt it loosen, the big test came. His mouth opened with the pressure on his shoulder and chest and his arm felt numb, but he worked another minute fraction of an inch of play and got his thumb over the needle against the side of his index finger.

He had to count slowly and forget his agony to keep that shaky grip, but he held on. Slowly, he relaxed, his shoulders slipping back into place, his muscles screaming for speed and easing with racking slowness. He was a set of fingers juggling a needle, nothing else in the world at the moment, making his body serve those fingers.

He did not try to use the needle immediately. It was enough that he was able to hold onto it. He lay quietly, twisted almost at right angles across Magee's body; and he waited. There was no sound from the other room and the door was still closed. He was wishing that the light had been turned out when his captors left. It wasn't serving him and it could embarrass him. Wishing paid no dividends; he bent his hand back and worked the needle into the cord that bound his wrists to his left ankle.

He was glad, once the needle bit into the cord, that Maxwell had bound his ankle and wrists together. He couldn't have reached his wrists with the needle. This way, he could make the cord hold the needle and rest his fingers, then resume work and drive the needle through with either hand. He worked it back and forth patiently, persistently, his ears straining for the sound of a footstep in the other room. The hole grew too large to hold the needle and he was afraid of losing it, so he shifted again and drove a new hole, taking care, as best he could by mere sense of touch, that the hole was close to the other. He resumed sawing. The house remained quiet.

Sweat was pouring from him and his labors forced him sideways across Magee until his cheek rested against the frigid chest of the corpse. He shrank from the contact and all but lost the needle. His breath came hard.

A heavy step shook the boards in the other room.

Rex Weimer was swearing petulantly, his high shrill voice echoing weirdly through the outer room and sounding through the panels of the door almost as the voices of two people. McNally gulped hard and kept plying on the needle, his body straining to ease the squeaky vibration of the bed. The double effort tightened his muscles and he felt his fingers stiffen. Too late, he realized that the hole had again become too large to support the needle unaided. He felt the piece of shiny steel slipping and his fingers grabbed stiffly, desperately....

He was too slow. The needle eluded the tips of his fingers and slipped on through the hole that it had made.

The catastrophe left him blank-eyed, breathing heavily, scarcely believing that his work was wasted. The sweaty cold of the corpse against his cheek sickened him and he squirmed away from it. The man in the other room walked up and down, his petulant voice keeping eery time to his heavy tread.

"Give it to him if you want to! Give him some more of what Jack did!"

The memory of Grenado's words flooded over McNally and he relaxed, resting to let energy flow back into his body. He did not believe that Rex Weimer had it in him to carry out the sentence but it was a sentence nevertheless. Neither Maxwell nor Grenado himself was squeamish and he had seen too much, heard too much. Men of their breed did not chance loose tongues. If he were still here when they came back, he couldn't hope for anything. He would be definitely through. He had the time between and the weakest—even if the crudest—of the trio to work on. He had nothing else.

And, just tantalizingly out of his reach, was the mystery of the numbers and the death of Snuffle Magee. He thought that he knew, but he had yet to test that knowledge.

"Eighteen sixty, ten twenty-nine, three."

**IT MADE** little difference when you reversed the order, he thought; particularly when you considered the fact that four men had kidnaped Ben Shuler and Herb Becker had died in a Fourth Street alley. The whole case was tied into numbers, a veritable mess of numbers and you couldn't get any place unless you considered them all.

You couldn't get any place either when you were trussed up like a turkey and had a corpse for a bedfellow. It was a deadlock and he couldn't even hope to sell his hunch for his freedom—if he wanted to. The hunch would ensure his death in quick order, correct or incorrect. And Rex Weimer still prowled the other room.

McNally squirmed. The suspense of that prowling step that approached the door and retreated, approached again and once more retreated, was getting him. The action was out of character. Rex Weimer was a vicious, cruel, blood-thirsty bully and he had showed it. He had wanted to strike and beat and torture even while McNally was unbound; confident in his own bulk against a cripple of uncertain age and certain habits. His eyes had gloated over the future possibility of having a victim squirming before him. Now the victim was provided and the victim was bound—but Rex Weimer was starving his appetite for cruelty. Why?

The corpse!

McNally answered his own question with a low whistle. The thought rocked him, but he knew that he was right. There was coward written right beside cruelty in every line of Rex Weimer's face, every move of his body. He could dangle a man over the borderline of eternity, perhaps, and gloat over him—but he couldn't face that man's body when the spark had left.

So he paced; a bloated, shrill-voiced slob who was torn with jealous rage because the other two had left him and he had been unable to stop them, with baffled desire because he had a victim that he lacked courage to approach—and with Lord knew how many other racking desires. He paced and swore and McNally lay helpless, knowing the man's weaknesses and unable to play on them; doomed if too many minutes ticked away on him and powerless to stay them.

"Damn! If only I hadn't lost that needle. I don't like this stiff any better than Weimer does and—"

McNally felt strength in his veins once more and he strained on the rope which bound him to his cold bedfellow. There was a soft, snapping sound and he almost cried out with the suddenness of his fall. His body rolled over and hit the floor with a thud.

The weakened strand of cord had parted under that last ounce of pressure and he was free of Magee at last.

## CHAPTER FOUR

## ONE HUNDRED GRAND

**FOR A** stunned second, McNally lay where he had fallen, conscious of the fact that the pacing in the next room had stopped. That thud had been loud enough to be heard in the other room and the parting of the single strand did little good unless he could borrow a little more time to work. Though he was free of Magee his own bonds were almost as effective as before. If Rex Weimer came in now, McNally was in no better shape than when Maxwell left him trussed up.

Slowly, hesitantly, the man in the other room approached the door. McNally pulled the air into his lungs. "That you, Weimer?"

His voice was the hoarse, whisky-bass of Needle Mike and he managed to get a note of terror into it. Weimer's footsteps halted. He was still slow about coming into that room alone, and he did not answer. He took another step. McNally called out again.

"What's the matter with you? Come on in here. This bloody corpse has fallen off the bed."

The floorboards creaked as Rex Weimer settled back hard on his heels. McNally grinned and bent his left leg under him. It had been numb from the tying but the blood was flowing in it again now and he discovered that he was not quite as badly off as he had been. He had the use of his legs. Jack Maxwell had taken that stiff leg too much for granted and he had merely looped the rope at the knee when he lashed the left ankle to McNally's bound wrists. The breaking of the bonds had loosened the loop and there was no other check upon the right leg. The left dragged a trailer of cord that was still fastened to the ankle, but there was no handicap in that. He could stand.

Weimer found his voice at last. He tried to put a snarl into it but the high-pitched, frightened voice wouldn't carry a snarl. "Whaddya mean, the corpse fell off?"

McNally had spotted the gleaming needle on the ground where it had fallen. He was bending over backward, his fingers feeling for it. "I meant what I said, you mug," he growled. "That corpse just fell off. Almost dragged me along. He's been kind of bending for the last half hour, muscles tightening maybe—"

He had his fingers on the needle now and he grinned when he thought of how this man would take to the idea of a stiff starting to bend and falling off a bed. Rex Weimer would want none of that show.

There was silence in the other room. McNally called out gruffly: "Hey, you! Come and get me out of here, I don't want to...."

"You shut up!" Weimer was moving away. McNally set his teeth. He was trying to set the needle up solidly in a crack of the bed so that he could work back against it and pierce the bonds at his wrist until they weakened. The needle wouldn't set rigidly. It wobbled each time and fell over.

A board creaked somewhere and he was suddenly aware that he had concentrated overmuch on the needle. He hadn't kept Weimer busy and he was making enough noise himself to be heard through the doorway. Weimer was trying to sneak up on him.

He straightened and the needle again fell out of the improvised vise. The door opened.

McNally had a glimpse of the gun in Rex Weimer's hand, the contorted, half-afraid set of the man's features. Then he kicked with all the power that was in his left leg.

Weimer wasn't expecting those tactics from a cripple and he was too big a target to miss. There was a flash and a roar as his finger tightened convulsively on the trigger and McNally felt the fanning breath of the bullet past his cheek as his foot sank almost ankle deep in the belly fat of Rex Weimer's waist.

They went down together; Weimer doubled in agony and McNally because the artificially stiff right leg wouldn't balance that kick. As he fell, McNally was conscious of glass tinkling and he twisted on the floor.

The mirror over the bureau had been shattered and the glass was still dropping.

Rex Weimer's breath was coming in great sobbing gulps and he was trying to curse. His fat hand groped for the gun that he had dropped. Fighting for balance, McNally kicked again and the gun spun out of reach. McNally lunged across the room.

**THERE WAS** glass scattered over half of the floor and McNally went down after some. He was racing against time and his fingers, trained to the brush of the artist and the needle of the tattooer, were nimble. They closed around a long splinter of glass and came up with it. Rex Weimer was crawling under the bed for the gun. McNally didn't know how far under it had gone and he needed time. He couldn't be beaten now.

With the glass clutched in his fingers, he took a step forward, balanced momentarily and kicked again. This time, he was not kicking at Rex Weimer who was on the opposite side of the bed. His foot landed hard against the petrified side of the thing that had been Snuffle Magee.

There was a sickening plop, a protesting creak from the bed springs and the corpse shot across the bed. For a mere fraction of a second, it hung on the edge; then it toppled off onto the fat shoulders of Rex Weimer.

The man's wild scream was enough to empty a cemetery. McNally, who had expected it, felt his hair rise. He staggered back against the bureau, held the glass in his right hand and jerked at a drawer with his left. The door opened and he closed it again with the glass wedged. It was a vise after a fashion and he was reckless of cuts as he sawed his wrist bonds against it.

The blood was flowing freely before the strands parted but he didn't care. Rex Weimer, wide-eyed, shaken and ashen-faced was backed into a corner of the room, his petulant lips slobbering. He had taken one kick where it hurt and he had been hit with a corpse. He was through.

McNally braced himself to be brutal. There was only one language that men like Weimer understood, the language that they used when they were on top. Hobbling across the room, all Needle Mike again, McNally braced himself before the cowering gangster with his hands on his hips, the blood running down his trouser leg. Between the two men lay the corpse. McNally spat.

"And you with a gun and me an old man!" he growled contemptuously. "Stand up and I'll finish ye—"

Rex Weimer crouched back, one hand at his belt line. He waved the other hand feebly. "Take that away!" he yelped. "Take it away."

He gagged hard. McNally bent way over and slapped him across the mouth with the back of his hand. "Shut up!" he said. "He's cleaner dead than you are living and he's none too clean."

He turned his back deliberately and walked around the bed. Still moaning, Rex Weimer pushed back against the wall and rose slowly to his feet with his back braced, squeezing every inch of distance possible away from the stiff thing on the floor. McNally went down to the floor on his limber knee and reached back behind the head of the bed.

When he came up, he had the gun in his hand.

Very deliberately, he examined it. It was a cheap make of automatic, but it was fully loaded save for the one shot that had smashed the mirror. He balanced it in his hand. Weimer hadn't seen the gun yet. He was looking at the corpse and he was more like an hysterical woman than like a man. McNally's lips twisted.

"I'm not a cheap cannon," he growled, "so I won't put a slug in your system unless I have to." He hefted the gun. "I ain't got a scruple in the world again banging you on the head with this, though. Not a one."

Disheveled, roughened up and with a streak of blood across his face where he had inadvertently passed his hand, he looked like a tough old pirate and there was nothing basically tough about Rex Weimer. Rex merely went with tough people. He wrenched his fascinated gaze from the body on the floor and stared wide-eyed at McNally.

The fat flesh of his cheeks trembled like wet and palsied putty. "Aw, Mike. I didn't do nothin' to you. I—"

"While ye were unconscious, I could tie ye up on the bed and sort of anchor poor old Magee there." McNally forced a harsh chuckle. "I guess maybe you've got enough weight to anchor him."

Weimer trembled back against the wall and the wall shook with him. There was a ghastly look on his face that told McNally that he had gone far enough. He shoved the gun away, took one step forward and shook his fist.

"You've got one chance, you cheap mug," he snarled, "and I won't fool with you. The first lie and I paste you. You three slobs put the snatch on Ben Shuler, didn't you?"

**REX WEIMER** was beyond speech. He tried to make his lips say "No." McNally reached slowly and deliberately for the gun. The gesture was enough. Weimer was bending at the middle.

"Please," he said. "I can't stand this. Let me sit down. You broke something inside of me. Let me sit down where

I can't see that thing. Let me have a cigarette. I'll tell you anything—"

McNally shrugged and waved to the chair. "Go ahead."

Weimer made heavy going of getting around the corpse, but his necessity was greater than his fear and he made it. He all but fell into the chair, a blubbering mass of flesh. "Yes," he said hoarsely. "We got Shuler. I didn't have anything to do with it. I just drove the car."

"Sure. Herb Becker was leading the crowd, too, wasn't he?"

A different kind of fear showed in the man's small eyes now. The eyes shifted. McNally balanced the gun, his jaw hard. Weimer gulped and drew back. "Yes," he said, "that's right."

"Sure. And you boys didn't like the cut, so Becker, he figures the hell with arguing and he just packs up everything in sight and moves out on you."

Weimer gulped, his eyes wide. "How'd you know that?" For a moment his fear retreated before his curiosity. McNally shrugged.

"It's always that way. Only the names are different. You monkeys never do anything new. Right after you got wise, all you gorillas could think of was to chase him and when you got all the cops in town on your trail, all you had time to do was shoot him and lam."

Weimer didn't have to answer. He was leaning back. He was off guard with the reaction to his shock and fear of a few minutes ago and McNally didn't give him a chance to recover. McNally was guessing out the logical sequence of things as they had come to him when he found the wadded clipping under the dresser with its implication that someone had been kept in this prison-like room who had an interest in that particular kidnaping. The rest of the way was still guessing, but that newspaper clipping had mentioned *four* men as the Shuler kidnapers.

"Sure," he said. "You monkeys cracked down on Herb Becker when he tried to ditch his car and make a run for it, but the cops didn't give you time to lift the dough, the hundred grand that Ben Shuler paid out. Becker had enough left to crawl up the alley but the cops didn't find any dough when they found him. That bothered you, didn't it?"

Weimer didn't have to agree to that, either. McNally didn't let him get set. He had his shot upon which everything depended. He hurled it with his chin out, his mouth hard.

"Which of you monkeys remembered seeing poor old Snuffle Magee in the headlights when you cracked down on Becker?"

Weimer jerked his head back. He all but ducked. "I... I...."

"O.K. You did. You remembered that later. You knew he was a cheap dip artist and you figured that if he saw a corpse that was carrying anything, he'd be glad that it was a corpse and not something that could fight back and that he'd take it...."

He'd found out all that he wanted to know. Weimer had told him nothing and everything. The rest was easy. Three dumb snatchers deprived suddenly of experienced leadership and getting along as best they could under the cold-blooded Grenado had gone on the prowl for Snuffle Magee, the one man who had been close enough to the dying Becker to grab the loot. And Magee?

The poor old crummy who had been taking raps in the pen for stealing a few dimes and dollars found himself suddenly with more money than he knew existed. And by

the irony of fate, he was a lamister from a charge of burglary with a sure chance of being picked up as soon as he
showed his nose. He had money, but he couldn't spend it
and there was a mortal certainty of its being taken from
him when the cops found him.

**IN THAT** spot, Magee had decided on a course of action
that would have done credit to a shrewder mind. He
decided to hide the loot, surrender to the cops and "go
up."

But Snuffle Magee had been afraid of more things than
one. He had been afraid that he would forget that hiding
place during the years in the pen. He didn't know St. Louis
as well as he knew East St. Louis and he tried to play safe.
The numbers, 1860-1029-3, were still on his chest to prove
that he tried to play safe.

McNally growled. Magee hadn't been any good to
himself or to anyone else, but in the end he had been a
tragic figure. "Why in hell did you mugs kill him?"

There was a new light in Rex Weimer's eyes and McNally
was slow to note it. The man's mind had been wrenched
violently from the terrifying aspects of contact with death
and he was physically comfortable in the chair. "We didn't
kill him," he whined. "The bird gave us a phony hiding
place and we thought he was square, see. We didn't watch
him close and he tried to dive outta the car... that was
before we found out he was a liar. We just let him lay."

"Yeah." McNally nodded. That cleared up the puzzling
fact that the trio had been on the hunt for Magee after
they had killed him. Once they found out that they had
been tricked on the hiding place of the money, they'd done
some second guessing once more and remembered that
they had picked the man up outside of the tattooing parlor.

They hadn't searched him for tattoos and they wanted to do it quickly if they couldn't get the secret out of Needle Mike.

Rex Weimer's eyes had filmed. He was breathing just a little heavily as though with suppressed excitement. His body tipped just a little forward. McNally's thinking aloud had led Weimer's shrewd brain along a logical path and he had jumped ahead. He no longer believed that the three numbers were code and that McNally knew the secret. He was picturing a poor old down-and-outer like Magee with a hundred grand that must be hidden quickly and, like McNally, he was suddenly conscious of the inevitable fact that Magee was incapable of figuring out a complicated hiding place or a complicated code. It had to be simple and he remembered where Herb Becker had died.

His face gave him away when the answer came to him. McNally saw the film drop from the man's eyes, the tensing of his muscles. It was more than the warning of impending attack, it was notification of the fact that Weimer *knew*.

McNally had been careless and he had no time to jerk the gun from his pocket. He met Weimer's charge with a straight left hand and as the man's fat fist whizzed by, McNally gripped the wrist and twisted. Together, they went to the floor.

The front door opened and there was a heavy tread on the stairs. Loop Grenado and Jack Maxwell had played a bad hunch and they were home empty-handed.

## CHAPTER FIVE

## NUMBERS' END

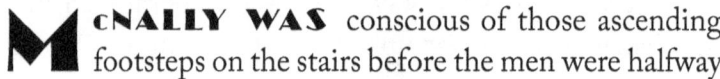 **M**c**NALLY WAS** conscious of those ascending footsteps on the stairs before the men were halfway

up. The sound filled him with desperation. Weimer was slugging and gouging at him like a veritable fury. The man was not strong, but he was vicious and bulky and hard to handle. McNally was flung against the side of the bed and Weimer's knee, aimed low, hit him in the chest. The steps on the stairs spelled doom and he had no time to be squeamish. He twisted his body desperately and his hand closed over the butt of the automatic.

Rex Weimer saw the weapon too late. He was plunging forward and the automatic was a shiny arc that came down fast. The fat man took it on the temple and McNally got the full benefit of the man's weight when he plunged forward. It was no time to bother about minor bruises and punished wind. With a deft roll, McNally extricated himself from the weight of his opponent and snaked to the doorway. There was no getting by the men on the stairs and he was not foolhardy enough to think of shooting it out with two of them. The outer room was fairly large and there was a davenport across one corner. McNally didn't even try to regain his feet. He rolled across the room and slid his body behind the ungainly piece of furniture just as feet pounded along the hall.

Loop Grenado and Jack Maxwell came to a dead stop inside the door. McNally couldn't see them but he knew that they had stopped. Grenado cursed and then stalked swiftly toward the little room. Jack Maxwell was right behind him and McNally could hear the volley of profanity that greeted their discovery of the prostrate Weimer. He waited only seconds after that.

Those men would be intent on their discovery in the first few seconds, after that they would be a poor bet. Those first few seconds were the important ones and McNally took them. He slid quietly out from the far end of the davenport, took one look at Jack Maxwell's broad back and sidled like a shadow for the door.

He wanted to make that door and he made it. Beyond that, he had no dream of concealing his movements in that creaky old house. Once in the concealing darkness of the hall, he bent low and released the clamp which held his right leg stiff; then he made a rush for the stairs.

His feet pounded on the worn boards and he heard the frantic start of the pursuit behind him. Crouched low in momentary expectation of a shot, he leaped for the front door as Jack Maxwell's feet hit the head of the stairs.

There was no shooting. These two were more discreet than the emotional Rex. When they shot, McNally reflected grimly, they would not just be calling attention to themselves; there would be a target on the other end of the lead.

He stumbled as his feet struck the pavement and the dark bulk of a sedan loomed in front of him. It was not the same sedan that had taken him away earlier in the evening, but it was the only sedan in the block and he knew the answer to that one, too. The other car had probably been "hot" anyway and it became a menace once it was connected with a crime. Grenado and Maxwell had merely gone out and lifted another.

With a lithe spring, McNally was in the front seat. He gave a grunt of satisfaction when he saw the keys in the ignition. They would be, of course. Auto thieves become as careless as their victims and this car probably had been prepared for a quick exit.

Just as Maxwell plunged from the front door of the house, the engine caught. McNally raced it in low, slapped it into second and lined away, cutting loops to either curb as he shot up the street. Two shots followed him but the zig-zagging had been effective and neither came close. He leaned back in the seat, swept around the corner and lined out for Broadway.

"The boys ought to keep bicycles around for emergencies," he said. "It's a long walk to where I'm going."

He was on Broadway now and heading north. He was not kidding himself that he had time to burn, but he held his speed down. He could not risk being picked up and he had to beat the gang to the treasure trove of Snuffle Magee. They'd be along, he knew, as soon as Rex Weimer came around enough to talk. He had seen awareness in the man's eyes. Weimer knew. He'd wake up talking.

**THE CITY** was asleep and his engine made a lonely roar in the night. Two blocks ahead of him the solitary light of an all-night restaurant gleamed. He braked down. There would be a phone in the beanery and what was the need of playing hide and seek with disaster any longer? After all, he'd had his thrill and he didn't want Ben Shuler's hundred grand. He had done his share and the rest was a cop party. Let them have it.

The decision did not quite satisfy him but it was common sense. Even if he could hope to shoot it out successfully with three armed gangsters, there would be the police to reckon with afterward. Needle Mike could neither hope to escape from underworld vengeance nor police suspicion. Nor could Needle Mike return one hundred thousand dollars with no questions asked. The only alternatives were to drop the character of Needle Mike forever or get out now with the cops making the last round-up. McNally sighed.

"It's like walking out on a show just ahead of the last act," he muttered. "But I've got to do it."

He braked down and slid to a stop a half block beyond the all-night stand. There were no customers and the solitary counterman was reading a newspaper. There was a stack of *Globe Democrat* home editions on the counter. McNally slowed and, as his eyes took in the headlines, he stopped.

GANGLAND TERROR SPREADS
Police Seek Tattoo Artist
Shooting of Detective Clune of Twelfth Blvd. Climaxes Night of Violence.

McNally forgot all about the phone. He dropped onto the stool instead. "Coffee!" he said.

The counterman looked at him curiously. In the mirror behind the counter, McNally saw his own bruised and dirty face with the streak of blood across it. He grinned and the counterman seemed relieved.

"Been in a fight?"

McNally shook his head. "Naw. I just rolled up from Little Rock. Hooked the back of a truck and fell asleep." He ran his hand over his face. "You Missourians make your roads rough."

The man behind the counter laughed and that was that. He'd think no more about it. He was the kind of person who believed what he heard. McNally let his eyes race through the front-page story.

The plainclothesman who had been on his tail was evidently named Clune. The bullet that he'd stopped had grazed his lung and he was in pretty tough shape, but he'd spotted the number of the car and he'd issued a statement to the effect that he had been keeping an eye on a character named Needle Mike when three of the man's friends had driven up in a big sedan, that he had stepped from the curb and challenged them; whereat they had opened fire on him and sped away.

The police dragnet was out for Needle Mike.

McNally found no comfort in that, but he was conscious of a vague relief that his common-sense plan had been knocked into a cocked hat. He didn't go over much for common sense and now he had to carry through alone. The police were out. He could imagine how they'd go for the story that he had to tell. At the very best, they'd round the gang up and send him over the road with them as an accessory. The Clune business damned him.

He got up from the stool, flipped a nickel on the counter and rolled out. He was glad that he'd obeyed the demands of caution to the extent of leaving the car a half block away from his stopping point. The counterman might shoot his chin a bit if the man who fell off a truck were to roll away in a sedan.

**BROADWAY WAS** still bleak and lonely. A battered flivver wending its way south at twenty miles an hour provided the roar of traffic. The street-car tracks stretched into empty distance. It was the zero hour. McNally kicked the throttle and woke the echoes as he sped northward. He wondered if Rex Weimer was still out.

As he approached the Free Bridge and the more populous section, he swung one block west to Sixth which paralleled Broadway. It was better driving and he would avoid passing his own quarters. He was moving into the dragnet area, a man sought by police and underworld—staking the long chance on the trail of three numbers. There was a tingle along the surface of his skin, a tightening in the corners of his mouth, a gleam in his eye. It was rough stuff, but it was living as one could never live when one sucked a silver spoon.

He crossed the long, cavern-like downtown streets and swung eastward to the river; down narrow streets that threw back the echoes and past buildings that had stood before the Civil War; empty buildings now, most of them, with the dust of many years of idleness upon window panes and sills and steps.

Just off Fourth he stopped. The rough cobblestones told no story, but there was a tire mark in a half moon on the curb where a hard-driven car had pulled to a fast stop. There had been ashes spilled on the sidewalk a few feet away and beyond that loomed the black mouth of an alley.

Herb Becker had taken his last dose here.

It was dangerous territory. McNally knew that the police were very likely to patrol this neighborhood more carefully than was usual after the rub-out. He couldn't help that. It was his starting place. The alley was halfway between Third and Fourth. The low-powered street light on the corner threw an indifferent light up the street. In view of later events, McNally could visualize what had happened here a few hours earlier.

There had been that hard-driven car that whirled around the corner with the roar of pursuit booming behind it. There had been the shivering figure of Snuffle Magee pressed back against the buildings; Magee, the cheap crook on the lam, who was probably venturing out for a bite to eat. Then the glaring headlights of the second car outlining Magee for a moment and passing on to Becker; the rattle of shots and the dying Becker crawling crablike for the alley. After that the police in pursuit of the killer car and Magee's moment alone with the dead.

McNally smiled grimly. He knew what a terrible moment that was for the man who was wanted. He was feeling a little of it himself and he wasn't in as bad a spot, nor he wasn't a Magee. The poor little crook had known that the neighborhood would teem with cops in a few minutes after that kill, a neighborhood usually so lonely and empty that it was safe. And by a stroke of chance, Magee suddenly had one hundred thousand dollars in cash.

What would he do? Run for it? Hardly. Magee wasn't the type that would make a run. Magee would hide. And Magee would hide damn close to where he happened to be.

McNally had turned off the ignition switch and switched to the cowl-lights. The feel of the automatic was consoling as he slid from under the wheel. So were the paper matches that he had taken off the counter at the eating house. There was no one in sight and he took it quietly down the block. Even the scrape of a foot made echoes.

Third Street was as ghostly still as the street from which he turned. The light on the corner fought a losing fight with the deep shadows halfway up the block. McNally strained to read the numbers on the bleakly deserted buildings.

*1860–1029–3.*

He believed that he was standing on the *3*. He walked slowly down the west side of the street. Stepping close to the building wall, he lighted a match. The number was faded but readable. *1025*. He felt a creeping in his spine. Two doors down he tried again. The building was shabby and decrepit but soundly built. A weather-beaten sign proclaimed the fact that a firm of drapers had once done business here. How long ago was it since there were "drapers?" McNally cupped the match closer to the door.

*1029.*

He had known that he was right, that he had to be right, but there was a thrill in the verification. Poor old Magee had hidden his loot somehow at 1029 Third Street and his simple system for writing the address down had been baffling enough to fool better minds than his own.

"Now what in blazes does 1860 mean?"

**THE THIRD** number, which Magee had been canny enough to put first, was still a mystery to McNally, but he didn't believe that it would bother him long now. He tried the door of the old building but it resisted stoutly. For a moment he was startled and taken aback; then he grinned. Of course, it would. The owners of these old places might let them stand idle for generations, but they would hardly leave them unlocked. And a lamister like Magee would hardly trust himself in a place without locks. The lock helped the illusion of desertion and kept the curious out. Somewhere, however, there would be a window or a cellar door or some other crack through which a man might crawl.

There was. McNally found a window low down against the scraggly yard in back. Dropping to his stomach, he wormed through, held by his fingers for a second and dropped. His heels thudded against the paved basement flooring and he stood for a moment in the darkness. There was no sound without or within. He could hear his heart hammering.

The scratch of a match was very loud. As the flame caught, he held the match above his head. There was no appreciable current of air and the flame held boldly. He was in a little basement store room; four blank walls enclosing a cramped cubicle. He was not disappointed. A man like Magee would neither live nor hide booty in a room so accessible. He moved on.

The next room was a little larger but, except for some dusty piled-up rubbish, as bare as the last. The third was a sort of corridor and a short flight of stairs led down. To the right, there was a fair-sized room and there was an indefinable feel to it, the feel that it had been lived in more recently than the rest; a feel and an odor of occupancy.

McNally's matches were nearly gone. He cupped a flame and held it. His blood coursed more rapidly. There was a lantern in the corner such as might have stood on a street excavation. One match sufficed to light it and the stone-walled room glowed redly. There was no cot, no sign of a place where a man might have slept or eaten, but there was a quantity of trash and a loose pile of lumber and of crushed cardboard containers, newspapers and general debris.

McNally held the lantern close and smiled grimly, exultantly. The stuff was dirty enough and dusty enough to have come down the ages—but there was no *layer of dust* over it.

That, of course, was the tip-off. Setting the lantern down, McNally went to work on the stack. He was very conscious of the stiffness and the soreness in his wrists now but he heaved the stuff aside recklessly. It came away easily and not like stuff that had been piled for years. There was no settle to it. When he had the space clear, he leaned forward.

At some time it had been necessary to drain this part of the basement regularly and there was an iron drain set in the stone; a drain thoroughly choked with rubbish. Etched into the block itself was a faded number, a forgotten number that might have stood for the date of quarrying or the date of installation, or almost anything.

*1860.*

For a few seconds, McNally just stared. He had worked this crazy crossword puzzle out, but now he didn't believe it when he had it. Slowly, hesitantly, he reached out and locked his fingers in the holes of the drain. The iron disc lifted easily and he laid it on the ground. The rubbish under it was as lightly sifted in as the rubbish on top.

Beneath it was a black satchel.

The red gleam of the lantern bathed the man and the satchel with a blood-like glow. McNally was conscious of it; conscious of the bitterly apt symbolism of this lantern in this place. It was the red lantern of danger and there had surely been danger along the trail of the satchel that he held in his hand. The light that glowed so steadily was the color of blood and there had been much blood in the history of the thing that he held in his hand. He snapped the catch and the satchel opened.

The money seemed to leap at him; stacks and stacks of it pent into such close quarters that it was almost human in its rush for freedom. One thick sheaf of bills dropped to the floor and bounced. McNally stopped another as it was slipping out. He wet his lips. He had not been born to the need of money, but he felt the tug of desire; he could picture the madness that would come to a man like Magee when he beheld a fortune like this.

As McNally crammed the money back and closed the satchel, his body stiffened. It came to him in a rush that he was in the same spot as Magee. He was in possession of money that could only be damning to him. Anything that he did with it would bring swift doom down upon him. He could neither give it to the police, give it to the gangsters, or let it alone. One way led to prison and the others to death. The red light flowed over the money mockingly.

# CHAPTER SIX
# SNUFF-OUT

**T**HERE WAS no time to sit down beside a light in this basement room and wrestle with problems. McNally knew that he had probably cut his time thin as it was. Weimer would not stay unconscious indefinitely from that tap on the head and it would not take three desperate men long to get a car. The trio would be down here and they would be a bad handful. Men who had kidnaped, murdered and robbed a morgue on the trail of one hundred thousand dollars would not be balked by one man if that man were foolish enough to get in the way.

Hefting the satchel in one hand, McNally picked up the light. It would be better than matches on the return trip and he wondered why Snuffle Magee hadn't used it instead of leaving it behind him; the habits of years spent in prowling, probably, had argued against it. A man like Magee wouldn't be comfortable moving through a house with a light showing. McNally didn't worry about that. He walked softly and kept his ears tuned for any sound that would indicate the expected arrival of Grenado, Maxwell and Weimer.

The house was quiet, spooky. He was climbing through the narrow basement window before he heard the first sound; the low hum of an automobile engine that was throttled down. Before the house the engine sighed off. McNally's muscles tensed and he slid into the yard. The front way out was impossible now and he didn't know if the back yard was a trap or not. He had to risk it.

As he glided toward a dimly seen fence, he heard footsteps in the paved areaway beside the house. His lips
tightened. A careless step now or the accidental kicking
of an old can would save him any future worry about this
black satchel he was carrying. He caught the hooded beam
of a flash.

The fence loomed just ahead of him and he sank down
into the shadow. The three men were blobs of black that
moved against the darkness of the house. The flash was
momentarily extinguished, then it came on again; a thin,
guarded beam. The man who carried it, by his build, would
be Maxwell. There was a low grunt of satisfaction. They
had found the window.

McNally did not stir. He was afraid for a moment that
two of them would go in and leave a guard outside. That
would have been bad. There was not enough of mutual
trust and confidence in the trio for that. The shadowy
figures merged for a moment as though a conference were
taking place; then, one by one, they dropped from view.

McNALLY WAITED a full minute after the last man
had gone in; then put his hands on the fence and went
over. He was in an alley; the alley, probably, in which Herb
Becker had died. How close the police and the gunmen
themselves had been to solution of a mystery if only they
had known it!

Out on the side street, McNally's borrowed car still
waited. There was no one in sight yet. He was conscious
of a mild surprise at that until he counted up. He could
not have been many minutes in the old house despite all
that had happened. He had moved fast. He hefted the
bag.

For a fraction of a second, he stood in the darkness of the alley mouth; then a hard, dangerous, gambling smile creased his lips and he swung out of the alley and across the sidewalk to his car. He moved swiftly on his toes with his body poised for a quick shift if necessary; his mind concentrated on the sudden inspiration that had come to him. The box in which he had been caught looked airtight, but he had found a small crack through which a man with nerve might squeeze. He was playing for that crack.

His foot went down on the starter and as the motor caught, he whipped the wheel over and U-turned back toward Fourth Street. Like many a man before him, he had found suddenly that his greatest safety lay in the thing from which he'd fled.

The milkmen and the other early risers were out and the brassy light of dawn was in the sky as he roared back on South Broadway. Twice he saw patrolmen on their beats but they paid no attention to him. He was not driving recklessly. He grinned at the thought of how quickly he'd be pulled in if he swung over and drove on the wrong side of the street.

All he was doing at the moment was transporting one hundred thousand dollars worth of grief and murder beside him on the front seat.

That hundred grand would be a big help if it were found in possession of a man already implicated in the shooting of a policeman. He looked over his shoulder. Pretty soon, there would be another car roaring out Broadway with three cursing gunmen who dared not linger downtown in the light of day. McNally's lips tightened.

When he dug a pit for himself, it was a darn big one.

**A FULL** block away and around the corner from the address where he'd been held prisoner, McNally pulled the car into the curb and left it. With the satchel in his hand, he strode down the silent block. The front door was locked and he rather expected that, but the third window that he tried was unlatched. He came into a living room downstairs. There was a deadly hush in the house and he was conscious of the thing upstairs. He grimaced and climbed the long flight.

The lights were out and he switched them on with no attempt at concealment. Snuffle Magee was lying on the floor still, half on his side and half under the bed. McNally lifted him gently and laid him on the bed. There was very little that he could do, but he did that little; pulling the sheet mercifully over the emaciated body.

"Poor old crummy!" he said. "They didn't give you much rest alive and about half as much dead. I'm as bad as the rest of them but I'm sorry about that kick."

He turned into the other room. There was a phone on the desk in the corner. He hadn't seen it before but he'd made a long bet that there would be one handy. Men who would stage a major snatch like the Ben Shuler thing would have a means of keeping in touch with the man who was left on guard. The stage was set. Let the trio appear!

He crossed the room, tossed the satchel carelessly behind the davenport and sat down. He rolled a cigarette and waited.

The cigarette was only half smoked when he heard the car. It came snorting up to the curb and the brakes squealed. The man who was driving was not in the cautious mood that had been his when he nudged the curb on Third Street;

there was suppressed rage in the way that car jerked in. McNally's lips were tight. His hand darted for the phone.

"Police headquarters!" His voice had snap and authority now. He heard the click and the buzz and a bored voice. He snapped through it. "Sergeant Corbin if he can come immediately."

"O.K. Corbin." There was a fractional second of delay that seemed a year with keys clicking in the lock, then Corbin's heavy voice. McNally dropped to a husky whisper and he was all Needle Mike now.

"Corbin? For Gawd's sake get this first bounce. This is Needle Mike. I been snatched. I'm at the same place they had Shuler." He rattled the address, conscious of the fact that the door downstairs had opened. "Magee's carcass is here and… they're coming back. Hurry, Corbin…."

He laid the receiver back gently, crossed the room well away from the phone and sat down. The cigarette was nearly gone but he nursed it. He heard steps on the stair and then a bedlam of voices.

"I tell you that damn dashlight was out…." Maxwell's voice was a snarl.

"Maybe…." Loop Grenado's voice was smoothly incredulous but the footsteps halted at the top of the stair. There was no appreciable sound outside there in the hall, but McNally could sense a tensing, a gathering of forces. Then he felt the stealthy approach.

The door opened with a jerk and Jack Maxwell came in crouched behind his gun.

McNally was completely Needle Mike again, even to the leg clip. He blinked at the tense man in the doorway. "Hello Jack," he said. "I came back…."

"Fer cryin' out loud!" Maxwell rocked back on his heels, his face a study in incredulity. The other two pushed into the door frame behind him. Weimer cursed and Grenado wet his lips. Grenado's eyes flicked around the room.

"Fan the joint, Jack. It's a plant," he said. "Nobody's this dumb."

He had his gun in his hand, his narrowed eyes apprehensive. Weimer had stopped cursing. Maxwell stiffened and crossed the room. He was half crouching again as he approached the door to the inner room. He went in again behind his gun, whipped the sheet off Magee and looked under the bed. McNally rocked patiently.

"You guys are plumb bugs," he said. "How'd this be a plant? Ain't you seen the papers? How'd I be going to the cops?"

**HE SPREAD** the *Globe* on the table top and pointed to the headlines. Grenado stepped close to him, his gun ready. The amateur leader of this trio had had a hard night and he needed sleep. His lips twitched. He looked at the paper and grunted.

"Yeah," he said. "You'd be in tough luck goin' to the cops." There was mockery in his eyes, contempt in the curl of his lips. He slipped the gun away and his right hand came booming back without warning. McNally had no time to duck and the blow took him across the room. He hit the wall and bounced. Grenado looked like a dude but there was steel in him somewhere. He was following up the punch now, his mouth drooping at the corner.

"You came to the right place all right," he snarled. His right clipped over again. McNally's stiff leg wouldn't hold him and he went down. Grenado bent over him. "Where's the dough?"

"What dough?" McNally shook his head to clear it. Grenado kicked him back against the wall.

"The hundred grand, slob! You beat us to it and then you come back here and try to song-and-dance us."

"Lemme have a poke at him. I owe him one!" Weimer's high-pitched whine cut through. He shouldered Grenado aside and McNally tried to get up. He took a roundhouse swing high on the cheek and then the blows came in a quick barrage. He was Needle Mike and not McNally now, so he covered as best he could with his arms and took it. Jack Maxwell stood in the doorway with a cigarette hanging from his lower lip and a sneer on his face. He was looking at Rex Weimer. McNally pulled his voice up from away down deep. It came muffled through the shower of blows.

"Hey, you mugs. I brought the dough back and—"

Maxwell was across the room in a flash and his fist came up like a piledriver. Rex Weimer never knew what hit him. He straightened up, spun once and went down on his face. Grenado pushed Maxwell's shoulder and spun him around, his hand moving to his gun.

"What the—"

"You heard that about the dough, didn't you?" Maxwell swung toward McNally. "I always wanted to sock that punk anyway to see what it felt like. You, Mike, what about that dough?"

McNally came up slowly. He was shaking his head. "I can't think clear...."

He was sparring desperately for time. Grenado's eyes were filled with rage and Maxwell wasn't reading the storm signals. There would be more killing over that hundred grand if these three had to divide it, but McNally knew that he wouldn't be around to see it. Jack Maxwell shook him by the shoulder.

"You spit quick, Mike. If you're stalling—" There was no clowning about the man now. He was the force in this mob and the killer-streak was uppermost. McNally staggered to a chair.

"I brought the dough back. I figgered maybe you guys would lay off me, help me to lam."

"Sure. That's all right. You figgered right. Where is it?" Maxwell was tense, his body half crouched. Grenado spat angrily.

"The hell it's all right. I won't even kid this mutt. He's going to come across and when he does he's going to get a load of lead in the guts for being smart!"

McNally shrank back. "Then I ain't going to tell. There ain't no percentage…."

Maxwell had stepped back, his hands on his hips; hot eyes on Grenado. With the reins of leadership once more in his hands, Grenado was riding hard.

"You'll tell if somebody cooks your feet long enough," he said. We'll try that candle trick some more and—"

McNally needed more time. He wet his lips, shifted his eyes to Maxwell. "You made me a better deal, Jack," he said huskily. "I'll tell you if you give me a break."

**GRENADO WAS** standing with his arms folded and his eyes slitted. He was looking at Maxwell as a snake looks. Maxwell took one look at him and his mood of a few minutes ago dropped from him like a blanket. He seemed to shrivel. He ran one finger inside his collar. Maxwell was bad on the charge or when goaded to a point; Grenado was bad all the time—and Maxwell didn't measure up. His eyes shifted.

"Sure, Mike," he said. "You'll get a break. Sure—" He kept darting glances at Grenado; glances that said plainly:

"I'm kidding him." McNally was straining his ears. Once he delivered that money....

He heard a motor that was muffled down, a few other significant noises. He wet his lips. He had to gamble. The men in the room were concentrated on him and on each other. Rex Weimer was sitting in a corner moaning; not yet quite into the picture. McNally rose to his feet very slowly.

"I'll get you the dough," he said heavily. "But I want a break. I won't squeal on you. I'll go on the lam...."

Grenado was satisfied with his victory over Maxwell. He played along. "O.K., Mike, O.K.," he said. "We'll take care of you."

Conscious of vigilant stares in the room and of a tightening circle outside, McNally moved to the davenport. He reached behind it and lifted the satchel. The two men strained forward and McNally dramatized his moment.

He snapped the catch as he slapped the bag down. The money, crammed tight, took its release and cascaded across the table top. Jack Maxwell swore throatily and Loop Grenado rocked forward. Rex Weimer came to his feet with a shrill cry. Two of the packages bounced and hit the floor and Weimer grabbed at them. Grenado kicked the man to one side and spun toward McNally. He was all snake again; quick enough to realize that this loot would never be divided peaceably and set to do what he had always intended to do, get rid of the threat of exposure.

McNally, set for an interruption that did not come, saw death reaching for him as the man's hand dropped to his pocket. Then Grenado remembered the angle of discipline. Maxwell had been in revolt. His eyes shot sidewise and his hand slid away from his pocket.

"Give it to him, Jack," he said. "In the guts!"

Maxwell had been staring at the money. His muscles jerked. He half straightened, then his shoulders bunched and he dropped into his crouch, his hand moving to his armpit

"O.K.!" he said.

Just then the front door went down and there was a crash in back of the house. A whistle shrilled.

Jack Maxwell, with his gun half out, spun around. Grenado swore. Rex Weimer gave a choked cry: "The cops!"

Feet pounded on the stairs. Grenado, his face a mask of rage, spun toward McNally and his hand came out of his pocket fast. He was just a moment too slow. McNally had Weimer's cheap automatic in his hand and he took Grenado in the shoulder and the man's gun flashed free. Grenado went up on his toes and spun. Rex Weimer darted to the light switch and as the light went out, Jack Maxwell charged for the stairs with his gun out and flaming.

There was a battering volley of sound and McNally did a quick dive into the other room where Snuffle Magee slept through it all in the long, long sleep. He left the automatic behind him in the outer room and he didn't try to get up when the cops moved in behind their guns and took over the place.

Jack Maxwell had never made the door. He lay huddled forward on his face and he'd taken his last knockout. Loop Grenado had not fallen fast enough and two of the bullets that Maxwell drew had knocked him into the corner. Rex Weimer had crawled halfway under the davenport and was sobbing like a woman. There wasn't a mark on him.

Corbin came to the door of the inner room and stood with his hands on his hips. McNally waved his hand feebly.

"Hi, Sarge," he said. "You come just in time. Them buzzards was goin' to bump me."

Corbin cocked one eyebrow, sniffed around the room and picked up the bloody cord that had bound McNally's wrists. His eyes took in the battered details of McNally's face. All of the evidence was here to support the story of a snatch and clear McNally from complicity in the shooting of a cop. In the other room was evidence galore in the matter of Snuffle Magee—plus a weak sister who could be made to talk and round out the story. Corbin sniffed, cleared his throat and spat.

"I don't believe it," he said grimly, "and I never will, but a bone-headed jury would!"

He shrugged disgustedly and turned to the other room. McNally rose slowly to his feet. He grinned painfully.

"Anyway," he said, "I made myself two bucks," and went out. Nobody made any attempt to stop him.

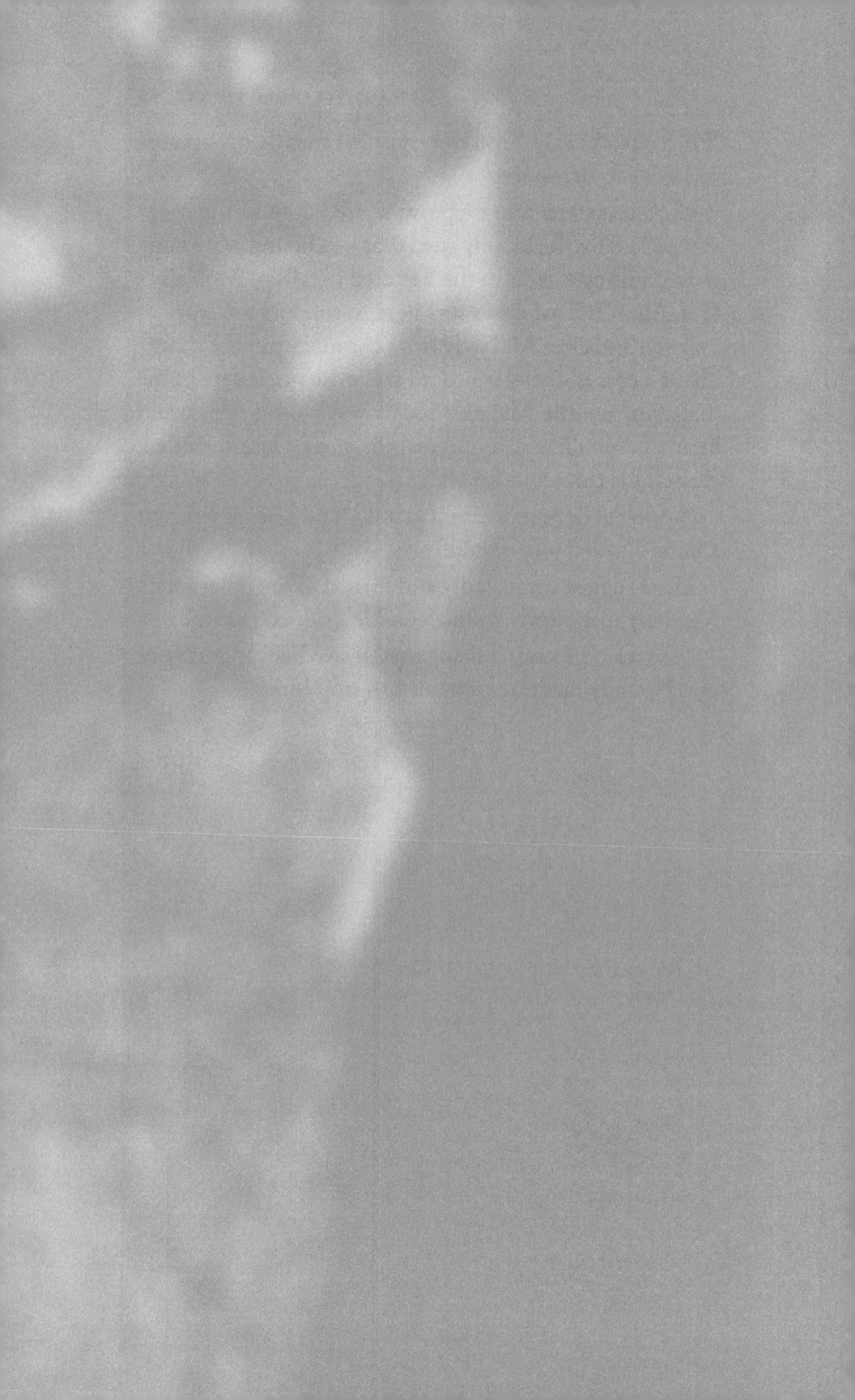

# THE TATTOOED COUNTESS

THERE IT GLEAMED—BLAZONED
BENEATH THE MILKY WHITENESS
OF HER SKIN—THE CRYPTIC
SYMBOL THAT INDICATED A
PRISONED WOMAN. WHAT EVIL
HAND HAD CAUSED IT TO BE
STENCILED ON THE COUNTESS'
THIGH? WHY HAD SHE WORN
IT WILLINGLY SO MANY YEARS—
ONLY TO HAVE IT ERASED FINALLY
BY A NEEDLE ARTIST WORKING
UNDER THE THREAT OF DEATH?

# CHAPTER ONE
## SINGING STEEL

**T**HE GIRL'S voice was low, intense, throbbing with earnestness. "Ken, could you trust me in something that was very, very important?" She emphasized her earnestness with a sudden squeeze of the hand she had held so lightly before.

Ken McNally missed the beat of the music and slipped out of step. Dancers in evening clothes jostled him. He looked down into dark eyes and felt tension in the slender body that was pressed close to his.

"The evidence is all in your favor, Sonia," he said lightly. "Tell me about it."

"You still haven't answered my question."

"How can I? You don't define 'trust.' You might mean one thing and I might understand something else." His tone was still light, bantering; but he was puzzled. Sonia Petroff was a friend of two years' standing and he liked her. On the other hand, she was engaged to Jeff Arnold who had been his friend since he was a boy.

"Please.... Come outside for a minute. We can't talk here." The girl gripped hard upon his arm. He noticed that she was biting her lip as he steered her deftly through the dancers and found chairs on the terrace. He laughed softly.

"How's this for solitude?"

From the chairs, they could see the lights in front of the hotel and the endless flow of traffic on Lindell Boulevard; but they could not see their closest neighbors except as cigarette ends glowing in the darkness. The terrace was a discreet spot.

"It's grand. A cigarette, Ken. Please." The girl's face was very close to McNally as she accepted the cigarette and waited for the light. In the flare of the match, he saw rigid lines that made a mask of her regular features. Her voice,

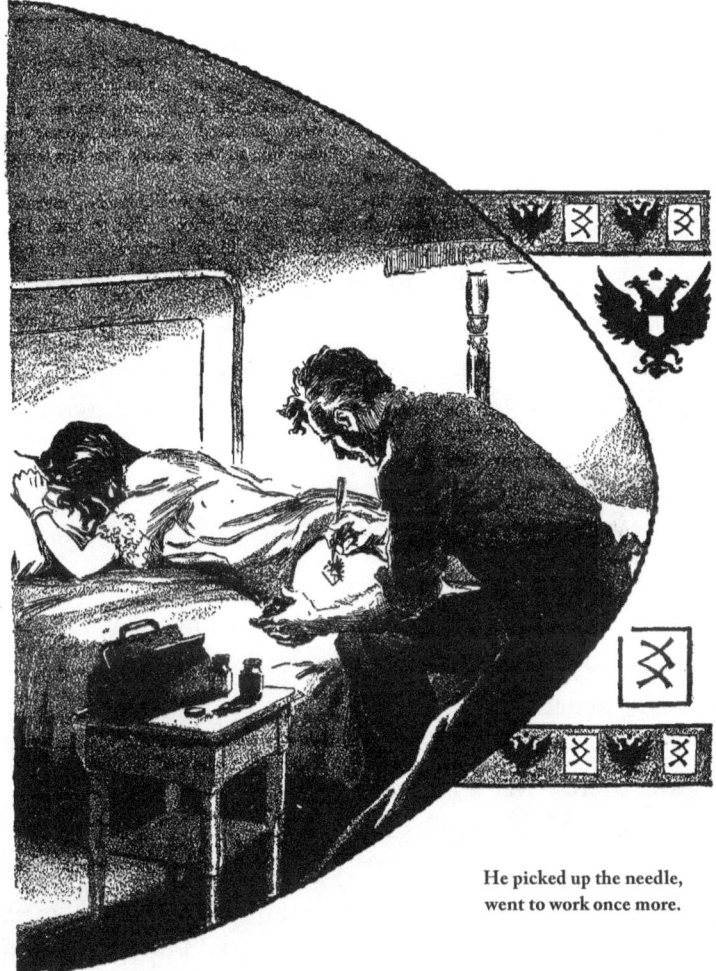

He picked up the needle,
went to work once more.

through the first puff of smoke, was tense; controlled, but
pulsing with the effort that that control cost.

"You've got to trust me, Ken. You've got to see a man
for me. You can't tell him who sent you. You've got to tell
him he's in danger, grave danger; that his only chance is
to go away, far away. You've got to convince him, Ken!"

McNally expelled his breath in a quick, gusty sigh that
would have been a low whistle if he had not been too

surprised to pucker his lips. He leaned forward. "One would think that you'd been in bad company, Sonia."

"Don't try to think, Ken. You'd think wrong. You couldn't guess right, not possibly—so don't guess. Just do as I ask, please."

McNALLY PULLED on his cigarette, his eyes narrowed. "Suppose that I do—and that this man thinks I'm talking rot?"

"You must convince him that you're not. You simply must. You can. I have faith in you. You can make him believe you."

"Thanks, but I'd be more convincing if I were convinced. You must excuse me, Sonia, but all this sounds like the talkies to me."

He caught the swift, heady fragrance of her as she leaned close to him. Her eyes glowed in the darkness like the eyes of a frightened animal. Her fingers gripped his lapel. "Ken," she said solemnly, "I give you my word. There's a life at stake. There's Jeff's happiness, my happiness—and this man's life. He must go! You must make him go!"

In spite of himself, McNally felt conviction in the girl's tone. She believed what she was telling him and she knew something that weighed on her heavily. He frowned at the winking lights of distant traffic.

"After all, why not?" Some gambling spirit within him sounded the challenge. "You've gone looking for adventure, McNally. Why turn your back on it when it comes seeking you?" His eyes turned again to the girl. She was relaxed in her chair, watching him. She had launched her most telling argument and she knew it; there was wisdom in her, a wisdom which told her when she had said enough. McNally sighed.

"Who is the man, Sonia?"

There was a quick rustle as the girl's hand delved into some mysterious recess. It came up with a folded triangle of paper which she pressed into McNally's hand.

"His name and address are on this sheet," she said softly. "He is Japanese."

"Japanese?"

"Yes." Sonia looked away, off over the rooftops on the further side of the boulevard. "Not an honorable Japanese, Ken; but one, perhaps, who still does not deserve to die. You must go to him immediately."

McNally's protest was silenced by one white finger that was laid lightly against his lips. "It is necessary and not too painful, *mon ami*. I know you. These affairs bore you terribly."

"They do. But I brought Laura Wheeler and—"

"She has neglected you shamefully for a sophomore that she is in love with. She deserves the scolding that she will get from her fortune-hunting mama for letting you get away."

McNally grinned. Sonia had put her finger on the big reason for his boredom with the society set into which he had been born; there were always mamas and matchmakers. He rose to his feet. "That argument is the clincher," he said.

Sonia's hand found his and gripped it with a warm clasp that managed somehow to be the kind of handshake that one man gives another. "I'll tell you sometime how swell you are," she said huskily.

McNally turned her toward the door. "Don't," he said. "Jeff Arnold is still a bigger man than I am."

McNALLY'S EYES were thoughtful as he shrugged into his dark overcoat. There was a warm glow of expectancy in his blood, but he was no Don Quixote. He didn't like tilting at windmills for a gesture. There were angles to this affair that he didn't like. With anyone else he would have stood adamant on a negative answer until he had more facts, but he knew Sonia. She was of the old aristocracy of a Russia that had been—and she had been born with the capacity for keeping secrets. She would not have told him more, and by insisting, he would have closed the channels of information. That wouldn't have been so good. For if Jeff's happiness and Sonia's and a human life were involved in this mysterious errand of his, he had to know more. He'd see what this unknown Japanese could be made to contribute.

Free of the lobby crowd, he looked at the folded piece of paper. His eyebrows went up and he whistled softly. "The hell!" he said. "I might have guessed, but…."

The name on the card was the name of a man who had been creating a mild sensation as a portrait painter to society—Jiro Sakamoto of Tokyo.

It was hard to tie that name up with any menace to the happiness of Sonia and Jeff. It was harder still to conceive of any argument which would make the man pack up and leave town in the face of the prosperity that was coming his way. Still, Sonia had been in dead earnest when she spoke about the danger to the man's life. She had said, too, that he was not an honorable Japanese. McNally shrugged.

"We'll have a look at him," he said. "If he's got to go, there ought to be more than one way of making him leave town."

**THE STUDIO** of Jiro Sakamoto occupied the top floor of a three-story house, west of Skinker Road. Originally a private residence, it had fallen into speculative hands and was now an apartment house of the type that caters to the studio trade. There was another artist and a writer of bad verse in two ground-floor apartments, a wealthy idler and a society surgeon on the second floor. The third floor, with its really splendid skylight, was Sakamoto's.

A very thin Japanese opened the door for Ken McNally. "Good evening, sar. You have appointment?"

"No appointment, but he'll see me. It's important." McNally passed over one of his cards and accepted the man's apology for leaving him in the hall.

There was practically no delay. The thin Japanese was opening the door again, his narrow face wreathed in smiles. "The master see you, thank you, sar."

McNally nodded and preceded the serving man down a short hallway into a large workroom that was hung with canvases; some completed and others in various stages of completion. It was the room with the skylight, the ceiling sloping with the angle of the roof and the skylight itself hidden by a black shade drawn tightly. A man stood before an easel in one corner of the room but McNally saw nearly everything else in the room before he saw him. For all of the life that he showed, the man might well have been painted on canvas; a stocky man with a pinched, scholarly face, a small black mustache and scanty black hair. The silk smock that he wore was pale blue and in perfect harmony with the color scheme of the room: hung against any wall, it would have merged into its background and been all but invisible.

For several seconds, the man endured McNally's scrutiny without blinking; then he nodded his head. "Misstair McNally. You wiss to see me, yess?"

The sound of his voice was a blend of hiss and lisp that hit the s's hard and grated on McNally's nerves. "If you are Mr. Sakamoto, I do want to talk to you—alone."

"Ah, yess?" One yellow hand came out of the capacious sleeve of the smock and waved dismissal to the servant. The other hand was not visible and McNally wondered what it held. It was all too obvious that Sakamoto did not consider him a possible client. The man was on guard, wary.

"You will sit down, yess. Your business wit' me isss—"

"To warn you. Your life is in danger. It is hazardous for you to remain in Saint Louis."

The man from Japan took that without blinking. "You are not the police?"

"No."

"But there are police here in Saint Louis."

McNally was inwardly cursing his own lack of facts; outwardly he was serene. "There are excellent police here," he said, "but the police catch whom they can—*after* something has happened."

"Ah, yess." Sakamoto adjusted gold-rimmed spectacles to the bridge of his nose. He seemed to be pondering something. Suddenly he smiled, a flashing full-toothed smile that somehow lacked mirth. "You would be from Miss Sonia," he said. "I hav' tried to interess' her in one of my poor paintings. She does not hav' money. The Jeff Arnold, he hass money, yess?"

McNALLY'S EYES narrowed. The man was suddenly very sure of himself. He did no fencing once he decided that McNally was from Sonia Petroff; made no attempt to confirm his own guess. Somehow, he just knew—and with the knowledge had come confidence, a feeling of power. The man was almost strutting now and his statement about Sonia's money and Jeff's sounded very much like a threat. McNally leaned forward.

"I didn't come here to talk about paintings nor about other people," he said. "I came to bring you a friendly warning."

"Your friendship is very much appreciate." Sakamoto bowed low but the eyes behind the glasses were mocking eyes. "Because it iss appreciate I show you the picture which Miss Sonia so like to possess. You will tell her you have seen it and that it iss safe."

Again that certainty that McNally came from Sonia. The man didn't even wait for a reaction. He was across the studio in an effortless glide. An ornately carved desk faced the room from the corner of the room that missed being under the skylight. Sakamoto came to a stop behind this desk. There was a chair behind the desk and another facing it from the room side. The Japanese waved to the second chair.

"If you will sit there, Misstair McNally, I show you."

McNally saw no reason why he shouldn't sit there. He changed places. His host was all smiles and affability now. With a gliding step he was clear of the chair; then a yellow hand moved a canvas that had been set with seeming carelessness against the wall. The soft light of the shaded desk lamp reflected from the polished metal of a safe door. The safe was built into the wall and Sakamoto's body shadowed the combination as his fingers worked. There was a sharp click and the door swung back. The Japanese reached swiftly within the strong box and when he turned, he had a rolled canvas in his hand.

"Unless some kind friend does lend the money to Miss Sonia, I am 'fraid she does not hav' thiss picture that she want."

He was all smiles but there was glitter in his eyes as he unrolled the canvas. McNally hunched his body forward with a grunt.

The painting was a nude. It showed a beautifully formed girl with her arm thrown before her face as she recoiled before the menace of a naming sword. The sword hung suspended as though the hand that held it were invisible. It was a broken sword; the point on a straight line from the hilt, but a jagged break severed it into two halves at the middle of the blade.

Compelling though the picture was in itself, it was not the girl nor the sword that rivetted McNally's attention. On the swelling curve of the girl's hip there was a mark that could be nothing but tattoo, a Chinese ideograph done in black ink. McNally, who had studied tattooing in the east for the sheer fascination of the art, could not be mistaken about that. The artist had caught the technique of the tattooer and had reproduced it on canvas.

For a long minute, McNally stared at the painting. The girl's identity was hidden by that shielding arm before her face; but it was likewise betrayed by that distinctive mark upon her body—if there was a girl who bore that brand.

McNally thought of Sonia and his lips tightened. He raised hard eyes to the glittering stare of the Japanese.

"What is the price of that painting?"

The thin lips curled beneath the trim mustache. "Fifty thousan' dollar."

**McNALLY'S MUSCLES** tensed. That price was the tip-off. By some manner or means, Sonia Petroff had become involved with this yellow man. That picture was the threat that she mentioned, the threat to her happiness and to Jeff's. She had not dreamed that the artist would show the picture to McNally and, knowing that she would not expect that, the saffron-skinned devil had crossed her up. Here was blackmail deluxe, the velvet touch. He took a step forward and the sharp voice of the Japanese stopped him.

"Care-ful...."

It was a threat and there was a world of confidence backing it. The man had slipped easily behind the desk while he was displaying the painting and he leaned a bit forward now with his hand on an innocent-looking bronze ornament. McNally, who had seen such desks before, stopped. He was more conscious now of the ornate scroll-work in the hard wood, of the writhing dragons and the target inlaid circular designs. Somewhere in the intricate pattern, there would be a target center in one of those designs that would be cut all of the way through. There would be a gun behind that design and a trigger connected with the innocent-looking piece of bronze. He smiled grimly, his eyes still hard.

"I'm still carrying the same message," he said. "You are in danger while you remain in Saint Louis."

The lips of the Japanese matched his own in a smile, but the eyes behind the spectacles were polished marbles. "I first will sell my picture. One man buys or another—"

He broke off suddenly. There was a slamming sound from the skylight and he crouched, one hand darting beneath the smock. The shade, suddenly released from the knot that held it had wound back upon its roller. McNally, startled himself, saw only black sky and distant stars through the paneled glass.

Something whined through the air and flashed past his left shoulder. Sakamoto, still looking up, took the singing steel of a thrown knife full in his chest. His voice welled out of him in a shrill squeak and, as his hand tightened on the bronze ornament, McNally flung himself to one side.

He was not quite soon enough. There was a slashing streak of flame from the ornament itself and lead tore through his coat. A veritable tornado crossed the room behind him and he was turning when a hand encircled his throat and something crashed down on his head.

It was a knockout blow and McNally felt his legs turn to rubber. There was a second of blackness as he slumped from the chair, followed by a period of stark paralysis during which he could see dimly without having power over his muscles.

He saw Sakamoto whirl with the hilt of the blade still sticking from his chest and slam the canvas into the safe. The man was falling as he closed the steel door and twirled the knob. Then a giant of a man hurdled McNally's body and McNally's vision dimmed. His head went down and he sank into the oriental rug and oblivion.

# CHAPTER TWO
# THE WAY OUT

**I**T HAD been a hard blow and McNally's head cleared slowly. He felt now like a beaten prize-fighter, his face in the nap of a fabulous rug rather than in powdered resin, but his body as inert as that of any chilled pug. There was swift and heavy movement in the room, a baffled shaking of the safe knob and hoarse whispers. For all of the two voices, McNally had a bewildering impression that there was only one man in the room. He fought to raise his head and strength flowed back into him slowly.

One knee came up under him and he shook himself. He was an athlete and his body was in good condition. Once the paralysis left him, his head cleared magically. He came to his feet in a half-crouch. There was a sound of movement but no antagonist before him. He whirled and his eyes swept the empty studio; then he looked aloft.

He was just in time to see a pair of legs disappearing through the skylight. A rope whipped up through the dark rectangle and the heavy trap banged into place. McNally swore softly and took a couple of steps toward Sakamoto.

A glance told him that he could do the Japanese no service now. The little man's glasses had fallen off and his eyes stared upward sightlessly. The smock had fallen off his chest on the right side but it was held in place on the left side by the blade that was still buried hilt deep between his ribs.

McNally pondered the fact that that blade had been thrown. He rubbed his head where, back of one ear, a lump the size of a plover's egg had appeared. The pain fairly sickened him.

Out in the hall there was a pound of feet and the sound of voices. Someone was knocking at the door and calling out some inquiry. It was the shot, of course, that had aroused the neighbors. McNally felt his side.

The bullet from the desk ornament had nicked his white shirt-front, torn his dinner jacket and plowed a thin, skin-deep furrow in his side. It was sore and it was bleeding. He grunted and turned toward the hall door.

Sprawled on his back in the middle of the reception hall lay the skinny little servant. He had been literally disemboweled with one thrust of a savage blade and he had fallen on his back with his arms thrown out wide. He was quite dead.

The full force of McNally's position came home to him then. The shot which had brought the neighbors had been fired at him. He carried the evidence of that with him. There was no one else in the apartment, the murder weapon was still buried in Sakamoto and McNally had no logical story to explain his presence in the studio.

He could imagine the reception that the police would give his story that he had been merely the carrier of a blind message of warning. Even if Sonia backed him up, it would be very thin—and there was plenty to contradict it. It might be even possible for the police to dig up an adequate motive. If it were proved, as it might be, that Sakamoto was a blackmailer, the world would accept that as an explanation. It would be assumed that McNally had got into a scrape and that the Japanese was blackmailing him; that he had murdered the man and the servant in a blind rage.

McNALLY WHIRLED and darted back the way he had come. The pounding at the door was more insistent now, but he had a few seconds. Private citizens rarely hammered a door down. Someone had probably phoned for the police and, with prowl cars on the loose, that call would be swiftly answered. He had seconds—a minute perhaps—

He looked at the skylight. It was closed from the outside and beyond his reach. Not even by jumping from the desk top would he be able to reach it. The murderers had planned well. In the event of detection or interference, they had the way of escape open; a way calculated to baffle investigators who would not think immediately of the rope-through-the-trapdoor expedient.

As noiseless as his own shadow, McNally sped through the other rooms. There had to be a way out; no matter how dangerous. There had to be.

He could not betray Sonia into a murder tangle no matter how guilty her knowledge might be nor did he want his own name dragged through scandal. There was a chink in his own armor that might put him on the gallows if the police broke in and found him. He might be finger-printed—and the police already had his prints.

As some rich men's sons go to Africa to hunt big game for their thrills, McNally had gone into the underworld of his own city. His had been the greater thrill. Living an alternate existence as Ken McNally, idler, and as Needle Mike, tattoo artist of South Broadway, he had found life far from tame. In one existence he was the confidant of those who possessed wealth; in the other, he rubbed shoulders with the shadow-pack that preyed on wealth. Tonight, for the first time, his two identities threatened to overlap.

If the police identified him with that grouchy old character on the fringe of the badlands—Needle Mike—then he'd swing for the Sakamoto murder. His explanation for his double life would be as fantastic as his explanation for being in the studio. The police mind rejects coincidence.

The thought of the fingerprints sent him scurrying back into the studio. He had touched a few things and he wiped off any surface that might betray him before he plunged again into the series of rooms that made up the apartment.

There was a scream of sirens now on Skinker Road.

The very imminence of his danger steadied him. He stepped over the body of the man in the reception hall and recovered his topcoat and hat. His eyes ranged the apartment swiftly. He had an idea that he was overlooking a detail but he couldn't think of any. Some monitor in his brain was shrieking, "Danger," but he couldn't put a name to it—and he couldn't linger.

The police were at the door. He could tell the difference in the tone of the knock. They would not knock long. The door would go down in a minute. He raced softly through the small rooms off the main studio. There were bars on the windows and he had a sinking sensation in his stomach. The kitchen remained and he took hope. He did not recall ever having seen bars on the window of an apartment kitchen. He didn't want to see them for the first time now, either.

Somebody had slammed his weight into the apartment door. McNally crossed the kitchen threshold and breathed deep. The window was narrow and set high, but it was unbarred.

He vaulted to the drainboard and swung across to the sill. He was not forgetting that he was three stories up. He'd need a few more breaks.

Below him was darkness; the black rear wall of the building and an enclosed yard below. A large tree stood in the yard but the nearest branch was well out of reach.

There was no cornice; nothing that a man might climb or walk. He looked up.

**THERE WAS** a drain running along the edge of the roof, a metal drain that he could grip with his fingertips if he stood tip-toe on the sill. To his left, the drain passed above the barred windows of the apartment; to his right it ran straight back for approximately fifteen feet before it crossed the fire-escape.

McNally didn't know if the old drain would support him but he heard the apartment door go down before a police assault and it was no time for nice calculations of tensile strength. Drawing the air deep into his lungs, McNally stretched out and gripped with his fingertips. For a split second, he paused and then swung; squirming to get a full finger grip.

Blackness was under him and it had the feel of a bottomless pit. McNally did not look down. Lips tight, he worked along the quivering drain that sagged away with his weight.

It was no stunt for a man in evening clothes. His collar rubbed his neck like a blunt razor and the stiff shirt robbed his body of mobility. There was an edged wind and it billowed the topcoat about him. His breath came hard but he fought for the inches and held on.

When his feet swung over the iron fire-escape, he gave a gasp of relief; but he didn't dare to drop. Pursuit was likely to be close and the noise would rumble into the apartment building. He had to keep on. It was a million miles to the ladder that led upward from the fire-escape to the roof. He gripped it at length and held on.

He wanted to climb to the roof and take a look through the skylight into the murder room. He wanted to search for possible clues left by the two men who had escaped from that same roof. He wanted to look for another way out by way of other roofs on adjacent buildings. McNally wanted, in fact, to do anything but go down; down the long black ladders past an aroused series of apartments and into a shadow-filled alley that might well be guarded by police.

But he forced himself to turn his back on the roof and start down. It was the wise course and he wasn't letting his fears get the upper hand.

His hands were sore from the drain; he rubbed them with his handkerchief and swore softly. His feet made a slight drumming sound on the fire-escape landings. He slowed his pace and the handkerchief slipped from his hands. As he grabbed for it, he saw something glint on the iron grillwork of the landing. Its visibility made him swear at his own stupidity in flashing a white handkerchief in the dark. He jammed the handkerchief away, pulled the dark topcoat closer about him and picked up the object on the landing.

It was a button; an odd button; black and hard but made of some composition fabric rather than bone. Where most buttons designed for masculine attire are concave or flat, this one was convex. McNally grunted and put it in his pocket. It was, he imagined, a possible clue if the murderers had escaped this way. Clue or not, he had no clear idea of what to do with it; he was no detective. He put it in his pocket and went on down the fire-escape.

**UNTIL HE** came to the last landing, McNally was in deep shadow against the side of the building; but the feeble light that flowed into the alley from a poorly lighted street was enough to outline him as he stepped onto the swinging ladder for the last flight. There was a screech of protest from unoiled hinges and McNally increased his pace. A bulky uniformed figure emerged from the shadows beneath him and he caught the blur of motion as the man went for his gun.

"Hold up there. Come down with your hands high!" the man called to him and McNally jumped. There was no setting of muscles, no pause, no take-off; he simply twisted with the challenge and let go, his body twisting in mid-air.

The policeman never had a chance. McNally's feet took him on the shoulders and bowled him over before his gun cleared his pocket. He gave a hoarse shout as he went down, but McNally did a tumble from his shoulders that would have done credit to an acrobat; and he gave his muscles no time to relax. Bouncing like a rubber ball, he came to his feet and cleared the fence on the far side of the alley with one leap.

It took him twelve seconds to reach the street beyond and less than a minute to reach his parked car. As the motor snorted from the curb, he wiped the back of his hand across his face and grunted with relief.

"A tough spot, my countrymen," he muttered, "and where do we go from here?"

He knew the answer to that before he put the poser to himself. He couldn't appear in public with a bullet-hole in his dinner jacket and the dirt of the fire-escape ground into his topcoat. He couldn't go home, either, where his parents might be alarmed and servants encouraged to gossip. The police dragnet would be out for a man in evening clothes if the policeman he had downed in the alley had got a look at him and—

It was then that he remembered what he should have recalled before making his escape from the apartment of Sakamoto.

He should have recovered his calling card. He had sent it in when he called on the Japanese—and the dead man still had it.

It was a fine lead for the police if they were looking for a fugitive in evening clothes. There was only one escape for Ken McNally. He had to pass out of existence. Some men had to die in order to do that, but McNally had only to become Needle Mike.

# CHAPTER THREE
# WOMAN IN PRISON

**H**E PARKED his car in the shadow of Eads Bridge, phoned to his garage for a pick-up and put another call through to his home. When he left the booth, he was officially on his way to Chicago for a visit with friends; actually, he was bound, in a hurry, for the shabby office that he maintained on one of the disreputable side streets that run down to the Mississippi.

He had retreated often to that haven. It was one of those buildings where the mere payment of rent was enough to ensure privacy. Nobody even bothered to sweep out his office. If anyone had, they would have found nothing but a shabby desk and a still more shabby filing case. These were both stage props; McNally used neither of them.

The filing case slid back and there was a loose-board arrangement in the floor. McNally hauled out a black bag. It took him less than five minutes to exchange the once faultless evening clothes for stained trousers, greasy blue shirt, tan brogans and a checked cap. These things were simple. By the light of a flickering gas jet, he went to work on his face.

There was a specially constructed dental bridge that fitted with clips over two sound teeth and provided an oversize gold crown which he pressed over a gleaming gold tooth in front. A few dabs with a special preparation transformed his tiny measle scars into blue-black powder burns. An irritant reddened his eyelids and gave his eyes a bleary look; a hasty touch-up touseled his sleek hair and touched it with gray. He grinned as this new man emerged. As he wiped a chemical-dampened towel over his face, the red tan of an out-of-doors man became the dirty yellow complexion of a sun dodger.

It was all so simple that it could stand inspection under lights. There was no messy grease paint, nothing to get out of place or to run or to get rain-spattered. A chunk of wax under his upper lip changed the contour of his face and he was ready except for the crowning touch.

From the black case that had provided the rest of his makeup, McNally brought forth a device of his own invention; an oval-shaped clamp of cork and rubber that fitted close to his leg at the knee joint. That stiffened his leg. That was his insurance of a distinctive walk that would not betray; he could not walk as Ken McNally even if he forgot temporarily that he was Needle Mike.

With a click, the case closed and went back under the floor. The filing case was pushed into place and McNally rolled out. He saw no one in the halls and that was not surprising. The tenants were few and furtive and the janitor was a drunkard. He had chosen his building well.

There was a bottle of particularly villainous liquor in the hip pocket of the gray pants and McNally reeled against a wall outside to take a drink. This operation gave him a chance to survey the block. Also it gave him the aroma of a ten-day drunk. He had chosen that brand of liquor carefully, too; there was no other with such a poisonous fume on the civilized globe.

Lurching just a little and setting the game leg down hard, McNally reached South Broadway and started for the tattooing parlor. A few men that he met grinned and waved. He nodded to them surlily and kept going. He knew what they were saying behind his back.

"There's the Needler again. Been off on another bat. He'll open up now, but he won't do a lick o' work for twenty-four hours."

The half-world understood men with habits, or thought that it did—and McNally capitalized on that. Needle Mike was a neighborhood character because he did the same things over and over again and always in the same way. In that lay safety. When the men who live in the shadows fail to understand something, they investigate. Needle Mike was an open book.

**THE TATTOOING** parlor was just ahead; a store-front window with a coating of dirt and a green shade that was pulled down when the place was closed. Between McNally and the shop was the Greek's place, a penny arcade where one could buy anything from a shoe shine to a set of biological postal cards. There was a big man talking to the Greek and McNally stiffened. The Greek had seen him and was suddenly nodding his head and talking fast. The big man turned slowly.

McNally wanted to look him over but it wouldn't have been in character. When Needle Mike came back from a toot, he wasn't interested in anybody. He had an idea, anyway, that the man had been asking about him. If he had, he'd be in. There didn't have to be any hurry.

As he fumbled with the key in the old door, McNally was conscious of the man who followed and watched him. He didn't turn around. The lock sprang back noisily and he pounded into his own quarters. They were as he had left them; shabby, broken-down chairs, a work table with a mirror, an instrument case and a series of lithographs about the walls—all starkly in character under the yellow light of the single, drop bulb. He lurched across the room and released the cracked green shade which rolled up with a loud squeak. As he turned around, he saw the man in the doorway.

The man was big, unbelievably big; over six feet in height and with a breadth of shoulder such as one usually finds in short and stocky men. His blue eyes were frosty and set well back under bushy eyebrows. There was a fringe of beard under his chin. For no particular reason, McNally thought of marching men in review before this tall chap. He looked like that.

"You work with the needle—art?" The man waved his hand at the walls. Speech seemed hard for him; as though he had to think of each word before he used it. McNally growled under his breath and stamped across the room.

"Naw. Come s'm'other time. I'm tired."

The big man seemed to grow taller. He had his hands behind his back. He didn't move but he had a thirty-days-in-the-guardhouse expression on his face. His voice came from way back in his chest. "You sit down. I talk to you."

McNally raised his head slowly; the belligerent expression of one, half drunk, on his stained face. "I own this place, mug," he growled. "Scram!"

The stranger didn't change expression, but he reached into a pocket and took out a thin roll of bills. He threw ten dollars down on the work table. "I have a job you must do tonight," he said slowly.

McNally was having a hard time in keeping up the pose of disinterest. The man before him was too obviously a Russian and there was something about the bulk of him and the power in his big frame that fitted into the drama that McNally had just left. The job that must be done tonight added up to a total which he could understand, too. He could make a guess at the job. His face, however, showed nothing except irritability. He threw himself down in one of the chairs.

"Nothin' doing," he said. "My hands ain't right. I ain't doin' no work for nobody. Yuh make my head ache—"

The Russian threw another ten on top of the one on the work table. He didn't speak. McNally eyed the money. He eyed it as Needle Mike was supposed to eye money. Twenty bucks was respectable cash on South Broadway.

"Whaddye want?" he growled.

The Russian's lip curled. He was the type of man who stands on a yes or a no forever. He might bring pressure on a man to change a decision but he never respected him for changing it.

"A person is tattooed," he said. "You must change the design. It must be something else."

"Gimme time and enough dough and I'll take it off entire and clean."

"No time. And you couldn't do it."

"Who says so?" McNally's chin stuck out.

"I do. No one has ever removed such tattoo. It is black. Japanese."

"Oh, that!" McNally shrugged and managed to look dejected. It called attention away from any traces of his inner excitement which might come to the surface. "To hell with it," he said. "That's hard work."

**THE BEARDED** man's eyes glowed with rage long suppressed. The lines deepened in his face and they were bitter lines. His face was that of a man who has been through hell and who has brought some of it back with him. One long arm shot out and a hand like steel pincers gripped McNally's shoulder.

"I have been nice. I have been polite. I bring this job to you as business. Bah to you! I will break your damn neck if you do not do this!"

McNally pulled the breath in his lungs. The grip of this man was torture and the menace which the man radiated was a tangible thing that he could feel. Here was a man who could kill and who would. A creature like Needle Mike would not be expected to stand up against so evident a threat. He blew his whiskey-tainted breath at the Russian. He didn't want to yield too easily even yet. The man must never be suspicious.

"I'm shaky. Mebbe I can't do it." He got the half-world whine into his voice. The Russian bared his teeth.

"I have look you up. You are the good artist in flesh. You can do it." His lips flattened and stayed flat against the strong teeth. "You mus' not shake—"

The killing grip of his fingers emphasized the threat and he shook McNally as a terrier might shake a rodent. McNally grunted. "You're too damn rough," he growled, "and I gotta have more money for a job like that."

The Russian stood up. He took the thin roll out of his pocket and slapped a twenty contemptuously on top of the ten. "Get what you need. We will go at once!"

"Hell! I work here."

"You work where I take you." The man stood spread-legged. He spoke clear English but always with that emphasis on each word that gave the impression of a recitation learned by rote. McNally got up and hobbled into the back room, cursing under his breath as Needle Mike might be expected to do. The Russian stood in one spot, his eyes still angry but his body rigid.

**AS LONG** as he was under that baleful glare, McNally moved slowly and grouchily. Hidden by the door in the other room, he became alert. Excitement pumped the blood hot in his veins. Events were shaping his way. With deft fingers, he whipped two folders from a battered wooden file. One was on Chinese ideographs; the other on Japanese tattooing.

He did not have to spend much time on the art of black tattoo. He had learned it on a trip to the Orient years ago when he was an art student and before he ever conceived the identity of Needle Mike. He did, however, linger for several moments on the doings of the *Nosatsu-kai* and on the file of ideographs.

It was as he remembered it. The *Nosatsu-kai* was an organization of hobby-riders like the stamp collectors and crossword-puzzle fans; Japanese who derived great enjoyment out of figuring new and unusual ways of writing their names in Chinese characters. His eyes raced through his own notes. There were many ways of following the hobby. Some Japanese made *nosatsu* of their names and left the characters on slips of paper before the shrines of the gods. That was harmless—as was the hobby of exchanging *nosatsu* with other hobby-riders. He paused at a paragraph.

Many Japanese have learned through experiments with

Chinese characters in combination that it is possible to use them for secret writing. Many seemingly innocent *nosatsu* serve to shield intrigue. Thoughts which a well-bred Japanese would hesitate to set down or to express in his own language can be expressed in Chinese symbols without shame—the *nosatsu* symbols being neither Chinese nor Japanese, but an expression of Japanese thought in Chinese characters grouped as the Chinese themselves do not group them....

McNally nodded and whipped swiftly through his collection of Chinese ideographs. He found the key figure of the design in Sakamoto's painting.

 a woman

Turning pages swiftly, he came upon the other symbol.

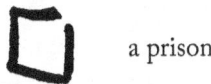 a prison

His eyes clouded. "A woman in prison." It didn't quite add up. But then it wasn't supposed to translate as it stood. That would be Chinese. The Jap had used the symbols to express a thought of his own. He shrugged. He didn't have a Japanese mind. He would have to ponder on that a bit.

Conscious of the waiting Russian, he slapped the files aside and started to assemble the equipment that he would need. Since he had to go outside, and particularly since he had to work over a Japanese job, he was not taking electric needles. The hand tools were slower and required more patience but they were better for this kind of a job. Then there was the matter of ink. Ordinary black India ink shows blue under the skin; he had to bring the imported Japanese grade. He frowned as he packed it into the little bag. He wasn't Needle Mike at heart and he hated to needle anything into a human skin that no one would ever take out.

There was a heavy footstep outside the door and the Russian stood framed in the doorway, his eyes narrow and suspicious. "We must not waste time," he growled. "You are slow."

McNally cursed in the fervent accents of Needle Mike. "There's them that's broke their necks with hurrying," he said, "and it's a wonder ye have a neck on you at all!"

## CHAPTER FOUR

## TATTOO

**T**HERE WAS death in the Russian. McNally could feel it as he limped along beside him down the dark side street that led away from the lights of South Broadway. The big man had taken stakes in a grim game and he was a man who played such games hard. He was worked up to a pitch now that he was away from the shop where passers-by might look in; the leash of his control was slipping. His heels hit hard and several times he muttered strange words that sounded like curses. In spite of himself, McNally felt a prickling along his spine.

This man was inhumanly strong and he was violent and quick. It was a bad combination—and McNally had an idea that he was being used as a pawn and that it was not intended that he should ever come back from this excursion to gossip about what he had done.

There was a dark car against the curb and two men in the front seat. The man beside the driver was sitting patiently and puffing on a cigarette; but he had a thick blindfold over his eyes. The driver growled something in Russian at the man who had brought McNally and got a hot retort in his own tongue. Then, without ceremony, the big Russian heaved McNally into the tonneau of the car, rolled after him and tied a thick black cloth across his eyes.

"It is not necessary that you see where you go," he growled.

McNally didn't answer him. There wasn't any good answer and a bad one would have been a waste of breath. Besides, he had enough to think about. He had had a good look at the back of the blindfolded man's head before his own blinders had gone on. There was no mistaking the bat-wing ears and sinewy neck above the soiled, tan shirt-collar.

The Russians had hired other specialized talent besides his own. The man beside the driver was Blinker Owen, box worker.

McNally had seen Blinker around the spots on South Broadway and he knew his story. In the days when yeggs were aristocrats in the underworld, Blinker had been a wizard at opening safes; a sure-shot with the soup when he needed soup but a better man at "feeling" the box and opening it by listening to the tumblers drop. Too many vacations in stir had dimmed Blinker's courage and he didn't try for any big stuff any more—but McNally could see a job that was made to order for the man tonight.

Sakamoto had closed his safe when he was dying and the picture of a girl with a black tattoo mark was in that safe.

**THE CAR** was rolling now, taking corners one after another and doubling forward and back to confuse the passengers. It took only a few minutes to lose McNally completely. He had no idea of direction any more, and he didn't care. He didn't expect ever to traverse the trail again—and he knew that the Russians didn't intend to give him the opportunity. They were merely being careful.

They rode for ten more minutes, then the brakes squealed and tires rubbed the curb. The big man shook McNally and cursed him for stumbling as he tried to get out. The man in the front seat said something in Russian and got a reply; then McNally was being hustled along with iron fingers on his arm. The car's engine raced a little and he knew that it was taking Blinker Owen to his job at another location.

They might have gone down an alley or a street McNally didn't know. He knew only that they reached steps eventually and that there was nothing gentle about the way the Russian helped him to mount them. He swore at him in the gruff fashion of Needle Mike.

"You bust that arm, mug, and you can whistle through hell for another tattooer in this town."

The grip relaxed somewhat and then there were stairs and a carpet underfoot, the soft opening and closing of a door. The bandage was whisked away.

McNally was standing in a deeply shadowed room. Before him was a low bed bathed in soft warm light from a silk-shaded floor lamp. A silent, grim-faced woman of middle age stood just outside the circle of light, her black eyes watchful, her attitude protective.

On the bed lay a girl, her head buried in the pillows and her body—save for one discreetly bared hip—swathed in soft, silken coverings. Gleaming from the warm flesh was the hideously disfiguring black symbol that the girl in the painting had borne; the symbol of "the woman in prison."

McNally sucked his breath in sharply. The scene was unreal, a bizarre stage-set moved into the room to confront his suddenly unbandaged eyes. The Russian gripped his elbow impatiently.

"To work, lout! You are not here to stare. You can change that design?"

McNally shrugged. He was back in character again. "I didn't know it was a woman. It'll hurt her."

"She'll stand it. You will make of that the Imperial Seal of Russia!"

McNally nodded. "The black, two-headed eagle? Sure."

The big man seemed surprised. He growled something into his beard. McNally was studying the design now, forgetting the woman and the bizarre setting. There were angles and angles to this mad night, but he had to take one hurdle at a time. Whether Ken McNally or Needle Mike, he had an idea that he was in sympathy with the scheme to change that Chinese ideograph. Changing it was a challenge to his skill.

"It's a big job," he grumbled. "You gotta give me lots of time."

The Russian muttered something. "Begin!" he said.

McNally was already in action. He spread his instruments, picked up the four-pointed needle and filled the reservoir with ink. His brow furrowed with concentration. There would have to be plenty of fill-in and that would be hard on the girl. He took a pencil from the case to make a rough outline guide.

AT THE first touch, the girl flinched and McNally could feel her flesh hardening in anticipation of the needle-thrust. The older woman who acted as guardian and chaperon moved closer to him as he spoke to the girl soothingly.

They were suspicious, these Russians, and he was in for a tough time of it. He turned with a snarl.

"You go to crowding me now and I'm likely as not to slip, not that it's my hide—"

The girl tried to call out without lifting her head from the pillows. Her voice was muffled but the sound of it brought a gleam to McNally's eyes. He felt the other two move back and then the needle bit.

The girl gave one sharp cry, her flesh quivered—and after that she lay like a statue.

Sweat covered McNally's forehead and the gleaming needle moved deftly, swiftly, surely, over the ideographs. He was used to this work and usually his patients were willing and made of tough stuff. But this flesh was soft and young and tender. He could feel the girl biting at the pillow in which her head was buried. But after that first cry, she was patient. Behind him the other two stood. They might have been furniture for all of the evidence they gave of life.

An hour passed and the eagle was taking form.

McNally put down the needle, flexed his fingers. They were not particularly cramped and he could have continued, but he wanted to give the girl a respite for a moment. The strain on her must have been terrific.

Furious at the interruption the huge Russian let out a string of curses in his native tongue and whipped an automatic from his pocket. "Get on with it!" he snarled. "Rest later—both of you—if you must. Now—there is little time—"

"Geez," McNally mumbled in his character of Needle Mike, "this's a tough job, mister." And with a show of spirit, "This ain't no ditch I'm diggin' an' if you don't like the way I do it—"

He broke off hastily and picked up the needle once more as the Russian started to advance on him, an expression of bitter, contemptuous hatred clouding the massive one's face. The Russian smiled mirthlessly, pocketed his weapon and stepped back in the shadows once more as the needle began its work again. Through it all the girl hadn't made a sound.

An hour and a half! Two hours! McNally's muscles really ached now from the cramped position, his eyes burned and he had to stop every few minutes to wipe his sweating hands. The girl had ceased to bite down and he had an idea that she was in a faint. It was better so. He cursed at length and rose groggily to his feet.

"That's it!" he said raspingly. The two behind him strained to see.

The girl's flesh was stained and swollen and discolored, but there was no blood. A craftsman in the ancient art prides himself that he spills no blood. McNally had not slipped once. He heard the Russian snort with disappointment and he shrugged.

"Looks blurry now. They all do. It's a good job. In a week or ten days, it'll flatten out—clean outlines—'s O.K.—"

The woman was bending over the girl and McNally felt the iron grip bite into his wrist again. He was spun around and pushed unceremoniously into the other room. There was a table in there with a small lamp on it. The Russian took a pen and a few sheets of paper out of the drawer.

"You will give me a receipt for the money I paid you."

"It wasn't enough."

The big man's eyes glowed. It was as though some other personality within him was glaring out. "You will not talk. You will write. Write it that you have changed a tattoo design on a girl's hip to a Russian eagle. Draw the design that you changed on the receipt."

The Russian still spoke slowly with emphasis on each word, but he got the idea over that he was not to be trifled with. It was not McNally's moment. He shrugged his shoulders, sat down and wrote rapidly. When he laid the pen down, he came to his feet. The Russian reached out for the receipt and McNally hobbled across the room to where he saw pale light reflected on tile.

"Bathroom," he muttered. "I'm all in."

**FOR A** moment, with the bathroom door closed behind him, McNally was content to rest and give his muscles time to relax into their normal position. Then he reached down and unfastened the device which kept his leg stiff. He had to work the leg up and down to get the blood circulating. His hands, too, were stiff and he let the cold water run over them. He clenched and unclenched them rapidly and turned to the door.

"Now, my Russian friend," he said grimly.

He stepped out and the man advanced to meet him. McNally took the first half dozen steps in the shuffling limp of Needle Mike, then he dropped into a crouch and moved with the lithe swiftness of a jungle cat. His right fist dropped to his waist, his left flicked out and then the right slashed over like a weighted lance.

The Russian had no time to cry out, no time even to be surprised. The fist took him squarely on the button and McNally's weight was behind it, scientifically thrown weight that was timed beautifully in the throwing. Rubber came suddenly into the man's legs and McNally saw his eyes cross. As he pitched forward, McNally put his arms out for him. The weight of the man almost crushed him but he let him down softly and stepped back. He was blowing on his knuckles.

"A glass jaw," he said. "I'd have bet on it. These big bulls can't stand it."

The receipt was lying on the floor where the Russian had dropped it and McNally picked it up. He didn't know why the man had wanted it, but there was no legitimate reason why he should have it. He tucked it away in his vest pocket.

"Just in case—" he said.

McNally made fast work of trussing up the Russian. He had the man tied tight with sailor knots and a gag rammed into place before the fog left the man's eyes. He stepped away from him and glided to the door that led into the other room. He had no indecision about what he had to do.

The police would already be making inquiries about him. If he had been able to return to his own home or to the dance, he could have explained the card with some story about consulting the Jap about a portrait. That bridge was burned. A man in evening clothes had fled the scene of the murder and had done violence to a cop. The police would not respect social position now unless he could offer something else. He didn't want to face a grilling with the kind of a story that he had to offer.

The only solution was to deliver the murderers up to the police in a manner that would leave him out. And he had to do that without involving Sonia.

That was the job. His brain had been busy on a plan while his needles were biting the black eagle of the Czars into the girl's flesh. If the gods were with him, he had a chance. His big card was the fact that he had recognized Blinker Owen.

At the door to the other room, he paused. Very gently, his fingers turned the knob. The door opened softly to a mere slit. He could see the bed and the broad back of the woman who bent over it. The girl was sobbing softly. The woman said something to her and turned. McNally closed the crack of the door and waited. He could hear the soft slither of the woman's feet across the rug and, for a moment, he was afraid that she was going to enter the room in which he crouched.

He breathed a sigh of relief when he heard the other door open. She was probably going downstairs for a drink or something that the girl wanted. He eased the door open softly once more, waited until he felt that the woman had ample time to put distance behind her, then called, softly: "Sonia!"

**THE GIRL** on the bed jerked upright, drawing the covers close about her with a frantic, alarmed gesture. Her face was a dead-white oval frame for her wide, dark eyes as she stared out of the circle of light into the shadows. McNally played those shadows. It was not time yet for the girl to see Ken McNally in the guise of Needle Mike.

"Stay where you are, Sonia," he whispered. "It's Ken. Can you get away from that woman? The big Russian is safe—"

The girl's hand had moved to her throat. She looked dazed, frightened. "Why, oh why? How—"

"Never mind the questions. I'll get a cab and cruise in front. You've got to get away. It's life or death, Sonia. Can you?"

"I can—yes—" Her voice was shaky. "But—"

"That's all I wanted to know." McNally faded back into the room. He wanted to leave her with a question on her lips. She'd follow him for an answer to it. He didn't pretend to know much about women, but he knew that much. She had recognized his voice, so she wouldn't be afraid to come. All that he had to do was to get out and get a cab.

He heard the woman reascending the stairs and he waited until she entered the next room. The house was unearthly quiet. The Russian was trying hard to wiggle out of his bonds, but McNally didn't think that the man would succeed in making much noise. The rugs were thick and the big body didn't have much freedom of movement. McNally tested the bonds once more to make sure before he left. The glare of the Russian was like that of a devil out of the pit. His face was distorted.

"Cheer up," McNally whispered. "If I was half as hard-boiled as I'd like to be, I'd crack your skull before I left you."

He remembered the gun the Russian had pulled before and reached in the big man's coat. McNally pocketed the weapon, then moved, as silent as his own shadow, to the door.

There was no one in the hall and he slipped down the stairs unchallenged. He was surprised when he stepped out on the street, to find himself less than a block from Forest Park; he had expected to be in some out-of-the-way corner of town. Within a block, he caught a cruising taxi. The hacker looked at him curiously and McNally did not forget that he was still Needle Mike. He had the leg stiffening device in his pocket but he walked with the limp that was characteristic of the man that he was supposed to be.

"I got a little dough and a little job, brother," he said hoarsely. "Are we together?"

The hacker spat. "Yeah. If the dough ain't too little and if I don't have to foul any cops."

McNally passed over the ten spot that he got from the Russian. "Maybe I don't want any change, maybe I do," he said.

"O.K. Your credit's good for ten bucks worth."The driver pocketed the ten. He was a lean, hatchet-faced youth with a hard eye. McNally climbed in.

"You got a tow line?"

"Yeah. We pick up a little extra sometimes pulling fellows that's stuck. You got a stalled bus someplace?"

"Naw. I just want to buy the tow line off ya'."

The hacker chewed on that. His expression showed that he was certain that his passenger was a burglar, but he shrugged after a moment of thought, and spat.

"Lift the back seat. The line's in there. And bang goes seven bucks of that ten."

McNally grunted as he reached under the seat and hauled out the line. It had a hook on one end and a loop on the other. As far as opinions went, he was even up with the man in the front seat. The hacker was a burglar, too. The line wasn't worth over three bucks. The taxi rolled slowly.

"Up to the corner and circle back. Keep doing it every two blocks till we pick up a lady."

The hacker nodded. It was an easy way to run up three dollars on the motor and it was none of his business if a crummy-looking old gimp in a ragged overcoat and dirty shirt wanted to be a gay blade. He got a shock, however, when McNally snapped him into the curb.

SONIA SLIPPED out of the shadows; a slender vision in light gray with a wisp of a hat sliding down toward one ear, dark eyes wide out of the pale oval of her face. There was the poise of an empress in the girl's carriage, an aura of something indefinable about her that the hacker summed up in one word—class. He threw a bewildered look back at McNally and sighed; then he opened the door. The girl drew back when she had one foot in the cab, a look of sudden terror in her face.

"It's all right, Sonia. Get in. I'll explain—"

At the sound of McNally's voice, she let her breath out in a faint, half-strangled "Oh" and stepped in. Her eyes were still bewildered, her attitude half defensive. McNally smiled. He leaned forward and gave an address to the driver, an address just one block from Sakamoto's studio. Then, very deliberately, he closed the glass partition that isolated the driver in his cubicle. Sonia was staring at him wonderingly.

It was no time for polite fencing. "Sonia," he said, "you wouldn't tell me facts the last time I talked to you. You can't afford not to tell me now. I want to know just why you sent me to Sakamoto and how you knew that he was to be killed—*now!*"

"But you—you—the way you are dressed—you are—"

"I'm Needle Mike, the tattoo artist. Yes. And I have just needled a Russian eagle on your hip."

It was brutally direct. The girl flushed and shrank back into the corner of the cab. Her white teeth gleamed for a moment as she bit down on her lip; then she tossed her head defiantly.

"All right. You're Jeff's friend. I can't stop you from telling him anything you find out. Maybe you won't think I'm fit for him. I'll tell you anyway, You know too much. Maybe you understand too little."

Her words were rushing out; bitter, disillusioned. McNally knew that she considered him a spy who had played her false. He gripped her fingers. "Hold it, girl. I'm in this with you; way in. Nobody in the world but you knows about my being Needle Mike. I'm matching trust with trust. I'm not judging you and I'm not telling anybody anything—but I saw that portrait at Sakamoto's. He wanted fifty thousand for it!"

She straightened slowly. "I never posed for that," she said. "He faked it! He was blackmailing me with it!"

McNally looked at her thoughtfully. "He had the ideograph right and he had it in the right place."

The girl's face flamed. "He should. He put it there himself."

McNally was startled. "Oh!" he said.

The girl gestured fiercely. "No. Not 'Oh' in that tone. I was a little girl, a very little girl."

She took a handkerchief and worried it between her fingers. Her eyes were savage. "My father was a general in the armies of the Czar, not a court general with a title—my father commanded troops." Her head was high now. "The revolutionists had no mercy. They—they killed him. I was a child and my mother was young, lovely."

The taxi rolled along through the streets of St. Louis, but the girl was far away; looking the long way back into the past. "It was a hard time for women, particularly women of officers. There was no hope for us at all. My mother would have been degraded by drunken beasts. A Japanese officer intervened. He had influence and he had men at his back. He took us away. He—he was better than the mob."

"That officer was Sakamoto?"

"Yes. He was not a bad man. He had queer ideas of what belonged to him—of what he could do to people—of what his rights were. He didn't marry my mother. He didn't want to marry her. He put the mark on me. I was to be his when I grew up. He wanted to marry me, I think. He did not want me to belong to anyone else."

**McNALLY THOUGHT** of those ideographs. He saw them suddenly with the meaning that the Jap put into them; not as "a woman in prison," but as a woman held safe within a stockade, locked away from others—*his*. Seeing them like that, he saw Sakamoto differently, too. The man would not consider his demands blackmail. If someone else was to have the girl—Jeff for instance—he would have to pay ransom for her, not blackmail. The girl was locked within a promise, or a pledge, or a dedication, or some such vague thing. The girl's voice broke a little.

"My mother sent me to school. She got a little money for me. Then she died. I learned English from American nuns. I came to America. I didn't see Sakamoto for years. Now he is—"

"Was." McNally nodded his head gravely. "He's dead. Didn't you know?"

"Dead?" She spun on him. "No. I thought the tattooing was to foil him, to make the picture meaningless. If he is dead, I—"

McNally frowned. "That's what I've been wondering about. They may have been worried because they didn't get the picture; but they are making a try for it themselves tonight and—"

The girl ripped her handkerchief into shreds. "The beasts!" she said. "They would betray me. Boris was an officer in my father's regiment!"

"The big one?"

"Yes. I fear him. He is not human. Michael is low-born, a renegade. He served Boris once. They pretend allegiance because I am who I am, the Countess Sonia, but—"

"You think they'll blackmail you if you marry Jeff?"

She was silent for a moment; then she sobbed. "Yes. But I won't marry him. They'd bleed him through me. Our people are like that. Women belong to men always and they serve them with money or with favors forever. There is no escape; not ever—"

McNally's eyes were narrow, brooding. He was thinking of Sakamoto. There had been no escape from him either, but the Russians had solved that in their own way. Russian flesh was as vulnerable as Japanese. His hand clenched into a fist.

It was clear to him now why the big Russian had wanted a receipt. It was in character with a man who planned an emergency out when he planned a murder. Failure to get Sakamoto's portrait would mean police publicity which would rum Sonia as an asset to blackmailers. They might not get the painting. If they did, McNally's receipt would still identify Sonia as the girl despite the reworked design. Their hold would be unbroken.

He swore softly and the hacker slid the panel back. The taxi slithered into the curb. "Three dollars and a dime," he said. "Yuh owe me a dime."

# CHAPTER FIVE
# UNDER THE SKYLIGHT

**T**HERE WERE two lighted windows in the studio apartment house in which Sakamoto had died, one on the ground floor and one on the second floor. The top floor was ominously dark. McNally and the girl strolled by on the opposite side of the street. The girl's eyes were glowing with a strange light. McNally, looking grotesquely fat by reason of the tow-rope that was wound around his middle under his coat, was trying to send her home. She lived only a block and a half from the spot at which they had left the taxi.

"It's no use, Ken," she said, "I'm going with you. I got you into this. If anything else is going to happen, it will happen to me."

"You'll get in my way. I don't know, myself, what I'll do. I want to catch those lads robbing the safe if I can."

"They may be gone."

"I don't think so. The police would be around for a long time. They'd have to wait till things quieted down." He took out the old turnip that was Needle Mike's timepiece. "About two thirty now," he figured. "Will you go home?"

"No."

He swore under his breath. If she hadn't known him in his adopted identity, he'd have been tough enough; but he couldn't take the hardness of Needle Mike into conversations with people who knew Ken McNally. It made him mad that he couldn't.

"All right," he said. "You asked for what you're going to get. In this show, you'll be just another man to me. I'll treat you like a male helper. No gallantry."

Sonia's white teeth flashed. "Perfect," she said.

They approached the alley carefully. It was black except for the pale overflow of light that seeped in from the street—and it took time to accustom one's eyes to that. Shadows in the shadows, they moved down the line of fences. There was no policeman back here to be knocked out this time. The skeleton shape of the fire-escape loomed above them. McNally looked at it thoughtfully and unrolled the tow-rope. The ladder was of the weighted type and remained on the underside of the first-story landing unless pressed down by the weight of an occupant.

McNally made three casts of the hook on the end of the tow-line. The third try hooked the ladder rung with a dull metallic *pinnnnng*. McNally held his breath and the girl froze to immobility beside him. They waited several minutes and there was no alarm, no sound of motion. Carefully, McNally hauled in his line. The ladder came down.

Sonia kicked her high-heeled shoes off and picked her skirts up above her knees. She went up the ladder with a fireman's skill and without any of a fireman's clumsy noise-making. McNally kept pace with her. The back of the building was dark, as it had been when he descended the escape a few hours ago. On the top-floor landing they both came to a halt.

They could, of course, go through the window into the hall and thence to the door of the apartment. If they were wrong in their guess, they might walk into the arms of a police guard. If they were right, they would have to crash the most direct way. McNally looked at the drain along which he had escaped. In the pale light of the stars, he could see the bulged places where his weight had pulled the metal out of line. He could go back over that route to the kitchen window, but he remembered that he had had to stand on tip-toe to reach the drain from that window-sill. It would be much tougher trying to get back onto it. The roof remained—and there were fewer arguments against that means of entry than against the others. He waved to the thin ladder that was riveted into the side of the building.

"All the way!" he said.

SONIA NEVER hesitated. A slim, boyish creature, she went scampering to the top—poised for a moment in outline against the sky and then slid from view. McNally slid over the roof edge after her and he was still carrying his tow-rope. He didn't have to warn her to be careful. She was flat on her stomach and creeping toward the skylight. There was a pale yellow light from below that gave a peculiar shine to the panels. McNally was shoulder to shoulder with her when she raised herself on her hands to look down into the studio.

One of the panes of glass had been cut out and that explained the banging of the shade before Sakamoto was killed. The Russian on the roof had had to cut through glass to reach the catch and he probably released the shade accidentally when he opened the way of escape for the killer. The missing pane was a card against him now.

Voices drifted up from below and the two on the roof could hear as well as see.

The shades were tightly drawn on the windows of the studio room and the small desk lamp was lighted. In the narrow circle of light, McNally could see Blinker Owen plainly and the blurred outline of the other man. Blinker had been working on the safe-tumblers but he was half turned around now.

"I don't like this can," he whined. "I don't like it at all."

"You can't open it?" The other man's voice was menacing.

"Geez, yes. I kin open it if you gimme time. I just don't like it. It's some furrin make and it's screwy somehow. I kin feel it, somebody's been duking it up."

"Bah! You open that or I cut your throat!"

The man's face was starkly revealed for a moment in the circle of light; broad, brutal, vicious. Sonia's fingers tightened on McNally's arm.

"Michael," she whispered.

McNally nodded. He'd had an idea that that would be Michael. From what he'd seen of him in the car, and from what he could gather from the man's crouched position below, Michael was short and thick-bodied and built like a junior-model beer truck.

Blinker Owen was at work again, beads of sweat on his forehead and an unintelligible whisper on his lips. McNally began to feel some of the man's anxiety, his sense of impending doom. To break the tension of silent watching, he amused himself by trying to pick out other details in the room below—beyond the soft circle of light. He did not want to intervene until the safe was open and the portrait in a position to be seized. Sonia no longer bore the brand of the "woman in prison" but it was better that the portrait pass out of existence. The trail from Sakamoto to Sonia might not be hard to follow if one got started on it.

Once accustomed to the light below, his eyes picked up objects easily. There was something out of place near the doorway that led into the reception hall, something that hadn't been there before; a low, dark something on the ground. It took several minutes of concentrated attention before it began to assume any recognizable form. When he recognized what it was, he had to choke down the exclamation that rose to his lips. The adventure had suddenly become more precarious than before.

The dark sprawled thing was the figure of a uniformed man, a policeman. It lay face down and it was terribly still!

He had been right, then, in his guess. The police had hung around and the two had had to wait before breaking in. Moreover, the police had left a man on guard. That poor devil on the floor was he.

McNally's train of thought was broken off by a sharp shrill exclamation from Blinker Owen. "Got 'er, guvnor. That's the click!"

Michael half straightened from his crouch, leaning forward impatiently. "Open it, fool!"

**BLINKER HALF** turned to the safe again. His face looked strained. There was an unnamed fear in his face. He hadn't felt right about that box and his was a superstitious craft. He rubbed one hand nervously against his shirt.

With an impatient snort, Michael gripped his shoulder and hurled him aside. One thick hand fastened on the knob. There was a jerk, a stabbing flash of flame, a thundering report.

Michael threw his arms out wildly and stepped back. He kept stepping back like a man off balance for several steps. His distorted face turned upward toward the skylight and all expression faded from it suddenly. For a moment the light reflected from the buttons on the man's coat and one of them was missing. McNally made an instinctive movement toward his pocket. He knew where that button was and where it had been lost!

Michael fell on his back and there was a round hole under his eye. McNally knew that he would not be getting up again. Blinker Owen was struggling to his feet, his eyes wide.

"Geez!" he muttered. "Geez!" He was paralyzed with the awful fulfillment of his hunch and he did nothing but stand staring at the fallen giant. McNally slid back the cover of the skylight, but he was slow. Sonia wiggled past him like a cat.

"Remember," she whispered, "treat me like a man."

Her body twisted through the skylight with swift dexterity and her fingers slid momentarily along the edge. She hung for a split second, then her body was turning as she let go.

Like a hurled sandbag, she came down on the shoulders of Blinker Owen—and Blinker folded.

McNally saw Sonia come to her feet like a cat and whirl toward the open safe. On the point of dropping through the skylight after her, he thought suddenly of his plan. That wouldn't do. The infernal racket in the apartment would bring intruders and it wouldn't do to be seen going up through the skylight. Even a dull-witted pursuer could head them off before they got off the roof. Besides, the skylight must be closed and the men in the apartment must bear the brunt of whatever happened in the apartment. McNally did not intend to remain a hare for the hounds all his life.

He slid the skylight cover back in place. Turning on the balls of his feet, he was across the roof like a sprinter. It was the work of a moment to fasten the hook of his towline into the drain above the kitchen window and less than a moment's work to swing over and down. His toe hooked the sill and he was over. He knew his way now and he went back through the rooms without hesitation.

On the threshold of the studio, he came to a dead stop.

Sonia had turned away from the safe with the rolled canvas in her hands but she hadn't gone far. Shaken out of his paralysis rather than hurt by the weight of the girl, Blinker Owen was on his feet. His criminal mind alive to the fact that the canvas must be valuable if men died for it, he was remembering that one Russian lived—

He had one hand now on the girl's throat while the other tore at the canvas. Voices sounded on the stairs, voices that changed into sharp yells of alarm, a terrified cry— Action and noise blended into one reel of high-pressure drama in which things seemed to happen instantaneously.

**McNALLY WAS** plunging forward when the broken door was heaved aside and a tornado seemed to burst upon the apartment. Blinker Owen spun halfway around, his face white in the half-circle of light. There was a whining sound and the light flashed on hurled steel. Blinker opened his mouth once—and only once.

A thin blade, travelling like an arrow, went to that open mouth as to a target. The point of the steel came out of his neck as he plunged forward and the man who killed by one mighty throw of singing steel, was charging behind the throw; charging as he had done when he killed Sakamoto—blind with the same lashing fury as before, the fury in which he had smashed McNally out of his way.

He didn't see McNally now at all. He saw only his dead partner, the man he had just killed and the girl with the roll of canvas. There was no crowd following him and McNally could picture the way this giant had ripped through the curious people out in the hall. They wouldn't be coming in immediately, but—

The sirens were wailing again on Skinker Road.

Boris was babbling curses and the girl shrank back from him. "Traitoress! You killed Michael!" His big arms reached for her and McNally shouted: "Stop! I'll shoot!"

He had the automatic up and the snarl in his voice got through the Russian's savage rage. The man's heels skidded along the rug and he pulled his head down against his shoulders with a swift movement that betrayed his anticipation of a shot in the back. He was turning as he stopped. At sight of McNally, his lips flattened against his teeth and something came into his eyes that was less like fear than like a wild animal's consciousness of impending death. Then he saw the gun.

From the look on his face and from the sudden shifting of his body, McNally was warned. He pressed the trigger, just in case. The gun clicked and there was no report. The giant hurled himself forward.

McNally had never thought to examine the weapon, but the Russian had known that it was worthless. Maybe he only carried it for a bluff or a club—maybe he had run out of ammunition. McNally didn't know and he had no time to wonder. He clubbed the gun and lashed out with it and the big Russian came in upon him.

The steel raked Boris down the forehead and brought the blood gushing—but it never even slowed him. One great fist caught McNally in the side and all but broke him in two. As he spun to one side, he lost his balance and went over a chair in a half-somersault. His brain was clear but there was pain inside him and he couldn't straighten up.

Boris was coming for him in a blind, slaughtering rage that took no account of possible police intervention or of anything else. Sonia had a vase and she hurled it, but Boris shook it off and kept coming. McNally tripped on the chair, reeled behind the desk of Sakamoto and saw death charging at him.

He was outweighed sixty pounds and even if he had not been, no boxing skill or ordinary strength would have prevailed against the insane strength of a giant like this Russian. The man hurled himself at the desk and McNally remembered something. It might be a one-time stunt or it might not. His hand closed on the ornament that graced the desk of Sakamoto. He tugged at it hard.

There was a thundering report and a flash of flame from the contrivance. Boris backed up one step and there was a look of ghastly surprise on his face as his hands dropped to clasp his middle. McNally didn't wait to see him fall. He vaulted the desk and gripped Sonia's icy hand.

"Let's go," he said.

There were pounding feet on the stairs.

**IT WAS** a swift and silent race through the apartment. The rope swung before the kitchen window. McNally boosted the girl up, but she shook her head—her lips white.

"I'm not man enough," she said chokily.

McNally didn't hesitate. He went past her and up—hand over hand to the roof. With a quick flip, he took the hook out of the drain and reversed the tow-line. There was a loop on the other end and he sent it curling down like a lariat.

Sonia caught it and he could feel her weight when she went out on the sill. He took two turns of the rope around a chimney and started to haul her up. His muscles creaked and there was fire in his aching side but he managed it somehow.

Together they sped to the fire-escape and down. The neighborhood was awakening and there were more sirens on Skinker Road. They hit the alley and all was dark and deserted. It was not time for a dragnet yet. The police thought that they had made the round-up in the apartment. The place was full of bodies and McNally had thrown the gun on the floor. He wore gloves, this trip, so there were no prints. It would look like a fight over the spoils.

Sonia still clutched the canvas to her breast. McNally steered her to the far side of the alley. "Over the fence," he panted. "It's less than two blocks to your house. We'll make it."

Wordlessly, she obeyed and when the door of her own home closed behind her, she fell against him and wound her arms hard around him.

"Ken—Ken," she said. "You were wonderful. If I didn't love Jeff so—"

He took her shoulders and held her off from him. "If I didn't admire that old world-beater, too," he said softly, "I might—but—"

She looked at him with something that glowed in her eyes. "You—"

He didn't let her say it. He felt suddenly foolish. It was all right to do things; it was something else to chatter about them afterwards. He shrugged his shoulders as though to shake off the load of praise that she had been about to heap on him.

"Sakamoto licked your Russians," he said, "I didn't. That lad was thoughtful. There was some gadget on that safe that disconnected the gun when he opened it himself, but—well, Michael never found it. The device in the desk shot Boris—"

Sonia turned away as though she would hide her expression. "We have a saying in Russia," she said slowly, "that one never knows when a Japanese is dead."

She walked to the open fireplace across the room and put crumpled paper and kindling under the canvas. There was a flicker of yellow as she struck a match, but she did not turn around until the flicker had become a roaring flame and the picture of the branded girl was ashes. Ken McNally was sitting in a big chair looking at her.

"I'm staying," he said, "until the neighborhood quiets down."

"And then?" Her eyes were wistful.

He lighted a cigarette. "Then I'm going to Chicago. Ken McNally is supposed to be there and I mustn't let Needle Mike make a liar of him."

# THE TATTOOED CURSE

THERE, FROM THE SMALL OF THE IRISHMAN'S BACK IT GRINNED— LEERING BLASPHEMY, BORN OF INK AND NEEDLE—THE WINGED SATAN. WHAT DID IT SIGNIFY? WHY SHOULD O'DOUL BEG FOR ITS REMOVAL—AND YOUNG BEN GODDARD, ON THE OTHER HAND, LIE PASSIVE, WILLINGLY SUBMIT TO THAT SHE-DEVIL'S CRUEL JABS, WHILE ITS GHASTLY TWIN WAS TRACED UPON HIS OWN LIVING FLESH?

# CHAPTER ONE
# THE WALKING CORPSE

**I**T WAS a dirty night. Ken McNally stood inside the door of his shabby tattooing parlor on South Broadway, St. Louis, and looked out into the sleet-beaten street. The sign on the frost-coated window read Needle Mike—Tattooing.

There was a faintly ironical twist to "Mike's" lips as he reflected that he might be spending a night like this in the warm library of his father's palatial home on Lindell Boulevard. There he would be Kenneth McNally, heir to a couple-odd millions.

He turned and hobbled across the dingy room, his right leg dragging stiffly. He wouldn't have that limp up on Lindell Boulevard. The limp belonged to Needle Mike and was accounted for by an ingenious little device of cork and rubber that held the knee stiff.

From the cracked mirror above his desk, the red-eyed, powder-burned, dirty face of Needle Mike looked out at him. That was not the face, either, that Ken McNally saw in his own shaving mirror. There was a mild irritant that made his eyes red and it was an easy matter to touch a few old measle scars into powder burns. The gray in his hair, too, was chemically induced.

The reason for it all? McNally had come down here to the fringe of the underworld with the same urge that other

rich men... men take to Africa, India, and the far places where they hunt big game. He wanted adventure and this was it; here in the half-world that lay behind the newspaper headlines.

**THE WIND** whistled in the distance, built up momentum and hurled the sleet like shot against his window. McNally heard his door creak and he turned. A shabby, coatless figure reeled into the room and stood coughing

She made a blood-rite of her work.

with his back to the door. A few evening papers fell from under his arm and made a sodden heap on the ragged rug.

"Mike, I gotta rest a bit. I can't take it like this storm can give it."

McNally grunted in the approved fashion of Needle Mike. True to the character that he lived, he offered neither welcome nor argument. Skeeter belonged to the neighborhood and that gave him a right to come into any place that was open. Broadway, south of Market Street was that kind of a place. His eyes followed the shivering newsboy as the lad crossed the room to the odorous little gas heater.

Not more than twenty, Skeeter was already an old man. He sold papers and he would probably never do anything else. He was thin and scrawny and cursed with a chronic cough. His features were a conglomerate blur and one eye seemed slightly lower than the other. On the social side, he was a problem that nobody could solve. Always pathetic, he had had more than his share of help. McNally knew of three different overcoats that Skeeter had had this winter; but anything that came his way was a crap-game stake and nothing else. He continued to be an object of pity.

Skeeter moved closer to the heater. "I'm sleepy, Mike," he chattered. "Hardly any sleep. Sat up nearly all last night with a sick drunk—"

"Yeah? Why?"

"He wouldn't go to sleep. When he did, he only had a dollar and a quarter."

McNally shrugged. Skeeter's morals, like his habits, were flexible. You could do nothing with them. Skeeter coughed harshly. "You'll be open for an hour or two yet, Mike. How's to grab a nap in your bed? I'm booked for a hallway tonight. No coupons."

McNally hobbled across the room before be replied— the perfect picture of a testy old sailor turned tattooer, a man who doesn't have to be polite to anyone. "O.K.," he growled, "but you better not leave any immigrants in it. I'll have your neck."

Skeeter laughed and made unsteadily for the back room. McNally rubbed his hands over the gas heater. It seemed strange to him to be living this way, to be swapping crude banter with crude people; strange, but exciting. His boyhood had been too sheltered. This was his Treasure Island and his Robinson Crusoe. Here, things happened to him—unpredictable things. He didn't worry about the bed. He might even leave Skeeter in it. He never slept in it himself. He did his sleeping on the long couch in this big room.

He rose to pick up Skeeter's sodden papers and stiffened as the door shook under a sudden assault. His eyes narrowed. Most people knocked reasonably or just walked in. Whoever was outside, tonight, went after a door like a rookie bull on a raid. McNally hobbled over and swung the door wide.

A BIG, red-faced man with a fur coat pulled up to his chin was leaning against the jamb. At sight of McNally, he straightened up. "You're the tattooer?" His voice was faintly tinged with the brogue of Erin and high-pitched for a man of his bulk.

"I am—"

"Then let me in for the love of God!" The man lurched forward and went past McNally into the room. There was an unholy urgency in him as though he had rested against the door to conserve his strength against this burst of energy. A flaky sleet of snow showered from the fur coat and sizzled when it fell within the heated area about the gas appliance. Words rushed from the man in short spurts.

"Ye can put on tattoo. Can ye take it off?"

"Most of it."

"Then I've a job for ye. It's a curse I have on my back, the devil's own brand—and work, man, as ye never worked—"

He fumbled in his pocket and came up with a bulging wallet which he threw on the instrument table. "Your fee's there! Whatever it is, I'll not argue—"

McNally didn't argue either. "Get your coat and shirt off," he growled.

"Lock the door first and let no one in till ye're through!"

McNally turned and threw the catch on the door. He did not look directly at the other man. He was busy with his own thoughts. The thing that he had always feared had happened. A man out of his other life had come to the tattoo parlor. He knew this big Irishman and he had to be on guard now that the man did not recognize him. The man had turned away and was removing his clothes with frantic haste, his breath labored. Some awful shock had done this to Tom O'Doul.

McNally opened the cabinet and selected his instruments and the reagents that he would use. It would be easier to change the design than remove it if the man consented. His mind raced. He knew the entire tribe of O'Doul. The man in the fur coat was a highly successful contractor, a widower with two sons in college. He had money and an enviable standing in a community that prided itself on its conservatism. He had twice refused a nomination for mayor.

McNally turned.

The big man had stripped to the waist and was lying face down on the cot, his fur coat wadded under him like a cushion, his hand pillowed in the crook of his arm. McNally swore.

"Hey, I don't operate over there. You gotta come over here by the table—"

"I'll stay here and will ye hurry, man—"

The "ye" of an Irishman under stress kept creeping into his speech and it told McNally as much as anything else that it was no time for haggling over details. He limped across the room and stopped short.

In brazen outline, on the man's back, was the grinning face of Satan, two wings spreading out behind it like the wings of a bat.

O'Doul's voice came muffled, "Ye see it, man. It's hell's own brand. I can't—" His voice choked. " 'Tis a curse. Remove it and be quick!"

"It's easier and quicker to work it over," McNally suggested.

"Change it, ye mean?"

"Yes."

"To what?"

McNally's lips tightened. "I'll put a cross over it and blot it out—"

The man on the cot shivered. "The crucifix. Yes. It's only right. The cross in the grinning face of him. For God's sake, man, do it now!"

McNally didn't reason with an Irishman's fear and his own fears had subsided. It was not likely that O'Doul in a normal condition would recognize him in his Needle Mike make-up; so, there was practically no chance of discovery with the man in his present upset condition. With a shrug of his shoulders, McNally set to work.

**HE WASHED** the surface with alcohol and with a preparation of his own, then selected a three-point Burmese needle. The extension on his electric-needle set would not reach to the cot but he rarely used the electric machine anyway, except for stencil work which he disliked. He was a fast hand worker and he'd been an artist of sorts before he'd studied tattoo.

The man on the cot never quivered when the needles bit. The long muscles in his back tightened, but he made no sound.

Swiftly, McNally boxed the winged devil under the sign of the cross. He derived a certain satisfaction out of the job and he worked at concentrated speed, his mind only vaguely bothered by the origin of the design and the possible "curse" connected with it.

The man under the needles groaned once. "Will ye be long now?" he asked.

"Not long. It's a big job. I've got the cross drawn."

"Ye got the face of him covered?"

"Not yet."

The man shuddered and lay still. McNally worked grimly. He was hurting O'Doul and he knew it, but he did not suggest a respite. The idea of speed was uppermost in the Irishman's mind and the Irish have endurance. With sure fingers, he worked a bleeding heart over the grinning face and spread the leaves of sorrow over the vicious bat wings. The sweat was dripping into his own eyes while the wind howled outside. Nearly two hours!

"Ye're done?"

The voice came muffled as McNally paused. McNally wiped the back of his hand across his forehead. "Done," he said.

"What does it look like?"

"I'll show you only it won't be clean for a week—"

"No! Tell me!"

McNally described the cross which he had drawn with a bleeding heart to represent the figure that he did not want to execute hurriedly in tattoo. O'Doul sighed.

"And he's gone entirely, the other one?"

"Gone completely."

"God be praised!" The man's body shuddered along its entire length. McNally wiped his hands, swabbed the design and tapped the man on the shoulder.

"Better get your shirt on."

O'Doul lay unresponsive, his head cradled into the crook of his arm. McNally tapped him again. He frowned and gripped the man's arm. A horrible suspicion came to him with that grip and he lifted the body to one side.

The fur coat was saturated with blood which had pooled under the man's body and a cruel wound just under the heart revealed the outlet for the blood. Thomas O'Doul's eyes were fixed in the unseeing stare of death and McNally let the body drop with a sudden revulsion of feeling.

The man had been a walking corpse when he came in; but, with the stubbornness of the Irish, he had refused to die with the devil's insignia on his back. He'd lain there, dying, and held his soul in his body by sheer will till the job was done. And now—

McNally turned swiftly as a foot scraped behind him. Skeeter was standing there on unsteady legs, his strangely matched eyes fixed curiously upon the body on the cot.

McNALLY STOOD dumbly above the body for several seconds, aware of Skeeter's measuring eyes but incapable of entertaining any thought but that O'Doul was dead. He looked down at his hands. There was blood on one of them and he fumbled with a handkerchief to wipe it off.

"He's dead, Skeeter." His lips felt a little stiff. Skeeter's mouth was puckered as though to whistle but no sound came.

"You're telling me? Why'd you do it, Mike?" There was no shock in Skeeter's voice; merely curiosity.

"You think I did it?"

Skeeter scratched his ear. "He didn't dutch it, did he?"

"I don't know. I didn't see any weapon."

The newsboy shrugged. "I wouldn't ho'd it against you, Mike. How much did he have?" His eyes wandered to the full purse on the table. McNally's jaw set. He'd been forgetting for a few minutes that he was Needle Mike. It would be fatal to forget now.

"I didn't give it to 'im, Skeeter," he said gruffly. "He must have got the shiv before he blundered in here. He didn't want to die with a curse on his back."

"O.K. You're in the clear. You better call the cops." Skeeter's eyes were narrowed. McNally looked at him sharply. He'd been thinking about that himself, remembering the past suspicions that he had stirred up; considering how badly his disguise would stand up at a police station. A man in disguise would have a swell chance if he were caught in a jam. The newspapers would have a carnival with that double life of his, too. He'd be convicted before he came to trial. He shook his head.

"I can't do that, Skeeter."

"No? You got a record?"

"Yeah. One that these cops don't know about yet."

Skeeter studied him for a few seconds, decided to believe him, with reservations, and whistled mournfully as he looked, at the corpse, a new interest in his eyes.

"Mike," he said, "it looks like this stiff did you a dirty trick."

McNally shrugged. "Never mind. He can't do a thing about it. We've got to get him outta sight for a while till I figure what's what. We'll shove that cot in the back room."

Skeeter hesitated, his lean fingers playing with his loose lower lip. He shook his head slowly from side to side. "I guess it's O.K., Mike," he said, "but I'll always swear I never touched him."

"Sure." McNally bent to the cot and, Skeeter helped him roll it. It had casters and the job was fairly easy except for the passage through the narrow doorway into the rear room. The cot had to be tilted there and the corpse steadied against a tendency to roll. They were both panting when they set the cot down beside the bed. McNally wiped his forehead.

**THE BACK** room was poor concealment; and concealment, itself, was a poor device. McNally knew it. His one hope was time. He knew the man's identity and he knew some of his associates. Starting from there, in his own identity as Ken McNally, he might be able to run down the mystery of that symbol on the man's back. If that connected up with the murder, then he had an outside chance of learning something before the cops tied him up with it and closed the channels to further investigation.

Skeeter coughed. "Mike, I—" For the first time, he had looked closely at the tattooed design. He cut his sentence in two. "What was that before it was a cross?"

"A winged devil—"

McNally whirled as he spoke. Somebody was knocking at the front door. Skeeter froze, his hand halfway to his lips. "Let 'em knock, Mike," he said hoarsely. "Don't let 'em in."

McNally felt a certain looseness in the hinges of his knees, but he moved slowly to the door. "No good, Skeeter. The light's on. It'd look suspicious. Some blamed fool might investigate. I'll get rid of 'em—"

There was a small puddle of blood where they had first tilted the cot, a few feet from the door. McNally picked up the soggy bunch of papers that Skeeter had brought in out of the storm and dropped them over the spot. Then he opened the door and took an abrupt step backward.

This caller was a woman!

She came in without an invitation while McNally hesitated; a young woman whose coat collar gleamed with the brilliant jewels of a winter storm. She shook the big collar with a graceful movement of her arms. She had quick, brown eyes that took swift inventory of McNally, flashed by him for a quick survey of the room, and came back to him with a sparkle in their depths.

"I am look for my hosban'. He is come here, no? A beeg man, beeg coat. All fur...." Her hand passed caressingly over the fur of her own big collar. Her accent was Spanish, her creamy complexion suggested the South Seas. McNally's nerves jerked at the description of O'Doul and this woman called him her "hosban'."

His face betrayed nothing of what he thought. He shrugged indifferently. "I never heard of him."

"No?" The girl was searching every cranny of the big room with nervous, darting glances while pretending to turn the full battery of her exquisite attention on the battered-looking hulk of Needle Mike. "Always when he is drunk," she said plaintively, "he gets the picture done on his skin. He weel look terrible does he keep on wit' the drink!"

"Yeah. I'll tell him that if he shows up." McNally tried to maneuver her to the door. He was conscious of the fact that her eyes kept coming back to the closed inner door. She pouted at him.

"You hav' done no work tonight for any wan?"

Her face was guileless but McNally's instruments and inks were in plain sight. Anyone could have told that he had been working. He growled under his breath.

"Sure. I done a job for a punk. He wasn't nobody's husband. He was just a punk. And you'll have to beat it, lady. I'm going to be in trouble with the cops if they see a woman in here, see?"

**SHE WENT** reluctantly. At the door, she turned abruptly and her fingers fastened into McNally's lapel. "Eef he comes, my hosban', you weel not put any more pictures on heem?"

"Naw. Not if he's drunk."

There'd been more than a bit of ham in that last request. The girl had tried to leave him with his suspicions lulled. McNally wasted no more time on her. When he had her safely outside the door, he closed it and threw the lock. He crossed the floor as swiftly as the game leg would let him and burst in upon the nervous Skeeter.

"Kid," he said, "I'm tailing that dame. I gotta hunch. Sit on the lid for me till I get back. Five bucks in it for you if—"

Skeeter grunted derisively. "Five bucks, hell! You'll give me a split on that stiff's dough or—"

"All right. Sit on the lid."

McNally hobbled through the big room, picked up O'Doul's wallet for safety's sake, grabbed a coat off a hook and lunged through the side door that opened to the left of the table into the adjoining locksmith shop which he used as a blind. It was dark in the shop but he knew every foot of it and went unerringly to the door. The lock was well oiled and slid back to his touch.

The girl was nearly a block away and heading south, her body bent against the wind. McNally hugged the shadows and swung off after her.

He didn't know, but the girl looked like a direct lead back to the murder spot. She had wanted to know too much. Now it was McNally's turn to be curious.

# CHAPTER TWO

# DANGEROUS RHYTHM

**T**HE SLEET sliced down at a dirty slant and stung McNally's eyes, made his face feel raw after the first few minutes of buffeting. Up ahead, the girl was having all that she could do to buck it. She did not look back. Either she was too preoccupied to think of the possibility of being followed—or she had a high regard for her own acting ability. Her "hosban'" who always got tattooed when he was "dronk" made a rank story; but how was she to know that it hadn't gone over?

She crossed the street and McNally stayed on his own side for safety's sake. When she came to the third corner below the shop, she turned left abruptly and hurried down the steep, narrow street toward the river. McNally increased his pace. The girl would make better time when she wasn't bucking the wind and she could not go far on that street. It was an old neighborhood and a few short blocks took one to the Mississippi levee.

He had barely turned the corner when she disappeared. Without a single backward glance, she veered sharply across the sidewalk and melted into the thick shadows that engulfed the ancient buildings. McNally's eyes narrowed. She might be brighter than she looked, but he doubted it.

Stepping lightly, he reached the point where she had vanished in a few seconds. There was no sign of life anywhere. The heavy, sighing sound of the river rose from the darkness ahead of him and there were pin-points of light along the levee. Behind him, the storm roared across town. Down here in this pocket between buildings, it was merely wet.

The buildings were a long, gloomy series of black fronts with weatherbeaten signs that were like tombstones over the graves of dead enterprises. The firms that had operated under these signs had flourished before and during the Civil War. The firms and the founders were long since gone and only the buildings remained—black fronts staring sightlessly into dark streets.

In such a spooky atmosphere it was possible to imagine that ghosts would walk or girls vanish, but McNally was hard-headed. He didn't know about ghosts, but he'd never known girls to vanish. Girls usually went somewhere.

He moved past doors against which frozen deposits of sleet had piled. It took no Sherlock Holmes to determine that those doors had not been opened within the past few minutes. Before an area-way that divided two buildings, he came to a halt, his nostrils widening like the nostrils of a hound on a scent. There was a cast-iron gate, but it was ajar and hanging on one hinge. A certain smoothness of the pavement indicated that not one, but many perhaps, had passed through that area-way since the storm broke.

He looked toward the curb. There were tire-tracks, quite a few of them; the spreading tread-marks, near the curb, evidencing slithery stops on the skiddy pavement. He did not step out of the shadows. The block remained black and silent, but he did not chance a hidden observer. He could see enough from the shadows. There was not a car parked in the entire length of the block. He felt a tingle of anticipation run along his spine.

**HE SHRUGGED** his shoulders, worked the stiffness out of his fingers with quick, grabbing movements of his hands and plunged into the areaway. Halfway down its silent length, he stooped over and removed the ovular device that held his leg stiff. There was no telling when he might need his agility more than his disguise.

The areaway was as deserted as the street and so were the small, fenced, rubbish-strewn yards behind the twin buildings. There was no light, but neither was there cover which would conceal a man. McNally had reached the center of the fenced space before he saw the light. It was low down, below the ground level; a thin, knife-edge of light that showed along the edge of a window that was otherwise tightly curtained. He stood silent, looking at it. There was no sound—only the narrow, yellow line that a man could not see from the areaway or from deeper in the yard. His eyes roved upward. The rest of the house was dead shadow against the grayish blur of the blowing sleet. He hitched his belt.

With most houses, a burglar would probably figure on working up from the basement. The treatment indicated, in this case, was to work downward from the roof.

There was a rotten-looking back porch with iron pillars and decorative grill-work. It wasn't a ladder for convenience but a man could go up it. McNally went, the noise of the wind drowning whatever noise he made.

The second-floor windows were shuttered and he let them alone except that they afforded stepping-stones to the floor above, where there was a lot of wood-and-iron gingerbread work that ran around the house like a ledge.

The windows on this floor were shuttered, too, and it was an easy boost on the shutters to the roof itself. There would be a skylight and McNally favored that. It would be sufficiently distant from the basement to make a reasonable amount of racket without detection.

He was cold and stiff when he found the skylight and the roof was slippery. He felt like the last man alive on the top of a frozen and inhospitable world. There was ice on the skylight and the rust and dirt of generations. Shivering in the wind, he tugged and hauled until he felt the gripping ice break loose. With a tug, he jerked the heavy covering from the dark hole in the roof, his nerves jerking to the shriek of old hasps.

Then, from the depths below him, came a screech that was not the protest of old iron, but the full-throated scream of a woman!

So unexpected was it that it almost toppled McNally over the brink. He gripped the rust-coated edge with blue hands and strained to the darkness beneath him, some primitive instinct reproducing the sensation of hairs rising along his back.

The silence had taken back the sound, muffling it, blanketing it, refusing it the dignity of an echo. Tense in the expectation of hearing it again, he reached around the inside edges of the pit. There was no ladder. He would have to drop.

He was wishing for a flashlight but he wasted no time on the wish. With the outside distance as a guide, he estimated that it would not be too much of a drop. He knew of one of these old places that had a stairwell, but he wouldn't risk that chance, either. He would swing his body as he dropped.

One... two... three....

He timed himself to a pendulum swing and then let go, his lithe body twisting. He was still in mid-air when it came again—that long, thin, drawn-out scream that raised his scalp and made his landing on the solid boards an episode without sensation.

**HE HIT** turning, and crouched in the darkness, the scream still beating at his brain. His nostrils quivered and a third shriek merged into the second. With that third cry, however, the shock went out of the sound. Ken's brain now had had time to classify it and he knew it for what it was; not the scream of agony, nor fear, nor terror, but a scream that springs from a woman's throat for no other reason than for the sheer sake of screaming—a shrill sound lacking timbre and tone.

With it, silence came again to the old building. McNally crouched there, while the seconds ticked away, but no one came to investigate; no stairs creaked nor did boards tremble.

The floor was covered with the dust of decades. It blanketed his steps on the stair. The floor below was as forgotten, as empty. Not till he reached the first floor did he smell occupancy. The rooms here were bare of furnishings but they had been swept. There was a definite feel of human life and less of history. A door barred him from the logical continuation of the stairway and he cursed softly. It would be ironic to be balked by locks now and to be forced to make a commotion that he had avoided by Herculean effort a few minutes before. He crept toward the front of the house.

There was another stairway and the door opened to his touch. A warm smell rose to his nostrils; the smell of heat and of humanity. The stairs led down invitingly toward soft light. Step by step he went down, his nerves keyed tight, until he stood in a doorway that commanded a view of the long flagged aisle that ran from the front of the building to the rear.

There were dim lights at either end of the passage, and doors leading off on either side into what apparently were rooms; but still no movement. In this basement, so obviously occupied, the absence of sound was more trying on his nerves than in the bleakness above. He stepped into the passageway and hesitated. There was another flight of stairs—a sub-basement.

Here sound dwelt. He could hear life and movement before he was halfway down the covered stair. Crouching back into the comparative dimness of the stairwell, he could hear the pad of slippered feet and could look across a lighted corridor at a doorway curtained in blue. The footsteps became more distinct and McNally pressed against the side wall of the staircase. He could still look out, and, as the slippered one came into his line of vision, he got a shock.

It was a man dressed in the brown habit of a monk, a cowl hanging back against his shoulder blades!

**THE MAN** in the monk's robe paid no attention to the stairwell. He paused, instead, before the blue curtain and pulled it gently aside, peering in with his body slightly bent. He was a thin, pallid man with bat ears and a head that was completely bald. McNally estimated that a good poke in the right place would put an end to that individual's usefulness.

It was a consoling thought to file for an emergency and he was consoling himself with it when the shriek battered once more against his eardrums; unmuffled now by anything save the thin curtain. There was something unnatural, inhuman about it and he recoiled instinctively. The man before the curtain swore plaintively in a high, sing-song voice.

For a moment the tableau held. Then the monk turned and, still swearing, padded down the corridor. His slippers were as loose as those of a Chinese and they made a distinct patting sound as he walked. McNally grunted.

"Nice of him," he muttered. "I hope all of these monkeys wear 'em. They might just as well carry bells."

He heard the steps pat away into distance before he ventured out. The corridor was clear and a glance sufficed to tell him that this sub-basement was laid out on a different plan than was the basement. The corridor did not run straight through, but angled off after a short distance; probably into other corridors encompassing the room with the blue curtain.

He didn't investigate the system. He was more interested in seeing the room which housed the screaming woman. A swift stride put him across the corridor as he pressed against the curtain, working himself into it between the velvet itself and the wood of the door frame.

He blinked in the soft light and his breath caught at the strangeness of the scene before him.

**HE WAS** looking into a ballroom in miniature, a room thronged with dancers; dancers who were all but naked and who danced with a sensuous abandon never seen on an ordinary floor. Writhing, whirling, dipping, they swept before his astonished eyes; the men clothed solely in sarongs whipped about their waists and worn as breech cloths. The women wore filmy, gossamer veils of cobwebby thickness.

On a dais, ignored by the other dancers, a woman danced alone. Hers was a dance of sheer madness; her body a white flame that flickered and flared, trembled and tilted in the grip of some frenzied emotional wind that only she knew. McNally stared fascinated at her for several seconds before he realized that she was stark naked.

Then she screamed!

It was the same wild, meaningless scream that he had heard from the roof; sound without soul, the explosion of vocal chords in a body whipped beyond endurance, by nerves that had gone amuck. As she screamed, the woman came to her toes, head and arms thrown back. She stood thus for a moment and McNally had the impression that she was little more than a girl. Then, madness blew on her again and she danced.

McNally's eyes swept back to the other dancers. They seemed indifferent to the girl on the dais, either as a screamer or as a dancer. They seemed, in fact, indifferent to one another despite the pagan abandonment of costume and mood. Their faces, as they passed McNally, were blank faces or faces upon which a single expression had set and remained. Their bodies moved in perfect time to the music, but—

Music? There was no music!

That realization came to McNally with a sense of cold shock. There was not a sound in the room except the faint, slithering sound that the dancers themselves made. Yet so perfectly did they time their movements, he had been unaware of silence. It was as though they danced tattle music of the spheres, some weird vibration to which they were attuned. He caught himself beating time to it—that music that no one could hear.

He became conscious of the lights, then, and he knew.

The lights played over the dancers in a rhythmic flow that made them less like light than sound; all of the spectrum colors and the shadings between. McNally, who had been so long unaware of them, found himself trying to pick out the pattern, to separate color from color and determine the frequency of each. He couldn't do it and the flow of light blurred in his sight until his brain translated it as music.

The melody crashed to a close in a dazzling flood of white light; stark glare for a moment, softening off into dim, yellow radiance. The dancers separated dully and McNally pressed back into the protection of the curtain fold. His hands clenched tight into fists.

Every man on the floor bore the same insignia that O'Doul had had upon his back—the tattooed image of the winged devil!

The yellow light of the ballroom was fading and the color of the room was shading to a soft pink. The dancers had withdrawn to the cushions which were strewn around the sides of the floor. Shadow blanketed them there and two cowled monks moved out upon the floor with tea tables upon which tall glasses of blue liquor were set.

McNALLY SHOOK himself. There was a hypnotic spell about it all; the strangeness, the stark unreality, the sensual contrast of cowled monk costumes in that sea of nudity. Some incredibly evil mind had woven this web and a man dared not linger too long in the spell of this room. He could feel the tentacles of languor stretching for him and he drew back.

Slippers slapped along the corridor and he cursed softly, bitterly. He had dallied and grown careless. He might have known that the man was a guard, that he'd be back after he'd made a report on the screaming woman. It had been obvious but he'd forgotten.

The thought of the man, to whom this guard reported, stirred him. That mysterious individual, whoever he might be, was the key to O'Doul's death. Without that key, McNally was in grave danger himself. O'Doul's body was back there in the shop and O'Doul's murderer, he was convinced, was here. He had to connect the two and waste no time about it. He wasn't giving any thought yet to the problem that the dead body represented. That would come later. For the present, regardless of cult secrets and screaming women, he had to concentrate on the man behind it all. He rubbed his knuckles into his palm.

"Wonder how many I have to smack over?" he said softly to himself. "I—"

He stopped his musing as the pattering feet came to a stop before his hiding-place and he heard the heavy tread of leather soles upon the stairs. There was a quick shuffle of slippers as the man in monk's garb evidently turned toward the intruder; then a husky voice.

"The boss, Bozo. Quick!"

"Why? Whatchagot?"

"Whadda you care? Think I'm wasting information on a greaseball like you? Be your age and shake it up!"

"What you got, like I said before?"

"I heard you and you'll be damn sorry you wasted my time if my info reaches the boss too late, to—"

McNally, tense and white behind the curtains, heard the deep sigh of the guard and the man's husky voice. "All right, but if he says throw you out, I'm glad to throw you out."

The slippered feet padded off down the stone corridor and the leather soles cracked along behind them. In the ballroom, the music of light had started again but McNally was paying no attention to it. His jaw was ridged hard.

He could have recognized that voice in a million. He'd been sold down the river. The man who had come with "important information" was Skeeter!

# CHAPTER THREE

# THE TATTOOED CURSE

**I**T TOOK a strong effort of will for McNally to proceed with caution down the long corridor after the retreating footsteps. Red rage blinded him and he wanted to charge rather than creep, to annihilate the man who had betrayed him and all of these who maintained this sinkhole of vice in which men were branded and men murdered; in which women screamed without knowing why they screamed.

The men ahead of him had turned the L in the corridor and McNally reached it in time to see them pass through an arched, curtained opening. He brought up short against the curtains, pressing as he did before, but not as hard. He'd have to take his chances on another guard in the corridor. There was more light behind this curtain than in the ballroom.

Skeeter and his guide had already passed through an anteroom in which another monk-garbed man was standing, his cowl over his head and his back to the curtains. Facing Skeeter, across a big desk, there was a huge, blue-jowled man in a scarlet robe, the cowl thrown back, dark eyes blazing. Leaning forward with his knuckles flat against the desk-top and his weight on his fists, he dwarfed the room in which he stood. His voice was a deep rumble.

"You're sure he's dead and he's at this tattoo place?"

Skeeter bobbed his head. "I wouldn't be here if he wasn't. I got something to sell or I ain't. You can easy check up. There's nobody in the dump now but the stiff."

McNally's palms were wet with perspiration from the intensity with which he clenched his fists. He wanted to leap in and knock Skeeter's teeth down his throat. He'd trusted the little gutter-rat and Skeeter was trying to knot a noose on his neck for a cash deal. The man in the scarlet cowl stared hard for a moment at the man who had brought him the information.

"Sit down," he said. He waved to the guard. "O.K."

The guard turned but McNally didn't wait to see him start toward the curtain. It was no time for heroics and for battles against odds. This bunch would truss him like a turkey. He'd have to pick a hole before he pounded through. Till he found that hole, he needed freedom and lots of it. He wasn't kidding himself about the jam. It was a tight one for even a Houdini to wiggle out of. Skeeter had just presented this murderous outfit with a complete "out." Now, they need only tip the cops off anonymously and the murder would have a home where the body was found. McNally's only possible witness was—Skeeter.

**HE SWORE** but he was not stopping to think things out; he was making time down the corridor. He turned the L before he heard the pat of feet on the flagged aisle as the guard emerged from the room behind the curtain. McNally's eyes swept the run ahead. He had the long arm of the L to turn before the guard covered the short arm and turned the corner. He knew suddenly that he wouldn't make it. The man would discover him and raise the alarm. He stopped and pivoted on his heel. The slippers patted louder and McNally crouched. He was remembering that skinny neck. It was a shame, but this lad would sleep soundly.

Then the man in monk's garb turned the corner.

His jaw dropped and his colorless eyes bugged. McNally saw the man's Adam's apple make a fast round-trip and he swung easily from the waist.

The guard didn't even have time to duck. He took it on the button, coming in, and McNally caught him as he lunged forward. They always fall forward when they are hit like that. With the man's body in his arms; McNally threw a swift glance over his shoulder. The long arm of the L was empty. There was a light down by the stairs which marked the location of the big ballroom. He decided that it was too far to go. There was another room that he had noticed on the way—while he was pursuing Skeeter. It opened off the corridor on the same side and it was only a few paces away.

He dragged the limp guard and, miraculously, the loose-looking slippers stayed on. McNally reflected idly that the wearing of them must be a knack like wearing a monocle. Englishmen, he had heard, were sometimes shot to death without the monocle slipping from place. He didn't know; he'd never seen a monocled corpse. He'd never seen a place like this before, either. Almost anything could happen.

He was opposite another doorway with the inevitable blue curtains. He paused and listened. There did not seem to be any sound from within. Easing the still limp guard through the curtain first, he entered himself, crouching close to the floor.

The room was dark—but it was occupied. Over to one side a man was intent on a piece of apparatus, outlined in unreal-looking light that was flowing through tiny port-holes at chest level. He was not wearing a monk's robe

and McNally watched him tensely. The man was concen-
trating, preoccupied. If he had noticed any sound, he did
not look around. That was all right as far as it went, but
McNally couldn't remain inactive. He was on the offensive
now and he picked his spots. The odds here were one to
one.

He rose slowly from his crouch and took two steps. The
man sensed his presence and turned. He took a step to
clear the apparatus and a ray of light fell across his swarthy
face. The snarl, with which he was prepared to greet an
interruption from one of his own gang, turned swiftly to
surprise. That was the extent to which the man's emotions
were expressed.

**McNALLY TOOK** two lightning-fast steps and his
weight moved in behind the right hand that he threw to
the other's chin. The man grunted and his eyes crossed.
He bent slowly at the knees and McNally hit him again.
It was no time to be soft. This man hadn't been built with
a skinny neck and McNally blew on his knuckles without
remorse.

"I can't use 'em dazed," he muttered. "They gotta be
cold."

The man hit the carpet with a soft thud and McNally
saw that the apparatus was a camera of formidable size.
There were plate and equipment cases on the floor and
they had what McNally needed—straps. He quickly
stripped them and went to work on the arms and legs of
his captives. The monk was stirring and McNally tapped
him again. He took the monk's robe off before he bound
him and by that time the other man was beginning to
come out of it. McNally worked feverishly. He had a couple
of short straps left and a wad of waste that had evidently
been used to clean the camera.

Torn in two, the waste made acceptable gags and the short straps held the gags in place. There was no time to be tidy but McNally rolled the two men to the darkest corner and straightened up to wipe his forehead. His knuckles were bleeding and he was warm. The gleam of battle was in his eyes, as he disrobed the monk, put on his habit. "Two less to worry about," he muttered. "Wonder how many of these monkeys there are?"

He was turning toward the camera. In a pinch, that camera would be a help. He could take the photographer's place if he had to have a hideout in a hurry. He took a step toward it and stopped; conscious of a low crooning from somewhere close at hand, a soothing sound like the voice of a woman who is lulling her child. His body tensed. That sound was too clear to be coming through a wall or a partition.

He circled the room slowly. It was very dark on the side opposite from the camera, where the faint porthole light did not penetrate. His hand, sliding over the wall, touched the yielding surface of another curtain. His lips tightened.

A man's laugh broke through the even, rhythmic flow of sound; a forced, unnatural laugh only one step removed from hysteria. Bending close to the curtain-edge, McNally looked into a room that swam in pink light. His fingers gripped tightly on the curtain and he breathed hard.

A man lay face down upon a bank of cushions. He was naked to the waist. Above him crouched the girl who had claimed to be the wife of O'Doul; her slim, provocative body cased in thin silk that clung closely to her, emphasizing every graceful line.

The man's head was turned to one side and McNally recognized him as he had recognized O'Doul. He was Ben Goddard, the son of a boot-and-shoe fortune and a personal friend of McNally's when he was not Needle Mike.

It was not the recognition—nor the girl—that froze McNally to startled attention; it was the deft fingers of the girl which were keeping time to the soft music of her crooning.

She was tattooing the symbol of the winged devil on Ben Goddard's back!

**McNALLY NEVER** knew how long he stood by the curtain while the man writhed and the girl wielded the needles. He lost himself for the moment in the spell of still another strange spectacle in this house of spectacles. Here was his art and here was a master of it—a woman.

Her body had the ripe, full curves of maturity and there was a certain magic in the soft, musical sounds that fell from her lips. The pink light lent her creamy skin a terrible allure, that even McNally felt, as her fingers moved with deft mastery and her body kept time with the weird melody. But her art was of the earth, earthly; the base art of tabu and of magic and of demon pacification. She did not draw on flesh as an artist in tattoo would draw—for design's sake. Where the American or the Japanese would pride himself that he did not puncture the true vascular skin, this girl made of the work a blood rite—drawing blood deliberately and wantonly, with sadistic joy.

Her body was a sensual poem, but occasionally she raised her head and her face chilled desire where her body warmed it. She could have been Polynesian, with the art of the needle born in her. McNally did not know. He knew only that, where he recognized her mastery and the deft sureness with which she wielded the needles, he was appalled at the expression in her face. She had tried to trick him and she had been beguiling, even with her body wrapped in heavy garments and her face stinging from the storm. Here, her body had full play but she was a woman indulging an appetite. She liked to hurt. She made a rite of it.

Ben Goddard was submissive. There was a stupid expression on his face and he mouthed nonsense while he tried, occasionally, to paw her. His mouth was slack and there was a dullness in his eyes that gave them a sort of glaze. McNally was puzzled for a few moments, then he swore softly.

It was all too apparent what lay back of the baffling elements in this house. The very circumstances answered themselves; the automatons in the ballroom, the over-stimulated, shrieking nude dancer, the blue liquor served by the cowled men—it all added up to an obvious answer—drugs!

They were all steeped in them, soaked in them. All of the materials for a pagan orgy were here; sex, mystery, weird rites, drugs—and behind it all, the big blue-jowled figure in the scarlet cowl to whom Skeeter had come.

THE GIRL suddenly finished her task. Leaping swiftly to her feet, she gathered her kit while Ben Goddard rolled over and grabbed at her clumsily. There was a strange light behind the glaze in his eyes and the girl laughed at him, laughed softly. Her body twisted sinuously and she danced lightly past his fingertips to kiss him tantalizingly on the ear as he turned. Then she was racing toward the door and McNally faded out of her way.

It was only a few strides to the camera and he took his place there as the girl swept out. She was still humming but the tune was a savage one now; such a tune as men might dance to about a jungle fire. McNally didn't look at her. He peered instead through the slot in which the camera was set. He could see the ballroom from a different angle, but the dancers were the same drugged puppets, dancing to music that they could not hear. On the raised dais, the nude dancer lay in an inert heap. She attracted no more attention thus than she had when she danced and screamed. This drug made people preoccupied with their own sensations.

To that ballroom Ben Goddard would "graduate" in the natural course of events, Ken thought. Every man in it was branded and, presumably, had known pain and ecstasy under the needles of the girl who had just gone out. Perhaps, too, they had been kissed lightly on the ear. McNally's lips curled.

There was a changing quality in the light that flowed over the dancers now. It was fading out like the last few bars of music trailing off into silence. He remembered the sudden white light that had impressed him before. A sudden suspicion crystalized in his brain and he jerked his eyes away from the floor.

Above the camera, a red bulb had lighted.

A signal to the photographer! For what? He was not ready yet to be uncovered. In the past few minutes he had been fitting Ben Goddard into a vague plan. He needed a little time free from interruption. What was he supposed to do when the red signal gleamed?

He made a swift survey of the niche into which the camera station was set. To the right of the camera there was an open knife-switch. His lips flattened against his teeth. An error here might be too bad, but no response to the signal would be equally fatal. His fingers moving with the thought, gripped the handle and the switch-blade plunged home. McNally's eyes went to the peep-slot anxiously.

The white light was on; a glaring, monstrously revealing light that was pitiless to the semi-nude dancers on the floor. Short and tall, fat and skinny, they all stood frozen for the moment where the light caught them—in the sensuous attitudes of the last step.

McNally's hand was hard on the switch. How many seconds? He tried to remember back to the previous flashing of the white beam, but it was easier to guess. As he jerked back on the switch, the yellow light flowed softly into the room, replacing the glare. The dancers were moving slowly off but McNally had no more attention for them. His forehead was creased with concentration.

**HE HAD** added another chapter to his knowledge of this layout. The camera could mean only one thing. Men and women were lured here by the unusual, the bait of a new thrill, disarmed by drugs and photographed. Why? He laughed harshly.

As a blackmail layout it was perfect. There could be no comeback. A person had to have money to get in. Probably the fees were so high that the customers never thought of any added charge. To sign, seal and deliver any unfortunate man lured into the net, there was the damnable tattooing. The camera-eye would catch that winged devil a dozen times in a single exposure. A man who bore that device on his back was bound to the sect which held its orgies under its sign. Any publicity for the sect was a threat to every man in it—and the man in the red cowl could use member against member to see that fees were collected and that the police were kept out.

The drugs and the woman, of course, broke down the reason of otherwise smart men. The pickings would always be easy as long as there were rich fools like Ben Goddard who sought thrills in strange places, drank strange liquids and laid themselves open to the blandishments of strange women.

O'Doul? Well, the contractor had been a big, full-blooded man and it was lonely for a widower. He'd paid for his indiscretion with his life.

McNally opened and closed his swollen right hand and turned toward the room with the blue curtain. They'd leave Ben Goddard alone for a while to recover from the shock of the tattooing. Well, he wouldn't leave him alone. He needed him.

The man was still lying face down but he was no longer kittenish. He looked sick. McNally shook him roughly by the shoulder.

"Snap out of it, Ben", he said gruffly. "You've got to get out of here."

"Huh—who says so?" Goddard's voice was heavy, almost drunken. McNally rolled him over. The man was listless. They had loaded him good. If he came out of this naturally, he'd have to have more of the drug to make the hangover bearable. McNally swore.

"You blamed fool! It'll be tough any way you take it."

He sat the man up and slapped the side of his face. Goddard perked and McNally slapped his other cheek. He kept on slapping him till the man started to fight back; then he spilled him and rammed a finger down his throat.

BEN GODDARD had a very sick and miserable time but McNally was merciless. Ben was a decent young fellow from a good family and McNally had known him for a good many years. He couldn't leave him in the hands of the fiends who ran this den. As long as he had to worry about him, he was going to get some help out of him.

"I'll let him worry, too," he said grimly.

McNally was giving him a treatment that was very much like first-aid in drowning cases and Goddard finally rebelled. He flailed out with both hands.

"Quit, will you? What is this, a Turkish bath?"

McNally grinned. He had won the first round of his battle. He stepped back and Ben Goddard looked up at him. His eyes were intelligent again even if they were a trifle bloodshot. He seemed puzzled.

"You've been calling me Ben. I don't know you—"

McNally passed his sore right hand over the unshaven jaw of Needle Mike and twisted his lips into a grimace. "You don't have to. You're in a gyp joint. You've been branded. Pretty soon you'd be photographed and—"

Ben Goddard blinked. He seemed aware of the soreness in his back and tried to reach the spot with one hand. His face twisted with pain.

"Gosh," he said. "That little yellow devil! We had a drink and the monk brought me in here and she—she—" His eyes lighted for a moment and he smiled reminiscently, the smile fading into a look of horror. His dazed mind was piecing things together. "She was singing to me and I was sleepy all of a sudden and—"

"And she tattooed a winged devil on your back."

"Tattoo? Devil?" Ben Goddard's eyes were big. He shivered. McNally's voice was hard.

"Tom O'Doul was in before you were. He's been murdered. You've got to get out. You've got to do what I tell you!"

Ben Goddard lunged to his feet and swayed weakly. "By God!" he said hoarsely. "By God! I know who you are. I know you now. You're Ken McNally!"

# CHAPTER FOUR
# A BARGAIN IN BODIES

McNALLY WINCED under the identification. He had hoped to avoid that. The intrusion of his other life into the affairs of Needle Mike meant the end of a great adventure. But wasn't it ended anyway? Didn't the shadow of the noose hang over Needle Mike? His shoulders twitched and some stubborn thing within him insisted that he would never run from an adventure because it had become hazardous. His face, however, betrayed nothing of his feelings.

He nodded grimly. "That's right, Ben," he said. "Now you know you weren't being kidded."

Ben Goddard ran his hand through his hair in bewildered fashion. He had had a series of shocks and his brain was reeling under them. It showed in his eyes; in the way he blinked at the faint, pink light in the room. Suddenly, his body jerked.

"Dorothy!" he cried hoarsely. "Dorothy! What did they do to her?"

It was McNally's turn to be startled. He shot out one arm and his fingers fastened vise-like on the other's shoulder.

"You brought a girl, a decent girl, to a hole like this?"

Goddard swayed a little. He was still passing his hand through his hair. "I didn't know, Ken," he said jerkily. "We heard about it. Dancing to light instead of music—all that stuff. Since the speaks closed there's no place exciting to go any more and—"

McNally shook him. "Who was the girl?"

"Dorothy—Dorothy Kelland—" It was a hoarse whisper. Ben Goddard was frightened. He was depending on McNally; his eyes fixed on him hopefully. And McNally was remembering—remembering an incident out of the past.

Dorothy Kelland was a deb of a year ago. He'd been at her coming-out party. He could picture her now. Blond, tall, statuesque. The Diana type and too wise to play the ingenue. She'd worn sequins; a metal sheath that caught lights and threw them back at you. Then another image blotted out the first; the image of a nude, blond girl, who'd shrieked and danced in the mad abandon of one whose natural dignity had been destroyed with drugs. The two images blended and he knew! He had thought that there was something familiar about the girl from the first, but he hadn't imagined—

The truth was too bizarre, too outrageous, too indecent! His fingers were gripping Ben Goddard's shoulder so hard that the man cried out. The truth bubbled on McNally's lips, but he strangled it. Ben Goddard had to be nursed along. He'd be no good if he knew. McNally shook his head, his lips stiff.

"She's probably all right. They're after the men mostly. Blackmail! But we have to clean this nest, Ben. I've got a monk's robe in the next room. There's a guard supposed to be down the hall. Go down there and stay. I'll need you—"

**HE WAS** hustling Ben Goddard into the anteroom now, but the red light was burning and he leaped across to the camera. The musical light was just fading. He grunted with relief and threw the switch hard. Fifteen minutes! They ran the dances just a quarter of an hour. He left the white light on for a little under three seconds and slapped the switch back.

He didn't wait at the slot to watch the yellow light flow on. The photographer was trying to make a noise by kicking on the floor. The fact that there was a fairly thick rug, and only stone flagging under it, was hampering the success of his efforts but McNally kicked him in the ribs for luck and the movement stopped.

The guard hadn't been doing any footwork. His slippers left his heels bare and that was too discouraging. McNally left him alone. He took off the monk's robe, flipped it to Ben Goddard.

"Climb into that. Take your shoes off and paddle down the corridor in those slippers. Shake it up!"

Ben Goddard did as he was told. The shock had worn off somewhat and Ben had managed to rout the remnants of the drug. He might have been thinking of the girl, Dorothy. His fingers were swift and sure as he untied his shoes and swapped them for slippers. McNally watched him slide out with a twinge of envy. He had needed that robe for himself. But he'd make out.

He had a few advantages of his own. He was younger than he looked and just as tough. This spot was closely guarded on the outside but a man could get around inside. The guards did not expect uninvited intruders in their midst and they were obviously servants rather than guards.

It occurred to him that he did not know if Skeeter had gone or not. He'd been busy and many people could have passed along the corridor. He didn't like to think about Skeeter. It gave him murderous impulses. But he wondered why there hadn't been a hue and cry, why they hadn't been searching the place for him. If Skeeter told them, as he undoubtedly would, that he had been trailing the girl—then they might at least have given him credit for being able to crash a dump like this. Or did they think that the girl had shaken him?

**HE LOOKED** through the slot. The dance was starting again. He tested his damaged right hand and found it sore but still serviceable. He'd stack it up as a fit instrument in an ordinary struggle. There had only been one guard outside the refuge of the scarlet-cowled monk. He took a deep breath and slid into the corridor.

It was as deserted as it had been before. The business of this place seemed to be conducted in little rooms, exclusively. He made his way cautiously to the turn in the L and still more cautiously down the short arm to the curtained doorway. His fists were knotted as he paused before the curtain and he drew his breath in softly. The odds were tough and—

He brought up short, balancing on his toes. He'd been stirred up, grim, swept by the success of his attack upon the other guard and the photographer. He'd been going after the man in the scarlet cowl as he had gone after those two—and then what? There was no step after that which he could take logically, safely, to anyone's advantage. The man with the scarlet cowl was safe behind his own ramparts of blackmail. He might be captured but capture would not eliminate him. It would pass a problem to his captor.

Cold logic erected a barrier almost like a wall in front of McNally. Crashing the curtain was easy; crashing through that barrier of logic was tough. His right hand dropped and, as it did, it brushed the pocket in which he had put the ovular device which provided Needle Mike with his game leg. His hand fell away.

"I'm nuts," he said softly.

He had been on the point of charging in, in the Ken McNally manner; just as if he had to be Ken McNally. He didn't have to be, he shouldn't be. In this adventure, he was Needle Mike. Needle Mike would not charge into anything. He was a man with a record. He would play an angle. His eyes gleamed. Needle Mike could do what Ken McNally couldn't do—now. Ken McNally could finish, later, what Needle Mike had started.

The body of O'Doul in his little shop was his big personal liability, his hostage to fortune. Woven through McNally's philosophy by the fingers of experience was the belief that a man's strength is always his weakness. If O'Doul's body could only be turned into an asset!

That was Needle Mike's job. That was the angle. If he could make a deal to have the body brought here—then Ken McNally, in his own identity, could finish the job. With his knowledge of this place, the security of his own position as Ken McNally seeking a vanished friend, he could lead the cops on a raid that would wipe out this nest in one fell swoop. The first step was Needle Mike's. He drew his breath deep, assumed the limp without the aid of apparatus and stepped boldly through the curtain.

A startled guard leaped up from a chair and McNally looked past him into the private room where the girl of the tattoo needles was sitting at the desk of the blue-jowled one. The man saw him as quickly as did the guard, and his ease of movement was the gauge of his strength. He neither leaped nor showed surprise. Only one hand moved and that one slid off the edge of the desk. His blue jowls were hard and there was a challenging stare in his eyes.

McNally grunted. "How's to talk a little business?" he asked huskily.

**THE MAN** in the scarlet cowl sat motionless behind his big desk. His features were as frozen as a mask but there was a slow narrowing of his eyelids as McNally limped forward. The eyes behind the slits glittered. Here was a strong man and a greedy one who found himself sitting atop a gold mine. He was letting no stranger in on it, under any pretext.

"I don't know you," he said flatly. "We have no business. How did you get in, huh?"

"That's where the business comes in. You want to know. I can tell you." McNally sat down, unbidden, grunted irritably, and started to roll a cigarette. Needle Mike was not supposed to be overawed by greaseballs who hit a good racket. The girl leaned a little toward the big man.

"It ees the man of the tattoo," she said. McNally cocked one eye at her.

"I know you, too, sister. Your line didn't go so good."

Her glance chilled. The guard shuffled in the doorway, hoping, McNally imagined, that he would not get orders to throw anybody out. The man in the scarlet cowl hit the desk with a hand like a catcher's glove.

"What do you want?"

"A deal. A guy that gets bumped off here wanders down to my place to die. I don't want him."

"Who tells you that someone gets bumped off here?"

McNally shrugged. "He does."

"You lie. I know different." The glitter in the big man's eyes was more pronounced now. McNally struck a match and lighted the scrubby cigarette. Anything that this monkey knew would be Skeeter's work. He growled under his breath.

"All right. He didn't tell me a thing. But he's got your trademark on his back. Maybe you'd like to have the bulls asking you questions."

"Nobody will ask me nothing."

"Maybe you'd like to have the bulls asking wrong as hell. My deal is that I'm the only needler in the business in this town. Your girl bites too deep when she inks that devil on. No medico is going to make a clean job of getting it off. Anybody that gets tired of that thing is coming to me for a workover into a new design, get me?"

"What do I care?" Blue-jowl was still keeping up the poker-face, but his eyelids were not so tightly drawn. His eyes showed interest. McNally made a rumbling noise in his throat.

"You know the answer. Some of 'em will get tired of it. That will mean that these bozos that try to get rid of your art are ripe to cut loose from you. How'd you like a tip-off, in advance, on guys like that?"

"Who gives me tips?"

"I do. This bird tonight came to me. There'll be more of 'em. How'll we trade?"

"How do I know this is not one big double-cross?"

McNALLY CAME up out of the chair in a bound that made the guard duck. He was Needle Mike in a tantrum. His fist hit the desk and made an inkwell jump and jiggle. His lips flattened in a snarl.

"Know? Why you big mug, you don't have to know. Do you think I'd be sitting here talking to a blue-faced monkey for the love of it? If I didn't have a record, I'd be down at headquarters telling the bulls about that corpse and about where I figure he got that way. You—"

"Aw right." The big man seemed to understand this kind of an approach. He raised his huge hand in a cease-and-desist gesture. However, there was something sinister in the sudden curl of his thick lips, and his eyes had gone back behind the slits. The terms "mug" and "blue-faced monkey" were too accurate to be comfortable. He laid one thick forefinger on the desk. McNally sat down again.

"What do you want?"

"I want you to haul that corpse out of there and stow it somewhere else. I can't explain it without dragging you in and if you think I won't, you're nuts."

"Yeah?" The man's coarse voice dropped to a purr. "How do you know you'd walk out of here to explain?"

The eyes of the two men clashed. McNally shrugged indifferently. "Be bright. Even a cop can still figure out that winged devil on the stiff. Cops remember like elephants. The first publicity break this dump gets is your neck on that kill—even if I don't show up."

The man in the scarlet robe was playing the sphinx again but that shot had gone home. McNally had an idea that the man had been way ahead of him and had figured that angle first. The big hand moved aimlessly around the desk. The other hand was still out of sight. That hidden hand suggested a weapon but McNally wasn't curious.

Finally the big man grunted: "If we take away this corpse, what about it?"

"Just like I said. I play ball. You get tips on any other winged devils I work on.

The room was suddenly very still. The blue-jowled man was thinking and McNally was letting him think. The guard was still in the background and he probably didn't bother to think about anything. Suddenly the big man nodded.

"Maybe we do it that way," he said heavily. The girl lunged swiftly to her feet with the speed of a jungle-cat leaping to the kill. Her body hung halfway across the desk. Her eyes blazed.

"Otero, look! Thees man is fake. Hees face is stain. Look at hees hair—"

**McNALLY CAME** to his feet. He had forgotten the girl, been too confident of his disguise. His suspicion that she was of some mixed race, not quite white, came back to him. Those with a touch of color are sensitive to skins. The skin of Needle Mike was a stained edition of McNally's. The big man rose half out of his chair. In that moment, McNally saw him as the headmaster of a degraded cult.

The sphinx pose was gone. There was raw brutality in the man's snarling face. Yellowish eyes flamed above a nose that had probably been hooked before many breakings had taken all shape out of it. Broad, thick lips curled back over badly matched teeth.

"Private dick," he growled. The hidden hand flashed from behind the desk and the light glinted on the long blade of a stiletto. McNally shoved the desk into him with one foot and whirled to the suddenly aroused guard.

The man was coming at him with flailing arms and not too much confidence. McNally had a swift version of a lumpish, peasant face distinguished by a black eye that looked almost like a gaping hole. He was shooting his right as his brain telegraphed the details and he had time for a follow-up left before the robed guard took a dive.

McNally hadn't bothered to throw punches for pictorial effect. He aimed for the button and he'd scored!

The girl had lunged for him and was blocking him like a speedy halfback. He swung her halfway across the room and wondered why his brain was frivolous in situations like this. He couldn't help thinking that the master had hired his ten-pin guards out of the crumb-bum line at some mission and that it had been a mistake on his part to throw cracks at this girl's sex appeal.

Then the man with the knife was over the desk and he knew how O'Doul had received the death stroke. There was the black eye and—

His brain ceased to function. The girl's hands slipped off his thighs as he twisted his body. The steel flashed and he was up inside it; up against a body that seemed built of steel girders and scrap copper. Otero was built like a battleship and McNally wasted no time hitting him. He had learned more than tattooing in Japan.

His hip twisted as his body collided with Otero's. His hands flashed, with the certainty of knowledge, to two points on the big man's free left arm. He ignored the knife and he seemed to exert no more pressure than mist against a window pane.

Otero's lips parted in a moan and his right arm jerked erratically out of the perfect downward arc of its swing. The knife nipped over in the air and hit the floor with a singing thump.

McNally slipped his grip and rolled his body past the suddenly unbalanced giant. He had given Otero a little touch of *judo*, the big brother of *jiu jitsu*, and the sudden paralysis of nerves had done what no shower of blows would ever had done. McNally had disarmed this human battering ram in mid-charge.

It was a bad bet for a repeat, though, and McNally knew it. Given room and a free play for his speed, he had a few more tricks in the bag but there was too much furniture to contend with, too many people. The girl was scrambling for the knife as Otero turned with a bellow.

**McNALLY SAW** the girl stoop at the instant in which he collided with the chair in which she had been sitting when he came into the room.

It was a light chair and he scooped it up with a running underhand swing that sent it across the room like a tea table on tires. The girl did not pick up the knife. The chair bowled her over like a toy soldier and Otero closed in, swinging.

McNally took two of those blows, rolling, but his head swam. He struck out wildly, himself, and Otero got tangled up in the chair that the girl threw away from her. The guard was getting up and McNally had three antagonists between himself and the door. The knife was lost somewhere underfoot but it would have taken a bold soul to have dived under that seething tangle.

Then, far down the corridor, a girl screamed!

# CHAPTER FIVE
# HOLOCAUST

**I T WAS** the same scream that McNally had heard four times that night. It came again and the woman in the room muttered something. She was a wild, disheveled creature now, stark primitive in her desire to bring McNally down. Her face was a cruel mask and her eyes were lighted with the same sadistic glitter that had been in them when she worked on Ben Goddard's back.

She had a bronze incense-burner in her hands and McNally ducked as she swung. Otero caught him as the heavy bronze zipped past his head and pandemonium broke loose down the hall.

Otero's voice thundered a command. "Benita! See what is that! Quick—"

McNally didn't see if the girl obeyed. Two big hands had closed about his throat. He looked up into the murderous eyes of Otero and there was hell-fire in them. Otero was savoring the sweets of revenge now; holding McNally's soul over the brink of eternity and letting it slip slowly... slowly....

His thick voice growled again as McNally felt the thud of some heavy object against his body. "Benita! Go! I take care of this!"

McNally didn't know if there were any more blows or not. He was looking up into those blazing eyes, raising his own hands slowly and using every atom of his will.

*A finger is weaker than a hand.*

Something within him whispered that as his hands crept up. His own eyes seemed to be popping out of his head. There was no air left for his lungs. The blazing eyes swam. Then his hands rested against the hairy, iron-hard hands of Otero. His will mounted triumphantly over his weakening body. He wanted to sneer into that brutal face.

He had found the man's little fingers, the little fingers of those throttling hands. There was still strength in his own hands; and, with the lights whirling in his brain, he exerted all of it in one sudden heave that put both hands into action at once.

Otero's little fingers were standing alone against two hands—and those fingers broke like matchsticks. The blue-jawed one moaned like a kicked cur. The blazing light went out of his eyes—and McNally breathed.

Kicking back, McNally freed himself, with a twist, from that relaxed grip and reeled against the wall. He heard the cursing sob of Otero, saw the unsteady blur of the guard's hesitant figure circling him. He was taking the air in big gulps and he was still alive.

His foot kicked against the bronze incense-burner and he picked it up as Otero kicked at him. He brought the bronze down against the man's knee and twisted toward the door. The kick had only partially missed him and he had a real limp now to go with the character of Needle Mike.

The guard was afraid to close with him and he heard Otero's pain-filled voice shouting: "The drawer, fool! Gun—top drawer...!"

Down the hall, women were screaming and men were shouting hoarsely. In here, there was less noise; but under the profane urging of Otero, the man with the black eye was fumbling for a gun.

**THE CHILL** of deadly danger helped to restore Mc-Nally's muscles. He was gulping air into his tortured lungs and his head was clearing. He saw Otero coming at him; an Otero bent with pain and mad with the rage of a wounded bull. There was no weapon in Otero's hands now, but somewhere behind him he was depending upon his man to come up with a gun. A mighty body to Otero was a good weapon only when he was top man. He had quit under pain and now he had only borrowed courage.

McNally measured him as he charged and, too late, Otero saw that McNally's right hand still held the incense-burner that was Benita's contribution to the melee. The broad, brutal face grimaced with fear and Otero turned his head back toward the desk.

He took it going away.

All rules were off and McNally hit whatever offered to him. The skull of Otero was a big target and the incense-burner jarred home. The guard was holding the gun and the muzzle was making erratic circles in the air.

McNally's lips flattened. "Drop it, you mug!"

"I'll shoot." The man's voice was thin, frightened. McNally straightened up, spat like a foc'sle bully and walked straight across the room into the mouth of the gun.

"You're a liar!" he said. He had the incense-burner poised in his hand and the man with the black eye could see the prone body of his chief. The muzzle traced bigger circles in the air and the man lost all confidence in the power of gun against bronze. The gun dropped to the desk.

McNally ducked then but there was no report. One more stride took him to the desk and he swept the gun into one hand.

McNally grunted: "Come here!"

The man cringed and it was brutal; but there was no time for gentleness. McNally dropped the bronze and swung. For the second time that night the guard went down and, out or not, he had the sense to stay down. McNally swung to the door.

The noise down the hall had increased but nearer was a patter of running feet. Benita whirled through the curtains and was halfway across the anteroom when she saw the grim, reeling figure of McNally. Her voice rushed up into her throat in a choked cry and she seemed to change direction in mid-flight. Before McNally could take a step toward her, she had slipped back through the curtains and was gone. He cursed and followed her.

He might as well have tried to catch one of the elusive light rays of the ballroom. The corridor was bare and he limped painfully down toward the bend on the L. He turned in full-tilt and skidded his heels to a stop.

**WHERE THE** stairs came into the corridor, there was a mad, milling crowd of semi-nude people, battling to escape. A few feet in the clear, two men in monk's garb battled while another lay on the flagstones in a heap.

Running madly toward McNally, her eyes wide and dazed, was Dorothy Kelland; her blond hair streaming wildly behind her, her nude body a white blur.

"Dorothy!"

McNally gripped her wrist and she struck madly at him without any recognition in her eyes. A scream trembled on her parted lips as if there was not enough lung power behind it to push it through.

It was with difficulty that he held her. She was insane with fear and his own strength was spent. A few yards away, the battle for the stairs was still in progress but the fight between the monks was decided. One of them was charging toward McNally. The latter swung the girl with an effort and his hand dropped to the pocket which held the captured gun.

"Ken!"

At the sound of that voice, his hand dropped away. Ben Goddard was panting and his features looked pushed around, but he closed in fast. His two hands fastened on the girl's arms. He talked to her; softly, soothingly. She relaxed and went limp. McNally threw a desperate glance down the corridor.

People were being trampled and clawed in that mad scramble and those stairs were a bad bet for two spent men with a girl to look after. Goddard had stripped off the monk's robe and was wrapping it around the girl. McNally swore dazedly.

"Did you start all that, Ben?"

"I guess. Dorothy screamed and I saw her and—my God, Ken!"

"I know."

"Well, I barged in and the bunch stampeded like cattle when those monks started jumping me. I don't know what happened—"

They were hurrying the girl between them now. McNally was not thinking any more of his personal problem. There might be a corpse in his shop to account for, and the hand of the law might already be reaching out for him, but there was now a problem on his hands that was more pressing because it would not wait for solution.

They passed the office of the blue-jowled one and there was another blue-curtained door beyond. That would account for Benita's swift disappearance. She would not tarry when she saw Otero down. She'd be making for the exit.

Leaving the girl to Goddard, McNally plunged through the curtain.

A hunch-backed man, whose hair stuck out from his head in wild, bushy disorder was pulling what seemed to be miles of film from the largest projection machine that McNally had ever seen. He screamed with rage as he recognized strangers, and, with uncanny nimbleness, vaulted to a raised platform just beyond the machine. He had matches in his hand and McNally's hand dropped to his gun-pocket. The man was shrilling abuse.

"Fools! Filthy spies! You think you can steal my secret. Fools! The film is the secret. It is the heart of the organ. Look—"

McNally saw the stairs beyond the weird figure but just then a match flared. It was too late. McNally spun and swept Dorothy Kelland off the floor with one heave. Gripping her tightly, he leaped back toward the corridor.

"Run, Ben, for God's sake! That stuff—"

There was a sighing sound like the birth of a great wind; then a long, shuddering, sizzling roar that threw flame through the doorway that they had just quitted and took down a section of wall with one blast.

McNALLY HAD no conscious impressions of that mad race down the hall ahead of the holocaust. He was spent and he was carrying a burden and his brain played him tricks. The image of that big projector remained fixed in his mind. The hunchback had called it an organ and probably he was right. It had never occurred to him that the play of light, that was so much like music, might be produced by the running of film. The thought was revolutionary. And the brain that held that secret was warped with suspicion, a set-up for dirty intriguers like Otero.

Or did any brain hold that secret? Did the flame wipe out its creator or did the hunchback make the stairs? He didn't know. His breath was coming in deep, sobbing gusts and the girl felt as heavy as a team of elephants.

Ben Goddard called out hoarsely. Instinct took over the job for McNally and he set the girl down as he turned, his hand moving automatically to his pocket.

Behind him, the flames were racing along the walls— great, red devouring tongues that crackled and crisped as they made their own music for an orgy; a music composed equally of sound and light and of a fury beyond the weak powers of man.

Against this lurid backdrop, Ben Goddard was fighting for his life; his face white and strained as he bent beneath the insane rage of Otero. The man in the scarlet cowl was like some nightmare demon conjured out of the flames that whipped behind him. His mismatched teeth flashed in the glare and his staring eyes were headlights of insanity. He had his knife again and it gave him courage. Ben Goddard's arm muscles creaked with the effort of holding the knife-thrust back —and Ken McNally stiffened wearily.

"Drop it, mug—" His voice cracked against the blazing orchestra of doom in the background. Otero's head came up and he snarled. With one surge, he heaved Goddard aside and leaped for the man who had been his undoing. McNally let him take one step—and fired.

**THE BODY** that was built like a battle-ship went down like a rag-doll. It hit, jerked and rolled over limply. McNally wasted no time on it. He saw where that bullet had penetrated and there was nothing mortal left to be saved from the charging holocaust.

"Ben, can you make it?" His lips were dry as he bent his body again to the girl. Dorothy Kelland was struggling to her feet.

"I can, too," she said dazedly. She didn't know what she was talking about, but she could move her legs. Ben Goddard reeled up and took her arm. It was very hot as they turned the corner of the L.

The fighting mob had cleared away from the stairs, spurred perhaps by the sound of the explosion. As McNally limped down the last stretch, he saw the curtains of the camera room billow out and two frightened men dashed into the corridor. One of them still had his hands tied behind him but they could both travel faster than the three that raced behind them to the stairs. McNally sighed gustily.

He had thought about those two prisoners and he had dreaded going in after them. That problem was off his mind.

The rest was a blur of smoke and heat and struggle. They dodged police and fire-men, ran through backyards in blanketing snow that had replaced the sleet.

On the edge of Chinatown, they caught a cab. Ben Goddard hung back after he had bundled the shivering girl in. There was a question in his eyes.

"You, Ken? You'd better—"

"No. Get Dorothy home! She won't remember much. Tell her she got tight and dreamed it!"

"But you?"

"Forget the disguise, Ben. That's all."

They shook hands and McNally watched the tail-light blink away. He shivered slightly and turned toward Broadway. He could run away from the character of Needle Mike and from the corpse in the shop, but he had always known that he wouldn't. Whatever he had to meet, he'd meet it.

IT WAS a short walk but it seemed endless. The black block on South Broadway opened ahead of him. There was only one light—his own. There was no excitement. His brow puckered and he speeded his tired legs.

In the big room, Skeeter sat huddled over the gas heater, his skinny body shaking. McNally paused on the threshold and the newsboy looked up with a twisted grin.

"So you got home? You've had time to get drunk."

"Yeah." The hoarse accents of Needle Mike came easily from McNally's smoke-tortured throat. "Yuh sold me out, you little rat!"

Skeeter rocked back. His eyes were mocking. "Why ain't you in jail, then?'

McNally didn't know the answer to that one himself. He came into the room slowly. Skeeter's eyes were sleepy. "It's goin' to cost you dough, Mike," he said. "I got rid of your stiff."

"Huh?"

"Sure. Two-way deal. I recognized that devil sign. I get around, Mike. Ask me something, sometime. I figured they wouldn't have chased that frail out after that mick unless they wanted him dead or alive—"

"You kidded them that you were doing 'em a favor?"

"Naw. I sold 'em a tip. Cash dough, Mike. They didn't want the cops finding any stiff with that sign on him. That mug, Otero, ran a speak before repeal smacked him into a new racket. He had a record, too."

McNally sat limply in a chair. "And the body?"

"Two greaseballs came over in a hot car. We took it out the back way. I went wit' 'em. They no sooner got in the dump when it blew up. The greaseballs came out, the stiff didn't!"

Skeeter was watching him with bright eyes, his hand out. "You can't buy brains every day, Mike. The price went up. I want *all* of that stiff's dough—now! Dig!"

Dazedly, McNally drew the wallet out. After all, he had to be Needle Mike in this spot and Needle Mike would pay. Ken McNally could send a check to the O'Doul estate and cover. Skeeter's hand closed greedily on the cash.

"Mike," he said, "you can't kill 'em too often for me."

There was nothing that could be done about Skeeter. He had absolutely no moral standards.

# THE TATTOOED COBRA

AROUND THAT SEVERED FINGER
IT COILED—THE HOODED HORROR
OF THE EAST—HIDDEN FROM
CURIOUS EYES BY A SLENDER
PLATINUM BAND. TO WHAT
GHASTLY SECRET WAS THE
NEEDLED COBRA A KEY? WHY
SHOULD EVEN THE CRAZIEST
MURDER MASTER ORDER SUCH A
SYMBOL INKED IN THE CORPSE-
FLESH OF HIS VICTIM'S HAND?

# CHAPTER ONE
# THE SEVERED FINGER

**A**GAINST THE green plush of the jewel case lay the neatly severed finger of a woman.

Ken McNally stared with horror in his eyes; a sick, all-gone feeling in the pit of his stomach. There was no blood, no ghastly touches; the finger lay like a creation of wax, in a setting of green; a platinum wedding ring pinched the slightly swollen flesh.

Maurice Dalton was breathing heavily, wheezily. McNally wet his lips, said, "Your—your wife's?" and nodded toward the open case.

Dalton twisted the fingers of one hand against the fingers of the other as though he were feeling in his mind the blow of the mutilation. He was a dapper man of medium height, his face pasty-white now; and his eyes were reddened from too much liquor. Blond hair hung damply, uncombed, upon his forehead.

"Yes," he said chokily. "There's no doubt of it. There's the ring and there's—there's something else. I'll tell you later. But tell me first what to do. I'm sick, Ken. I—"

Ken McNally didn't doubt that he was sick. He was feeling ill himself and the horror hadn't happened to anyone who was dear to him.

Dalton was fumbling with the whiskey bottle on the library table. He'd already had too much, but McNally didn't have the heart to argue with him.

"You'd better tell me about it from the beginning," he said. "You've been shooting disconnected fragments of the story at me but I can't connect them up."

"What are you trying to do— send us all to hell?"

"It's all my fault." Dalton gagged a little over his drink. Sweat was heavy on his forehead. "If I hadn't passed out last night—"

"Forget that. The beginning, I said!" McNally's voice was sharp. Dalton stiffened, wanted to be resentful but failed.

"There isn't a beginning," he said. "Everything started and ended the same way. I always drank too much and at the wrong time. Ethel drank too much. We had too much money, too much time on our hands. If we hadn't had so much, we'd have been happy. We loved each other, Ken. We just never got the chance to really prove it."

**McNALLY SETTLED** back. He didn't know if this were the beginning or not, but Dalton was going to have to tell his story in his own way. The man's eyes were haunted and he kept fumbling with the half-filled liquor glass, sloshing it around noisily.

"Ethel was always superstitious, fearful. Maybe she knew, somehow, that this would happen some day." Dalton's eyes were wide. His voice rose. "Out on the Coast, five years ago, she went to one of these Yogi fellows. She had an idea that something would happen to part us. He told her a lot of stuff about snakes, about the cobra and a circle of eternity; all that kind of rot. She believed it. She was awfully pathetic, Ken, when she believed something—"

The man's voice broke. There were tears in his eyes. He sloshed the drink but didn't raise it. Instead, he extended his left hand and pushed a signet ring off the third finger with his thumb. McNally stiffened.

There was a hooded cobra tattooed on his ring-finger in delicate miniature, the coils running around the finger and the ugly head upraised almost to the knuckle.

"I had that done to please her," Dalton said chokily. "She believed the Yogi. He said that it would keep us together—eternally. It was no harm to believe it. She had the duplicate—"

He swallowed hard and his eyes went to the white finger in the case. McNally's gaze followed his. The ring, however, was wide and it was no time to interrupt the man's narrative. McNally restrained the impulse to examine the finger. Dalton, of course, did not know of McNally's passionate interest in tattooing. That interest belonged to the other side of McNally's life; to the world in which he was known as Needle Mike, tattoo artist, and not as Kenneth McNally, wealthy idler. With an effort, Dalton lifted his eyes from the case.

"It didn't work," Dalton said huskily. "We quarreled a lot. Lately she took to worrying about her looks, looking in mirrors and brooding. She said that she was getting old before her time, that her eyes were puffy and all that sort of thing."

McNally frowned. "Was she right?"

Dalton choked a little. His face reddened. "She looked all right to me," he said evasively. "We drink a lot. Hangovers do things to you—"

"I understand. Then she disappeared?"

"Yes. We had a quarrel. She left a note that she was going to visit her sister. I didn't worry. It was an all-right note. Look!"

**DALTON PASSED** over a double sheet of fine stationery with a trembling hand. McNally hastily read through the short note. It was nicely written, in a firm hand, without haste or apparent nervousness. It seemed like the kind of letter that a woman might write to a man she loved but with whom she was slightly peeved.

"What did you do?" McNally asked.

"I got drunk. That was Monday. Tuesday morning I got this in the mail."

He passed over a single sheet of rough dime-store bond. There was a message typed on it—

Mr. Dalton:

188 THE COMPLETE CASES OF NEEDLE MIKE, VOLUME 1

Yore wife has been kidnapped. We have her. She is safe
if you do this. Get twenty thousand dollars from yore bank
in small bills. Don't take the numbers. At ten tonite, drive
yore car to the levee near the Steamer J.S. Drive north to
point marked on this map. Park car at X and get out. Walk
north till you meet a man carrying overalls under his arm.
Give him the money and yore wife is safe. Don't do this
and it is too bad. Forget the cops or that is too bad too.

Tug.

McNally was frowning intently, his jaw hard. "You didn't
do it?" he asked incredulously.

Maurice Dalton sloshed the liquor around in his glass,
threw a deep draught back into his throat and choked on
it. "Ken," he said hoarsely, "I could shoot myself. I got the
money. Then I was all jittery. I didn't dare tell anyone. I
called Louise, my wife's sister, but didn't tell her anything.
Ethel hadn't been there. I kept drinking—"

The sweat was heavy on his forehead, his eyes haunted.
"Ken, I could drink all day once. That was once. Not now.
I must have passed out. It was damn near morning when
I came out of it—too late—"

He gulped and looked with gray intentness at the finger
in the case. "That came this afternoon. There was a note."

McNally took the second note. It was like the first except
that there was no map and it was shorter.

You had better bring the money tonight, or we'll send you
the other fingers tomorrow.

McNally was not unduly squeamish nor was he a ten-
derfoot in matters of violence. Reading that curt note,
however, and looking at the grisly evidence in the case was
a little too much for him. He stood up and reached for

Dalton's bottle. Dalton stared at him with popping eyes. The man's face was a deathly white and had the wet look of fresh paste.

"I can't—can't trust myself again, Ken," he said faintly. "I need your help. I'm going to—"

His eyes seemed to pop almost to the bursting point. His voice liquefied until only a gurgle reached his lips. McNally took a swift step toward him and threw out his right hand. He was too late. Maurice Dalton came halfway to his feet, twisted grotesquely past the outstretched hand and plunged, face down on the rug, before McNally could close the gap between them.

"Maurice!" McNally dropped on one knee and lifted the limp body partly off the rug. Glassy eyes stared at him but the man's lips twitched and there was a faint, erratic pulse. McNally gently rolled him over on his back and elevated his feet. Ordinarily there might be virtue in the administration of whiskey for a case like this; but McNally knew that Maurice Dalton had had his share of whiskey—and more.

"Maurice," he said huskily. "If you can hear me, I'm going for a doctor. Lie quietly till I come back—"

**HE GOT** up and whirled toward the door. He felt particularly futile but this was no spot for amateur medical attention. Dalton was too perilously on the brink and he remembered that there was a doctor on the floor below, a specialist of some kind.

There were two phones on the nearby desk; an outside phone and the apartment house-phone. McNally passed them up. There was a dust storm outside and a doctor from any distance away would be too slow; he had an idea that he could get the doctor on the floor below before he could explain what was wanted to the apartment staff.

Moving with the swift speed of a man in training, he took the stairs three at a time.

A slim, curly headed, languid youth of the matinee-idol type answered the insistently rung bell of Doctor Felix Borne's suite. He seemed annoyed at such vulgar haste. McNally's voice cracked.

"Doctor Borne?"

"You have an appointment?"

"No. There's a man dying upstairs—"

The youth didn't move. "I'm sorry—Doctor Borne doesn't—"

"He damn well will!" McNally's shoulders twitched and he pushed past the startled guardian of the door. A tall, military-appearing man, who wore a Van Dyke beard, was standing in a doorway off what was obviously a reception room. McNally's eyes sought his.

"I believe you heard what I said to your assistant, Doctor. There's no time to lose. The man has collapsed. He had a shock. Heart, I think—"

The doctor's lips tightened. "I do not go in for that sort of thing—"

McNally's lips flattened against his teeth. His eyes blazed. "Doctor," he said ominously, "you'll come in a hurry."

Doctor Borne read something in McNally's face that told him he was not facing a bluffer. A determined man with money and time could make things unpleasant with the medical associations. He shrugged slightly.

"Just a second," he said curtly.

He stepped back into the office behind him and came out with a black bag. He handled it with seeming distaste.

McNally spun on his heel and stalked swiftly past the still startled youth at the door. He heard the medical man's footsteps behind him and flung over his shoulder: "It is Maurice Dalton. Perhaps you know him."

There was a break in the steady pace of Doctor Borne's footsteps. McNally looked back. The man looked startled. As his eyes encountered McNally's, his face became a mask again.

"I treated his wife a few weeks ago," he said. Then they were at the door of the apartment and McNally pushed in. Just over the threshold, he stopped short.

Maurice Dalton had not stayed where he left him. The man had struggled to his knees, evidently, and gripped the outside phone with his fingers. It now lay, with the receiver off the hook, just beyond his outflung hand. Dalton himself was kneeling like a Mohammedan at prayer, his knees drawn up under his stomach and his forehead resting on the rug.

Doctor Borne made a sharp, clicking sound with his tongue and crossed the room slowly, brushing past McNally. The house phone rang shrilly.

For a moment, McNally let it ring; then, as the doctor dropped to one knee beside Maurice Dalton, he crossed the room and scooped the phone from the desk. An excited voice came over the line.

"This is the clerk, downstairs, speaking. Is anything wrong up there? There is a police officer on the way up. He says there was a call—"

"I'll let you know." McNally dropped the receiver back into place and turned around. He was a little dazed at the idea of Dalton struggling to the phone for help. The man must have forgotten McNally, must have imagined that he was alone. The telephone girl, of course, would notify the police and the call would go out to the prowl cars by radio. It was fast work.

Knuckles rapped against the door and McNally was conscious of the open green case with its ghastly secret. He picked it up mechanically and snapped it shut; then he crossed to the door. Doctor Felix Borne straightened up from his examination of Maurice Dalton. He rubbed his slender hands together.

"There is nothing I can do," he said. "The man is dead."

Borne snapped shut the catch of his emergency case as the young copper from the prowl patrol entered the room. The medical man's face was grim.

"There's no case for the police here," he said crisply. "The man had a weak heart and he'd been drinking too much. He's dead now and he was dead before I saw him. You might have the medical examiner stop by. He wasn't my patient. I don't want to make out the death certificate—"

The patrolman removed his cap and wiped the sweat from the inside of it while his eyes took swift inventory of the room. He was a young man of the alert type usually found on prowl-car duty.

"I guess that's right, Doctor," he said, "but I've got a report to make and I'll need a few facts."

He took a notebook from his pocket while the medico exhibited a testy impatience. "I'll have to have your name, Doctor, and—" He moved across the room to the desk and stopped. The two ransom notes were lying there where Maurice Dalton had laid them. McNally had been very conscious of them since the policeman entered the room. The cop saw them now. He broke his question in half and picked the top note off the desk.

"Oh, oh," he said softly. "Maybe you better have a seat for a moment, Doctor." He wheeled to the phone. It was the house phone; the outside one was still lying on the floor.

"Hello—desk? Give me police headquarters. Right.... Yeah.... Kane? This is Prescott.... Yeah, this Roney Apartments call.... Guy's dead.... Heart disease, maybe.... Better have homicide take a look.... There's angles.... A snatch mixed up in it.... Yeah? Corbin? Swell. Have him over.... Better send the doc out, too...."

He hung up and looked quietly from McNally to Borne. The doctor's cold stare did not intimidate him. He was the law and he knew it.

"I'm sorry, gentlemen," he said, "but you'll have to wait a few minutes. It will save misunderstandings. Sergeant Corbin is only a few blocks from here on another matter. He'll be right over. Let's get the facts down."

**HE HAD** the book out and he was starting after the facts with questions aimed at the tight-lipped Doctor Borne. McNally fumbled for a cigarette and looked longingly at the half-filled whiskey bottle. He was not much of a drinker but this was one case where he felt that he needed it.

Dalton's death was a shock and somewhere Ethel Dalton was facing further mutilation unless something were done. To top it all off, Corbin was coming over.

McNally knew Corbin all too well. The hardboiled sergeant had been on several cases in which Needle Mike, the tattoo artist, had played a part—and Needle Mike was McNally's other self.

The crisp young patrolman was shooting incisive questions and an angry medical man was answering them. The mills of the law were grinding and it would be McNally's turn soon. His brow furrowed. Like the highly incensed medical man, he had not wanted to walk into anything like this and now that he was in, he was not sure of his own position.

If the police decided that Ethel Dalton had been really kidnapped and that Maurice Dalton had died a natural death, the McNally reputation would be proof against annoyance; but if the police suspected another angle involving Ethel Dalton, it might be tough.

The patrolman was writing in his book and Borne had risen to lean over the desk and inspect the written record. For the moment, McNally was screened behind the doctor's back. It was an opportunity that he had hoped for and he didn't miss it. He reached out and picked up the green plush case.

There was one thing that he had to know and, as the lid snapped back, he reached in and slipped the ring down a bit. Where the ring had been, there was a tattooed cobra!

His lips tightened and he started to slip the ring back into place; then something about the tattooing arrested his attention and he took a closer look. His lips pursed and for the moment, he was rigid; his body bent forward.

The door into the hall opened and McNally sensed it rather than heard it. He straightened and he was closing the green case as he turned. He was too late. Detective-sergeant Pete Corbin was staring at him, his eyes narrowed. A cigar was balanced aggressively in the corner of his wide mouth.

"I'll look at the case—" Corbin's voice was harsh. Doctor Borne turned around, startled. The young policeman looked up.

McNally shrugged and handed over the green case. "It came with the second of those notes," he said.

Corbin grunted and pressed the catch. His eyes widened and the cigar all but leaped from his mouth. He shot a venomous look at the uniformed copper.

"A swell job you're doin'," he growled. "Everybody paws the evidence before we print it and...." His voice trailed off in a disgusted growl. He set the case down gingerly and took a chair, his eyes straying indifferently over the body on the floor.

"Let's have it from the beginning," he said. Doctor Borne drew himself up.

"I've given all the information that I can give already," he said. "I'm Doctor Felix Borne and the man was not my patient. I must insist that—"

Corbin waved one heavy hand. "O.K., Doctor. Sorry you were bothered. We'll call you if we want you."

He ignored McNally and bent a hard look on the suddenly flustered cop at the desk. After a moment of hesitation, the doctor turned and walked stiffly from the room. The patrolman was summing up tersely and McNally followed the medico. Nobody stopped him but he sensed the fact that Corbin watched him go. He knew how Corbin worked. The dick wouldn't let anyone go far if he didn't think that he could pull him back.

**BORNE STARTED** for the stairs and McNally caught up with him. "I'm sorry if the delay inconvenienced you, Doctor," he said, "but if you knew the Daltons, you—" He broke off, aware of the fact that Borne did not intend to pay any attention to him. Ken's lips tightened. When the medical man turned to descend the stairs, McNally stopped him with a hand on his forearm.

"Doctor," he said, "the Daltons were my friends. Ethel Dalton is still missing. Will you tell me if there was anything serious the matter with her when you treated her?"

Doctor Borne's eyes were coldly expressionless. "A reputable physician does not discuss his patients," he said.

McNally stepped back. "Just like that," he muttered. "Well, maybe I asked for it." He turned back into the room, a feeling of inferiority rankling him. He was out of his element; outranked, in this case, by both police and medical men. His eyes clouded. He was merely the man whose aid Maurice Dalton had asked. Well, it was enough. As he turned back into the apartment, a man got off the elevator, followed him in.

The new arrival was the police medical examiner and McNally stayed in the background until he was through. There were other technicians on hand now—a fingerprint expert and a photographer. This wasn't a murder case but the background of kidnapping and extortion gave it murder rating.

Corbin was chewing his cigar grimly. He was on the homicide squad and always ready to entertain ideas of foul play in a mysterious death. His eyes stabbed McNally.

"I've seen you someplace," he said bluntly.

McNally didn't change expression. "I wouldn't know where," he said.

Corbin didn't know, either, but he had a reputation for remembering faces. He wouldn't be looking for Needle Mike in expensive tweeds and minus the traditional limp, the scars and the dirt. McNally didn't care to be around, however, when the matter of the tattoo design under the ring was discussed. Sheer association of ideas might put Corbin on the trail. It was a ticklish spot.

McNally turned to the medical examiner, a keen-eyed man of middle age who was studying the finger in the case with professional interest. "Can you tell, Doctor," he said, "if that finger was amputated from a living body or a dead one?"

That question focused even Corbin's attention. The medical examiner tilted the case thoughtfully. "It was cut from a living body," he said. "Yes. The tissue looks healthy. No signs of decay."

Corbin's jaw snapped. He reached out one big hand and pulled the telephone to him. When he got headquarters, he barked his report into the transmitter. "I've got a hunch this is the same gang that got the Gerspach and the Stone women," he growled. "Keep the lid on the press and we've got a chance. Clamp down on everything till I get in."

**HE WHEELED** around again and leveled one thick finger at a man in gray who stood inconspicuously in the doorway. "You, Carmody, get downstairs and grab that doc, also the guy on the desk. Tell 'em to button up and talk to nobody—"

The phone rang and he turned back to it without completing the sentence. He listened for a moment, his face reddening; then he hung up with a curse.

"Somebody's already tipped off the papers," he growled. "They're sniffing around headquarters and they'll be here any minute." He slashed through a quarter arc with his big fist. "That clerk downstairs, the triple-plated, blinkety blank—"

McNally rose and laid his card on the desk. "I've told you all I know," he said, "but if you want me, you can get me. I've got to go along now."

Corbin merely grunted. There was no charge that McNally could be detained on and one doesn't hold material witnesses to death from heart attack. McNally turned to the door.

He'd be followed, of course. He expected that and it would be up to him to shake the trailers. He was going to do just that. For one thing, he was going to have to be Needle Mike again and for another, there was the matter of locating Ethel Dalton in a hurry.

He was not quite so sure, as was Corbin, that the clerk at the desk had tipped the papers—and he had one puzzle in his mind that hadn't even occurred to the cops as yet. Dalton had identified the ring and the tattoo as his wife's, and the medical examiner had declared that the finger came from a living woman. But Ethel Dalton had had her tattooed cobra for years and McNally was willing to wager Needle Mike's professional reputation that the cobra on the amputated finger was only a few weeks old.

## CHAPTER TWO

## THE JADE RING

**I**N THE shabby little office that he rented on a side street east of Broadway, Ken McNally slipped out of his stylish tweeds and climbed into shabby gray trousers and blue shirt. After a few deft touches, the measles scars on his cheeks became blue-black powder-marks, his sleek black hair became tousled and streaked with gray, his eyes reddened and bloodshot, his tanned face a dirty yellow.

McNally grinned into the propped-up mirror and Needle Mike grinned back. There remained the adjustment of the especially made dental bridge which clipped to two sound teeth and held a gold cap over one of his canines.

There was little of McNally left and the chunk of wax under his upper lip removed that trace. Needle Mike's mouth was slightly awry.

McNally stood up. Rolling back his right trouser leg, he adjusted an ovular device of cork and rubber that fitted snugly to his knee. With that in place, there was no fear that he would ever forget to walk with the characteristic limp of Needle Mike; he could walk no other way.

It was done. Whistling softly through his teeth, McNally turned and hobbled out of the office. He took a pull from a bottle of particularly villainous whiskey and spilled enough of it on his clothes to give him the odor of ten tough days on a bat. He was now ready to come home to South Broadway; home, as he always came home, lurching and slightly tipsy and in a rile mood. The half-world knew a man only by his habits and Needle Mike had established a tradition.

The usual thrill of exchanging identities was missing tonight. Ken McNally felt no glow of adventurous spirit in his veins; instead, he felt a sense of foreboding. Ken McNally might make blunders and still get by on his reputation; Needle Mike could make no mistakes because Needle Mike had only a shady reputation to fall back upon. Needle Mike was a dweller in the shadows, a seemingly drunken old vagabond whose tattooing business and locksmith shop had often enough come under police suspicion.

Yet, upon Needle Mike's shoulders rested the responsibility of saving Ethel Dalton from her captors. Doors opened for the Needler that Ken McNally could never crash in fancy tweeds; men who would whisper carelessly where Needle Mike lingered over a whiskey, would sit stonily silent in the presence of one who was not of their world.

He had been away and he could not plunge back into his role immediately because he had never done it that way. He would have to follow his accepted custom and he would have to putter when he wanted to rush. The underworld is never hurried and it distrusts people who have to have quick answers.

Then, too, there were the police. Once let Corbin learn that the tattooing on the severed finger was new—there would be hell to pay. Tattooing in St. Louis meant Needle Mike—to the police. Only McNally himself, and a very few others, knew that there was another needle artist in the shadow-world; and McNally could not prove the existence of that other. It was that knowledge which had sent McNally to South Broadway and the role of Needle Mike. Now, if only he could scare up a lead before the cops fell on him!

**DOWNTOWN ST. LOUIS** was blacker than usual as Kansas dust settled like a fog over the city and dimmed the street lights. McNally hobbled along with his head down, his face grimly set. Music blared from a tuneless radio in a corner restaurant and he found some frivolous part of his brain fitting words to an old drinking-party dirge. It was *St. Joe's Infirmary Blues*—

> She gone, let 'er go,
> Gor blyme 'er,
> Wherever she may be....

He swore softly. The words were too pat, fitted too well into the pattern of his thought. Ahead of him he could see light streaming from the penny arcade that was only a few doors south of his tattooing parlor. He was nearly in. He'd have to stop at the Irishman's for a whiskey to announce his return, if there were no cops hanging around.

A hoarse voice hailed him from the shadows. "Mike?"

He slowed, turned toward the hail. There was a dark hallway leading back from a door opening flush with the sidewalk. McNally caught the flash of a hand that beckoned, the darker shadow of a man in waiting. He felt an uneasy prickling of his scalp but his shoulders twitched irritably. It was probably some bum trying to make a touch.

"Whozit and whaddye want?" He turned to the doorway with his jaw jutting. The man who had hailed him coughed harshly.

"Never mind gettin' tough, Mike. Get on my tail and off the pave—"

"Skeeter!" McNally felt a stir of interest as he limped into the hallway. He'd recognized the voice and the cough and he didn't need anything else. If Skeeter had a deal, it would be worth a few minutes' delay to hear it. Down the hall, a door opened which shed a pale yellow rectangle of light for a moment. McNally hurried toward it and the door closed until he reached it; then it opened hurriedly to admit him—and closed again. Skeeter stood leaning against it on the inside, a strangely gaunt figure in the pale, flickering gaslight.

There was no describing Skeeter and no explaining him. At twenty he was an old man with stooped shoulders and a chronic cough. He sold papers on a South Broadway corner, in all weather, for a few pennies, yet time and again he had had big stakes which he flipped away at dice tables. He had no conscience to torment him and no moral code, but he managed, somehow, to be likable in the face of his utter worthlessness. His blurry features were twisted now in a knowing smile.

"Mike, you were walkin' right into a pinch."

McNally turned. "What fur?"

Skeeter passed one bony hand caressingly across his loose lower lip. "Don't kid me, Mike. I flagged you down and saved you the ride. I want in."

"Are you nuts?"

"Not me." Skeeter was studying him. "There's dough in a good snatch racket if it's worked right. I want a cut."

McNally was far from forgetting that he was Needle Mike. He cursed fervently and with emphasis, jerked a flimsy chair out from the wall and flopped into it.

"You're a dirty little chiseler, Skeeter," he snarled, "and you're spotting me for somebody. Whatinell's it all about?"

For the first time, Skeeter looked doubtful. He also looked startled. Moving more slowly than McNally, he straddled the only other chair in the room. "Mike," he said, "you maybe ain't a liar. You ain't—on any evidence I've got, anyway. Kick in. Are you on the snatch or ain't you?"

McNally grunted explosively. "Not me. You're just as nuts as I figured."

Skeeter seemed deflated. He took a shabby crumpled cigarette from his pocket and lighted it. "I still saved you from a pinch," he said. "That ought to rate something."

"Yeah? Tell me about it."

Skeeter exhaled. "Rafferty, the big harness bull was watching your dump. I couldn't figure it. Nothin' in the paper tied to you any. And I remembered that it was time for the Scientific Sleuth program on the radio—he was the guy that spotted you, Mike."

"Yeah?" McNally was smoking and slumped back in the chair. He seemed uninterested but there was a tingle in his blood. He knew about that radio program. Some smart-aleck had tapped a leak at detective headquarters and was scooping the newspapers every afternoon on police news under the name of the "Scientific Sleuth." Skeeter was nodding his head.

"The guy says, Mike, that the cops have information that the guy behind the snatching of all these women is a tattoo artist. Is that a kick in the pants?"

"It's worse! What else?"

"Well, Corbin is talking to Rafferty when I come down the street and they're both sore as hell when somebody tells 'em about the radio program. They figure that maybe you won't come back now and—"

McNally's eyes narrowed. "You were the guy that told them about the radio program!"

Skeeter grinned. "O.K. They'd a' heard about it anyway. It don't hurt a guy in my business to do a cop a favor."

There was tension in the room. McNally felt trapped, a little smothered. He had just thought of something that brought the sweat to his forehead. He'd been criminally careless. It wasn't just the tattoo design that had put the cops on his trail—it was worse than that. To cover his sudden feeling of panic, he took the whiskey bottle from his pocket and drank. It took all of his fortitude to keep from gagging. Skeeter reached out his hand and McNally passed the bottle over. Skeeter tilted it.

**FOR SEVERAL** moments the scrawny newsboy coughed his heart out. He raised streaming eyes to McNally and spat across the room. "You win, Mike," he gasped. "Nobody that had a big-dough racket would be drinkin' that kind o' rowboat paint. Wow—"

He wiped his thin hand across his lips and stiffened suddenly, his eyes narrowing. "That's one damn nice ring, Mike," he said slowly.

His voice was ominous. McNally looked down at his own hand and cursed inwardly. He was slipping badly. This was colossal blunder number two. The jade ring on his hand was the gift of a Japanese nobleman and it belonged in the life of Ken McNally; it had never come before into the haunts of Needle Mike. It did not belong on South Broadway.

Skeeter held out his hand. "The ring, Mike," he said, "for telling you about the cops and"—he paused—"for not telling the cops about you."

There was friendliness in his voice and no hint of threat, but, because he was Skeeter, he did not have to threaten. He was an ally to be bought and he had never pretended otherwise. In that policy lay his strength. McNally looked him in the eye and cursed with all the vigor of Needle Mike.

When he had finished cursing he passed the ring over. Skeeter put it in his pocket and rose. "I'm still in if you've got a snatch racket, Mike," he said.

McNally's jaw was suddenly hard. He reached out swiftly, as he rose, and gripped the skinny arm of the newsboy. "Skeeter," he said, "forget it. I haven't. But I gotta find who has. Do you know where that Polynesian girl, Benita, went to when—"

Skeeter's eyes widened. "The one that was in that cult business?"

"Sure. Can you find her?"

Skeeter's eyes went back behind slits. "For how much?"

"Twenty bucks."

"Make it fifty."

McNally hesitated as Needle Mike would be expected to hesitate. "You're a damn robber. I won't do it."

"I'll make it forty, Mike."

McNally grunted. "O.K., but it's still too much. Find her and let me know. I'll be at the public lib'ry. Newspaper room."

"Check. Watch out for cops."

Skeeter slid from the room as though anxious to be on the trail. McNally took a deep breath. It was a long shot but he was in no position to complain about the odds.

He'd pawed the green plush case and its metal fittings like a raw yokel while the cops were waiting to fingerprint it—and he'd closed the doors to all explanations and alibis when he did it. Ken McNally could never claim those prints, now, and the arrest of the kidnappers would not clear the logical suspect.

The police had the prints of Needle Mike on file.

# CHAPTER THREE
# INFIRMARY BLUES

**T**HE NEWSPAPER reading room of the public library is the most democratic spot in St. Louis. McNally, in his role of Needle Mike, was not conspicuous among the businessmen, students and down-and-outers who lingered over the out-of-town newspapers. McNally, however, was not interested in the papers of other cities. In a corner of the room, he searched carefully through ten issues of the *St. Louis Star*. The first headline of interest was exactly ten days back.

ST. LOUIS WOMAN KIDNAPPED

Leaves Home to Visit Mother, Disappears
Husband Receives Ransom Demand

That was the Gerspach case. The detailed files running down to date gave a running narrative of police efforts to locate the kidnappers, and of the husband's despair at his failure to hear further from the people who had taken his wife.

The second case was only six days later and the headlines shrieked—

## SECOND WOMAN KIDNAP VICTIM

Kidnappers Break Faith With Husband George Stone Appeals to
Police After Paying Futile Ransom

The bald facts in this case were much the same as in the first. Mrs. Stone's husband was a well-to-do businessman and she had disappeared after first announcing her intention to visit relatives in Illinois. There had been no evidence of violent abduction, no clues. With the Gerspach case still in the public prints, Stone had taken no chances of notifying the police. He had paid the twenty-thousand-dollar ransom demanded and kept his mouth shut. His wife, however, had not been returned.

McNally frowned thoughtfully as he read hastily through the accounts. They checked in all the essential details with the case of Ethel Dalton. Apparently there had been no violence in that case, either. She had written a neat, unhurried note, then vanished. The ransom demand had also been for twenty thousand. In only one particular did the Dalton case differ.

No other husband had received his wife's finger in the mail.

McNally watched the library clock. Skeeter was taking plenty of time and the library was not the best place in the world for a wanted man. The police made regular checkups of the floaters who hung around there. The papers were barren of any startling facts and McNally craved activity. He flipped the pages over impatiently; stopped to con a story by the Star's regular crime writer.

RUMOR MANY WOMEN SNATCHED HERE

The police are reported to be in possession of information on other kidnapping cases similar to the Gerspach and Stone cases. According to rumors current today, many prominent St. Louis men have paid ransom....

It was a vague story and it betrayed the fact that the writer had few facts to go on, but the germ of an idea was there. It was easy to believe. The technique of the kidnappings was smooth and the ransom demanded in each case was comparatively light in comparison to the resources of the victims. But if there had been other cases in which the women were safely returned, why was Stone double-crossed after paying the ransom? Why didn't the women, who were previous victims, come forward and tell their stories? And why the mutilation in the Dalton case?

That amputated finger bothered McNally. If it wasn't Ethel Dalton's—and it wasn't if her tattoo was several years old—then whose finger was it? Why did the snatchers cut the finger from another woman after going to the trouble of duplicating a tattoo mark? If they were going to mutilate, why use one woman rather than another?

There were too many questions to answer and they couldn't be answered by anyone who sat around in libraries. McNally got up in disgust. Skeeter was taking his own sweet time and, meanwhile, the dragnet was out for Needle

Mike. Logically, the quickest escape from that was a quick switch back to the identity of Ken McNally—but that, too, had its dangers besides imposing definite limitations upon his activities. The police might get the idea of taking McNally prints to eliminate them from prints found on the ransom messages or the jewel case.

A direct link between Kenneth McNally, Needle Mike and Maurice Dalton, at this stage of the game, would be hanging evidence.

**EYES ALERT,** McNally hobbled toward the main entrance of the library. A sharp-eyed youngster of eleven or twelve came up the Olive Street steps, two at a time. When he saw McNally he slowed his pace and a wide grin lighted his pinched features.

"Gotta message for yuh…" he panted.

McNally stopped. He was wary of messages. "Who from?" he growled.

"Skeeter." The youngster held the grimy envelope tightly. His young-old eyes were suddenly calculating.

"I gotta have expense money. Taxi," he said.

McNally looked at him more closely as he put a seemingly reluctant hand in his pocket. It was thus that Skeeters were developed. He brought out a quarter and the youngster surrendered the envelope. There was a single slip of paper inside and a scrawled line—*Thanks for the tip, Mike. Skeeter.*

For a long minute, McNally stared at the message while a blue vein danced on his jaw line and fury gathered in his eyes. He'd been sold out. Somehow Skeeter had stumbled across the path of the girl, Benita, and the path led to the snatch ring. Skeeter was declaring himself in; he was a body and a soul for hire. McNally cursed.

"How about a taxi back? My feet hurt."

The youngster who had brought the message was shifting nervously from one foot to the other, his eyes bright. McNally glowered at him. The kid had probably never ridden in a taxi in his life and didn't intend to ride in one now. It was a gouge. Ken McNally wouldn't care but it was Needle Mike's cue to be good and sore about it.

"You got two bits. Beat it!" he growled.

The youngster stopped shifting. "If I take a taxi," he persisted, "I ain't goin' to run into any cops. If they see me, they'll maybe ask me did I see you someplace and if they catch me lying to 'em—"

He broke off as McNally reached into his pocket. Needle Mike's growl was fervently deep. "How much?"

The youngster's eyes glowed. "A buck," he said.

"Here. Beat it!"

McNally passed the bill and watched the youngster scurry away. It was the Skeeter proposition all over again; a shakedown. The underworld lived like that, declaring itself in for a cut on every deal—and from the youngest to the oldest, the clippers took their toll.

"Damn Skeeter!"

McNALLY TURNED back into the shadows of the library pillars. He was more alone than ever, now; and the man that he had depended upon was playing his only card and playing it for personal gain. It was something, however, to know that his guess was good. The tattoo clue led to Benita and Benita led to the mutilating snatchers. But how to pick up the trail?

"If I could circulate around!" McNally shrugged There was no sense in thinking about that. He couldn't circulate. He'd last about ten minutes in downtown St. Louis before he was picked up. There had to be another trail out of the library and into the heart of the mystery. Break the Dalton case and he had a fighting chance for his freedom; fail and—

Unbidden, the dirge-like melody of *St. Joe's Infirmary Blues* echoed in his brain; silly words to a bad tune.

> She's gone. Let 'er go,
> Gor blyme 'er,
> Wherever she may be....

Then suddenly, out of the maudlin song, he had the answer. His body stiffened and he snapped his fingers. He had a hunch, he had an idea—and there were three phone booths to his right.

He thumbed hastily through the directory and jotted down the phone numbers of Harvey Gerspach and of George Stone. As he waited for his connection on the first number, a crazy jumble of words ran through his brain.

"Infirmary... hospital... hospital... doctor... gone... let 'er go... amputation... hospital... doctor...."

There was a click in the receiver and then a voice at the other end of the line said, "Hello." McNally's shoulders twitched. He had Gerspach on the line.

Fifteen minutes later, after getting George Stone on the third attempt, McNally stepped out of the telephone booth with a gleam in his eye and a hard slant to his jaw. He had asked each man four questions about his wife and his wife's disappearance—and he had received the answers that he hoped to receive, the answers that Maurice Dalton would have given if Maurice Dalton were alive to answer questions.

The trail led out of that booth to the lair of the snatchers and he was betting his life and his liberty on it. He hummed a doggerel tune under his breath and choked it off when he stepped out into a St. Louis night that was heavy with Kansas dust. He had slipped off the leg clamp in the booth and the telltale limp of Needle Mike was gone. A cruising cab poked up Olive and he whistled to it.

## CHAPTER FOUR
## THE BITE OF STEEL

**THE BODY** of Maurice Dalton had been removed and the police had departed. Life was going on as usual at the Roney Apartments. McNally had left his taxi two blocks away and had walked up on the far side of the street from the apartment house. There were good-looking cars around the entrance and a party of people in evening clothes had just emerged. McNally slipped further back into the shadows.

A man who wore the tattered outfit of Needle Mike would look strange as he walked through that lobby—if he got that far.

McNally didn't put the matter to the test. There was an alley and a tradesman's entrance. The Kansas dust had created a light-dimming fog even in this, the higher part of town. The alley was a black pocket and the one bulb over the service entrance was weak. McNally picked three empty bottles and a paper bag from the receptacle inside the alley fence and walked confidently into the basement. A colored woman looked at him curiously but the package sidetracked any possible questioning. Repeal had not stopped nighttime bottle deliveries at the Roney.

McNally didn't bother with the elevator. He ascended the back stairs slowly and carefully. At the fourth floor he reconnoitered before leaving the stairwell. There was no one around and he could see the dignified metal plate on the door of Doctor Felix Borne's office from where he stood. Something glowed in his eyes. He was only a few steps away from high hazard and something wild sang in his blood. His fingers dipped into the bag and shifted the position of the bottles. They were a gag, so far; they could be used as weapons.

The same slim, languid, curly-headed, young man opened the door. There was a faint fragrance in the air about him and he was beautifully marcelled. His eyebrows lifted inquiringly. McNally lapsed into the gruff speech of Needle Mike.

"The doctor in, buddy?"

"No. He is not. Are you sure that you have the right address?"

"Sure I'm sure. I got three bottles." McNally pushed the package at the matinee idol so abruptly that the man's reaction was instinctive. He put his hands up and McNally gave him the bottles. The youth looked startled. For a few seconds, he held the package as though he had never had a package in his hands before.

McNally stepped in, closed the door behind him and leaned against it. "Buddy," he said, "we're going to swap talk." A hard grin crossed his lips. "Just try screaming and the roof will fall on you."

The guardian of Doctor Felix Borne's door took a backward step. There was swift panic in his face but no resolve. He was the kind of youth who has things happen to him; he was not the type to make things happen. And he was looking into the fighting face of Needle Mike. Even in the rougher dumps along South Broadway, nobody went out of his way to make passes at men who looked like the Needler.

"Anybody but you in this dump?" McNally's voice matched his looks.

The slim youth swallowed hard. "Nobody. But—"

"Never mind the repartee. Just back slowly into that reception room." McNally thrust his chin out belligerently and followed that chin. He was not packing a weapon and he was conscious of the lack—it would have been a help. Lacking a gun, he needed courage, lots of courage.

**THE YOUTH** backed across the reception room and, still holding the bottles, sat in a corner chair. His eyes were wide and there was perspiration on his high, white forehead. McNally stared steadily at him.

"What's the doctor's business?" McNally growled.

"Er—why—he's a nerve specialist."

"Whose nerves? Women?"

"Why—er—yes. Of course." The elegant secretary seemed relieved at the easy questions and his face brightened. McNally studied that face. It didn't take a Sherlock Holmes to guess that Felix Borne's specialty was women patients. The sweetly scented male attendant was the tip-off on that. A man with bad nerves wouldn't be able to stand it. McNally balanced his weight forward.

"What's his other specialty—besides nerves?"

Fear leaped into the man's eyes. He moistened his lips. "I don't know what you mean," he faltered.

McNally took two swift steps, jerked the man out of his chair and slapped him back into it with his open palm. The paper bag crashed to the floor and the empty bottles rolled.

"I've got no time for waltzing. You answer my questions." The words snapped from McNally's lips. "I asked you what his other business was!"

The fashion plate cowered. He had been hired to greet nervous women, not to confront roughnecks from South Broadway. He put his hand before his face in a protective gesture.

"He—he's a plastic surgeon—" Fear surged whitely into the man's face. "I'm not supposed to know."

McNally hid his elation under a scowl. "You mean that he's a face-lifter? He makes old women look young? That sort of thing?"

"Ye-es. Sometimes—"

"Sure. When that's what they're nervous about." McNally couldn't keep the scorn out of his voice. Legitimate surgery was one thing; undercover rackets was another. He drilled the cringing man before him with hard eyes. "Where's his hospital?"

"I—honest—please—" The man gagged, his eyes terrified.

"Please, hell! You've snooped. If you don't know what's going on, you suspect." McNally's fists were iron balls. He took one step. It was enough.

The marcelled youth pressed back against the upholstery, his face putty-gray. "Don't! I'll tell you! He'll kill me! It's down near the barracks...." He whispered the address hoarsely and he was too frightened to lie. McNally grunted.

"How much staff has he got?"

"I—I don't know—really—"

There was a clicking sound behind him and McNally whirled. He was not quite quick enough. The door had opened and closed again. Doctor Felix Borne was standing with his back against the panels, a heavy cane in his right hand.

One glance was enough for the doctor. His cold eyes swept from the frightened man in the chair to the roughly dressed, aggressive figure of McNally. His thumb pressed on the handle of the cane and the sheath fell to the floor. A long, slender blade glittered coldly in the light.

"Make one move, my friend," he said grimly, "and you'll regret it. I am an expert—" A slight motion of his wrist flashed the blade. He nodded his head slightly to the man in the chair. "What is the meaning of this, Winkler?"

Winkler put one slender hand to his throat. The coming of the doctor had not relieved his fright; it seemed to intensify it. He choked over his words. "I don't know. This man forced his way in—"

"What did he want?" Doctor Borne's voice was cold, metallic. He had advanced from the little hall into the reception room and he held the long blade with practiced ease. McNally admired the man's nerve while he cursed his own helplessness.

**THE DOCTOR** had had to rely on his own wits and his powers of observation for his assumption that the blade would be a valid threat. A gun would have made it useless, but he had evidently reasoned that McNally would have had the gun in evidence if he possessed one. McNally had witnessed miracles of speed on the part of fencers in the past and he knew that, in expert hands, a sword was only a shade less effective than a gun.

Winkler was still pressed back in the chair. He seemed to be trying to force a lie through his trembling lips, but it wouldn't go. "He wanted to know about your business!" he blurted.

Borne's face betrayed cold, inflexible purpose. The beard gave him a devilish appearance. His lips curled. "You didn't know anything, of course…?"

"No—no—"

"You're a liar. It's written in your face." Borne's eyes drilled past the cowering Winkler, held hard on McNally. McNally had not dropped his role of Needle Mike. He was standing in a half crouch, his face sullen. His mind, working at top speed, grasped at an excuse.

"The monkey's O.K.," he growled. "I coulda tore him apart. I'm just outta stir, see? A feller told me you could fix me up; new mug, new fingertips, see? I'm goin' lamister on the parole and—"

Borne's face told him the story was going to miss. That was one branch of criminal surgery, evidently, that the plastic man had not yet touched. The doctor's eyes blazed.

"Who told you anything like that?"

"A feller. I ain't namin' no names."

It was terribly still in the room, graveyard-still. Something had come into Felix Borne's face that had not been there before; something that followed hard on his first expression of disbelief. His racket was hot, judging from the events of the afternoon, and McNally's visit was too pat. There was death in his eyes.

"Tie him up, Winkler," the doctor said harshly. "I'll take care of him!"

Winkler got up unsteadily. "The police?" he faltered.

"No, not the police. There'd be unfortunate publicity, a lot of bother—" Felix Borne almost purred. The blade was held very stiff but the man's body had relaxed into a catlike pose. Looking into his eyes, McNally saw two purposes.

The man expected him to object to the tying and that would call the steel into play—or, if he submitted— McNally shook his shoulders. There were too many things at a medical man's command; deadly things that could be pressed to a tiny cut with swift and horrible death as a result. He could not afford to be helplessly tied.

Winkler stepped up behind him and McNally moved.

With a quick collapse of all his muscles, he hit the floor, tensed and scooped for one of the bottles. He had it in his fingers but he had no time for a throw. Felix Borne's body seemed to flow behind the blade. It flashed like silver lightning and McNally felt the prick of steel against his throat.

A thousandth of an inch away from bloody death, he looked up into the blazing eyes of the surgeon who was facing the ruin of his career and his life. The motive and the will to kill were there, but something had checked the plunging rapier, something that drove the blaze out of the man's eyes.

"Don't make a move!" Borne's voice was cold. He held the point of the blade where it was. McNally felt the sweat on his forehead. He crouched, stiffly motionless. He could hear the smothered breathing of the perfumed Winkler somewhere behind him. The room was terribly still; then Felix Borne laughed.

"Winkler," he said, "it's all right. We won't mess up the rug. I know this fellow."

RECOGNITION! THAT fear had walked long with Ken McNally. It was a much older fear than the fear of steel against his throat. For a moment he forgot the threatening blade as he stared up into the burning eyes of Doctor Felix Borne.

"I know this fellow," the doctor had said.

That one statement cut right through McNally's dual life. It hung him—a man without an alibi—on the hooks of crime. The public thrills to the sins and the weaknesses of the wealthy and the successful; and the public always gloats when a proud name goes down into the mire. McNally's name meant something in St. Louis and who was going to believe that Kenneth McNally became Needle Mike and lived in a slum for a thrill and for a feel of raw humanity's elbow touch? There would be a smell of scandal in the story, a heavy smell—and Ken McNally would not be around to answer the whispers.

He could read that in the eyes of Felix Borne. Alive, he was a menace to the doctor; dead, he would still be a menace and a problem, perhaps, if it were not for the double-identity. The mystery of his death would be overshadowed by the revelation of secret chapters in his life.

Doctor Borne had seen him only once as Ken McNally. And now— The whole puzzling sequence of thought passed through McNally's mind in split seconds; the cold touch of death was on his throat and the threat of recognition in his ears. Then Borne's lips curled.

"This fellow is the tattooer that the police are looking for, Winkler. There's a picture of him and a description in tonight's paper. I read it coming up—" He flipped a rolled paper out of his pocket with his left hand. "See if I'm right, Winkler."

McNally almost sighed aloud with relief. He had not considered the possibility of being recognized as Needle Mike because Borne had never seen Needle Mike. The danger had been in being recognized as Ken McNally while he wore the garb of Needle Mike.

"Stand up, you!" Doctor Borne stepped back a few feet, the blade poised carefully. His manner was suddenly contemptuous. He was not dealing with a disguised cop and the knowledge steadied him. Winkler clucked his tongue excitedly.

"It's the same man!" he said. "Indeed, it is!"

McNally had risen. He looked with interest toward the paper. There was a front-page picture. He remembered that. It was probably the only picture of Needle Mike in existence. A bone-headed news cameraman had made it when he came out of police headquarters the time that he was questioned about the death of Snuffle Magee. As a likeness it was too good, but it had had its good points. It looked nothing at all like Ken McNally. His disguise had been perfect that day.

"My gun out of the drawer, Winkler!" Borne snapped the command, his eyes still on McNally. Winkler, his confidence returning swiftly, was anxious to please. He made fast work of getting the gun out of the drawer—but he did not make the mistake of passing within reach of McNally. The surgeon took the gun and his hand fitted it like a hand accustomed to guns. He laid the blade aside and sat down.

"Put that back in the sheath, Winkler," he said.

"How about me, boss? You know who I am." McNally dripped an East Market Street whine into his voice. "You know I spilled you a fact. I'm lamister from the cops and—"

The face behind the Van Dyke might well have been cold-chiseled out of hard wax. There was the hard surface gleam of polished glass in the doctor's eyes.

"I understand and I sympathize," he purred softly, "but I do not, of course, operate here. I will take you to my private hospital." He beckoned to Winkler. "You will bring out a clean shirt and one of my suits, the blue with the pin stripe will do, for our patient. He must not occasion comment when he leaves."

**WINKLER WAS** goggle-eyed. He bobbed his head a couple of times and gulped. He was not the kind of young man who retained his composure upon encountering the unexpected. He needed women nerve patients around to be at his best. As he scuttled away, the eyes of McNally and Borne met.

They were not kidding each other very much and they were only going through the motions of trying to.

Somehow, Borne had grasped at an idea into which he had fitted Needle Mike. He was not taking seriously the claim that anyone would look him up for change-of-identity surgery; and, since he had gained the upper hand, he wasn't caring much what purpose McNally might have had in mind. He was concerned with his own purposes. McNally couldn't guess at those.

But McNally was figuring the blue suit as the uniform of a one-way ride—and he wouldn't have bet a dime on Winkler's chances, either. If Winkler were going along, it would be Winkler's first trip to that "hospital." A first trip for such a weak, babbling slob would be a last trip.

The atmosphere of the room oozed murder. "Here you are, sir. I brought a necktie and socks, too, sir." Winkler was back with his bright air of willingness to please. The doctor nodded.

"Very good. Get into them, you!"

McNally grunted and was suddenly glad that he had always been thorough in his characterization. When he became Needle Mike, he was Mike from the skin out. The underwear of the tattooer would not have looked well on a Lindell Boulevard line. He was glad, too, that he had discarded the knee-clamp. A doctor might have been curious. The clamp was in his pocket and nobody had been interested enough to search him.

He undressed and dressed in silence. When he was ready, the surgeon rose briskly and put the gun into his side pocket. "I am taking you at your word," he said, "but you can't expect me to trust an avowed criminal. If you attempt the unexpected on the way out, I'll shoot you in your tracks!"

"You won't have to." McNally nodded surlily. There was nothing more said. They went down the elevator and out to the doctor's car without drawing a curious glance.

"You may drive, Winkler." Borne edged McNally into the back. "I'm riding with you," he said.

"O.K." McNally sat back. Winkler turned his head.

"The address, doctor?"

Borne's eyes seemed to glow in the darkness. His body was stiff, rigid. "You know it," he said coldly. "Drive to it!"

**WINKLER SHIVERED** perceptibly but he did not argue. He put the car in gear and they rolled out into the evening flood of traffic. A policeman on a motorcycle passed them without a glance, his predatory gaze fastened on a flivver full of carousing Negroes who were doing about thirty-five. McNally's lips twisted in a wry grin. Life, at times, was full of laughs.

It was a laugh, too, that they had to pass the darkened quarters of Needle Mike when they wheeled into South Broadway, but that was all the comedy there was. The long, dark stretches of South Broadway, as they sped toward Jefferson Barracks, were in the mood of the grim company. No one spoke.

Some distance short of the Barracks, they turned off and an old-fashioned stone house loomed ahead of them. There was yellow light behind discreetly drawn shades and, when Winkler silenced the motor, there was the deep sighing song of the Mississippi.

> She gone, let 'er go,
> Gor blyme 'em,
> Wherever she may be....

Some frivolous side to McNally's mind sought to fit the words of that doggerel dirge to the ageless melody of old Mississip', but they wouldn't go, somehow. Felix Borne stepped carefully out of the car.

"Either I am very careless or you are very alert, Winkler," he said. "You didn't waste a mile."

There was a deadliness in his tone that the words themselves didn't carry. The doctor beckoned to McNally. "Step out!" he said.

McNally heard a door open somewhere. He rose from his cramped position in the corner of the car and bent over as he stepped out of the low car door. He was off guard and a setup for slaughter. He sensed, too late, the shadow of the upraised gun and he had no hole into which he could pull his head.

White light crashed upon his brain and spread out to all the crannies in his skull. He felt his body plunging forward from the running board of the car, felt his own terrible inability to check its fall—but he felt no impact when he hit. From some immeasurable distance he heard a cold voice saying: "You may carry him in, Winkler. If he is too heavy, McBain will assist you."

# CHAPTER FIVE
# TATTOOED COBRA

**M**cNALLY CAME back to consciousness slowly with a subtle perfume in his nostrils, a throbbing pain in his head and sharp stabs of agony in his hand. He shrank from the effort of opening his eyes but he became increasingly conscious of the pain in his hand, pain that was now centering in one finger. It was like the pain in a tooth under the dentist's drill. He opened his eyes.

The Polynesian girl, Benita, was crouched over him and she had his left hand flattened against a board while she worked on it with a glittering needle.

She was not immediately aware of his eyes on hers. Her small features were set in the hard mask of cruelty. Her lips were very red and she kept touching them with the tip of a tongue that was, itself, too red. Her teeth gleamed whitely in the intervals when her tongue disappeared. They were small teeth. Her eyes were shiny brown and there was glitter in them.

The needle flashed in and out, stabbed wickedly, savagely, but with an unholy, deft skill. The light in the room was soft and, under it, the girl's skin was creamy, maddeningly seductive. Under her skin there were smooth muscles that moved with sensuous rhythm. She wore few clothes and there was no single line of her ripe figure that was blurred or broken by clothing; the few wispy things she wore flowed to the lines of her body and merged with them.

"You're a butcher!" McNally's voice was harsh, husky. The girl's head jerked up. She smiled wickedly.

"I should butcher you good, no?"

Their eyes dueled and they were both remembering. McNally, as Needle Mike, had broken up the obscene love-cult racket in which this girl had been a prominent figure. Benita had been outwitted, in that case, and her vaunted allure had been flouted. She had cause to remember and she did.

"I do on you a serpent. It is proper, yes?"

McNally's eyes focused on his flattened left hand. It was hard to see because he was bound securely with tape. Even the left arm was fastened. His shirt had been removed and rolls of thick tape held the arm against his body above the elbow, leaving only the forearm and hand free for the girl's manipulation.

On the third finger of his left hand, she was working the design of the hooded cobra.

McNally cursed. The curse was fervent and came from deep inside him. He was not slated to get out of this mess alive, of course, but if he did get out, they were ruining him. Not only was he damned by the prints of Needle Mike on the jewel case, but now they were engraving on his skin the indelible sign that made a dual role impossible. He could never again jump from the role of McNally to Needle Mike, and back again, while he bore a mark that proclaimed the two as one and the same man.

The girl was looking at him. "You do not like?" she said. "I show you one trick. See!"

**SHE HAD** a moist pack in a bowl. It looked like a mess of pressed leaves. She took it out and laid it against his finger holding it there. "It is quick tattoo," she said. "This heals verra fast. Makes verra clean picture. See!"

She whisked the pack away. McNally was startled. The part of his skin that had been rough and swollen, with the blurred design, had smoothed down. The design had come up. He knew, now, that she had been treating the finger at intervals as she worked. It was a native trick, a trick that he didn't know.

"You put that thing on a woman recently!" he said.

The girl stabbed him viciously with the needle. "Yes," she said. Benita was almost dreamy about it and the savage pain-lust was in her face again. "She screamed and hollered. She did not like it." The girl raised her left hand. "Once she bit me. See!"

There was a healing mark on her forearm. Her eyes met McNally's and there was something unholy and unclean in them, something that chilled him. "For what she did," she said softly, "the doctor let me help him when he cut that finger off."

McNally was scarcely conscious of the cruelly driven needle as it jabbed his own skin. He was thinking of that other scene and trying not to think of it. This girl was scarcely human. Even in her tattooing, she was a fiendish sadist. Where a tattoo artist prides himself that he does not puncture the true vascular skin nor draw blood, this girl stabbed deep and gloried in the blood. Before her, on a little table, he noted the model from which she worked.

It was a set of two photographs which showed the hand of a woman; a hand that had the third finger circled by a tattooed cobra.

McNally stiffened. That photograph made many things clear to him. Borne, of course, had spotted that tattoo when Ethel Dalton came to him for treatment weeks ago. With an eye to the future, he had photographed that hand. There were many excuses he could have used, X-ray or what-not.

But who was the woman that he had turned over to this little fiend of a torturer—the woman he had mutilated? It had not been Ethel Dalton. She had already had the cobra on her finger and it would not have been necessary to put one there. The only excuse for it at all was to provide identification to Maurice Dalton and frighten him into action.

It was all guesswork, of course, but it excited Ken McNally and made him forget the biting needles and the pain in his head. The girl was softly humming and he turned his head away from her. With an effort, he controlled his sudden surprise.

The door to his left had opened without a sound. Swift as a shadow, a man glided through the opening. His arm went back and a bottle flashed across the room.

Benita never knew what hit her. Her body stiffened and a choked cry died on her lips. The needle in her hand once more bit viciously into McNally's hand; and then her body became a slumped heap on the floor.

Skeeter closed the door softly and grinned as he leaned against it. "Howarya, Mike?" he said softly. He was carrying a five-gallon can which bore the label—*Gasoline.*

**SKEETER CROSSED** the room in quick, awkward steps, put the can on the floor. He bent above the girl, swiftly flipped a black case open and took out two rolls of adhesive tape.

"Handy stuff, tape," Skeeter grunted. "I'm goin' to stick up her kisser first. She's got a screech like a hoot-owl. That's why I had to bop her."

McNally was staring at him. "You could have busted her conk that way," he said bluntly.

Skeeter looked at Needle Mike and his mouth twisted wryly. "Hell, Mike," he said, "it was an *empty* bottle."

He was working with amazing speed and rolling the girl's body around as though it were a dummy. He had each hand lashed to the sides of her chair and her legs fastened at ankle and knee before he stood up. McNally wriggled.

"O.K., how's to cut me loose?"

Skeeter considered that. He was grinning faintly. "No can do, Mike." His voice was pitched to a confidential whisper. "I muscled in, see? They think there's two of us; one on the outside and one on the inside and that we know the racket. That gives 'em no premium to bump me if there's a loose squawk to trip 'em up."

"Sure. Tell me how bright you are some other time. How's to cut this tape?"

Skeeter rubbed his hands together. "I was telling you. It's harder collectin' my way than crashing in. I got another angle. There's a dame in here they been holding for a twenty-grand squeeze. It's too much, I tell her. I'm takin' her out of here for ten grand. Cut-rate, Mike. That's why I conked Little Bo Peep. I'll fix her up so she won't do any hollerin', and no runnin' around, neither! She'd better be careful or you'll be—"

Skeeter stopped talking, went to the door to listen. Satisfied that there was no one within hearing distance, he began emptying the can of gasoline on the floor of the room near the unconscious Benita and the now frantic McNally.

On a table, in the corner, stood an unlighted kerosene lamp. Skeeter carefully lighted it, turned up the flame and balanced it in the tightly taped lap of the unsuspecting Polynesian.

McNally raved: "What—what are ye tryin' to do—send us all to hell? Fer God's sake, Skeeter, I'll—"

Skeeter cut in: "Shut up, Mike! If you an' the bimbo don't move—don't interfere wit' me—ye won't get hurt. Otherwise—" He added: "The gal's got some keys I kin use, an' I t'ink they're in here." Skeeter frisked Benita's purse which lay on the corner table, turned to McNally in triumph.

He held the keys up in one hand, then shoved them into his pocket. "I gotta leave you out, Mike. You're a souse and a stumble-bum and you got a bum prop. I can't have a gimp stumbling around this shanty and raising a hell of a noise."

McNally stared at him hotly. "You double-crossing little tramp—"

"Pass it, Mike. I'll cut you in for five percent when I collect. Clean gravy for you, Mike, if you live to collect." He grinned crookedly as he turned to the door. "Treat the little girl like a gentleman, Mike."

Benita had passed out with her needle in McNally's flesh. During the few moments in which she had been a limp heap beside him, McNally had worked his fingers around the needle and palmed it in frantic haste. He had it now. The girl must not awaken before he could free himself! After that, he'd be all right!

Exerting all of his strength, he brought his left arm up across his chest and forced the long tattooing needle into the tape that went across him there. Once he had made the initial tear, it was swift work. He ripped the tape in a dozen places and broke it with the bulge of his muscles. There was a hard smile on his face when he stood up.

The girl was coming out of the fog, but her eyes weren't focusing well yet. She looked cross-eyed. He felt her pulse and decided that she would do as she was. He carefully removed the lamp from her lap, extinguished it, and turned to the door, working the stiffness out of his limbs as he crossed the room.

**OUT IN** the hall there was an eerie silence. The house was well lighted but the hushed quiet and the faint medicinal odor was a tip-off to what it actually was. Legitimate or not, this was a hospital.

From somewhere downstairs there came a faint hum of conversation as hushed and indistinct as voices from a radio that is turned down low. McNally stole like a shadow along the upper hall. He did not know how many men might be downstairs, but he had an idea that they would remain down there until Benita had had time to mark him with the sign of the cobra. He didn't need any diagrams for that play.

The sudden police activity, following the death of Maurice Dalton, had Borne and his outfit scared. They had to head the police off from the tedious, damning, piling-up of evidence that they would engage in once the case loomed up as mysterious. McNally's disfiguration and death had been intended for an easy solution—to mislead the police.

A known tattoo artist and already on the broadcast sheet as wanted, he was the logical suspect. If his body turned up, somewhere, with the same mark on his ring finger as that on the finger in the jewel case, the kidnapping might still be puzzling but the police would have a solution of sorts that would throw them off the real trail.

There might even be another body found with McNally's—the body of one of the kidnapped women.

Well, that little act was temporarily postponed. McNally tested one of the doors opening off the hall. It was locked and he could detect no sound from within. The knob of the third door turned under his hand. He pushed it slowly inward. It had opened barely a crack when he heard Skeeter's hoarse whisper.

"Naw," Skeeter was saying, "that's the only thing you can be sure of. I ain't trappin' you. I ain't in with 'em. They just think I am. The reason I'm on the loose in this dump is, I know this mug, Otero. He thinks I got an outside lineup like maybe I have and he knows me. He knows I don't spill to cops. No marbles in that for me...."

McNally slid away from the door. He shook his head dazedly, choked back the curse that threatened to crack through his stiff lips.

"Otero!"

He remembered the big, blue-jowled man very well; so well that he would have figured him in this play, when he found Benita in it; would have figured him in for a certainty, only for the fact that the man should have been doubly dead.

Rigged in a scarlet cowl, Otero had run a poisonous blackmail racket that had destroyed lives and reputations galore. Needle Mike had wrecked that game and Mc-Nally's mind still carried the vivid picture of Otero crumpling before him as he pumped a bullet into the man's body—was still capable of recalling with horror the terrible wall of fire that had raced down the corridors of the blackmail den.

And Otero had escaped!

It was hard to credit. Only a bulletproof vest and a quick recovery from the shock of the slug could explain that. McNally backed slowly down the corridor. He was not interested in explaining anything. If Otero were still alive, explanations didn't matter.

**THE NEXT** room, beyond the one in which Skeeter conspired with some captive of the ring, was likewise unlocked. McNally slid the door open, listened for a moment and stepped into the black darkness of the room. He had no plan. With Skeeter and Otero added to the odds against him, his alternatives were few.

There was no percentage in crashing in on Skeeter. McNally didn't know which of the kidnapped women had bargained with the newsboy. If it were Ethel Dalton, he'd be safe in crashing; but a woman who was a stranger would trust Skeeter more readily than she would trust Needle Mike. A scream now would ruin everything.

He tried to create a mental picture of Ethel Dalton. She was the keynote of any plan that he could evolve. If he reached her and got her out of this place, her story would bring the police in with a rush. Alone he would encounter suspicion and delay and there would be time enough for the gang to clean out. He passed his hand across his eyes. His mental picture of Ethel Dalton was dim. It was a long time since they'd moved closely within the same circle; the Daltons had traveled much.

Slim, vivacious, pretty as a girl, Ethel Dalton had looked a little hard and more than a little tired the last time he'd seen her. She had been rather bulgy; not merely with a fullness of figure but rather with a deterioration of body, the lines coarsened and sagging. It was that fading of her beauty that had led her here, led her to clutch desperately at plastic surgery for rescue from the sea of habit, from careless living.

He seemed to hear Maurice Dalton's words ringing in his ears. "She had an idea that something would happen to part us." McNally's fists clenched. "I've got to find her," he muttered. "Got to get her out of—"

He stiffened suddenly and turned. There was a rustle in the room behind him.

For several seconds he held himself motionless, staring; then the rustle was repeated and he located the source. It was on the far side of the room. He crouched a little and held his breath and it was seconds before he heard the sound again. The element of surprise was gone now and he could analyze the sound. There was nothing dangerous in it. It did not seem like the quick, furtive movement of a stalker; it was slower, dragging, helpless.

Tense against the possibility of an error in judgment, he crossed the room with quick strides. The sound quickened as he approached but it was not menacing. He made out the blurred lines of a cot and he fumbled in his pockets for a match. He was still wearing the suit given him by Doctor Felix Borne. He had taken time in the room, from which he had escaped, to put on his shirt and coat again. In the breast pocket of the coat, there was a paper of matches. He struck one and pale light glowed.

There was a cot—and there was a man lying on it, a man whose hands were securely tied behind him with tape and whose mouth was cross-taped with narrow strips. Agonized eyes pleaded with McNally and McNally whistled under his breath.

The man on the cot was Winkler.

With recognition, the tiny flare fizzed out. McNally dropped the matches in his pocket and bent over the cot. "This isn't the worst thing that could happen to you," he said. "You could be dead. You've still got a chance—"

**HE DIDN'T** think that Winkler deserved any more encouragement than that. After all, the man had known about this slimy racket and had kept his mouth shut; greeting women and playing the gigolo while he knew the fate that awaited them.

The gang had evidently delayed knocking him off until they had a means of ridding themselves of his body. It gave the man a chance and he didn't rate any more than that. McNally turned to the door.

"There's no way I could use him," he muttered to himself. "The sap would doublecross me to get back with Borne and he'd get himself killed anyway."

He was halfway across the room when some instinct speeded his stride. He had heard nothing that could be definitely defined as sound, but some alert monitor in his brain warned him of movement in the hall. He opened the door to a thin slit.

The stairs were within his line of vision and he had a swift vision of Skeeter as the newsboy turned to descend. There was a woman half hidden from McNally by Skeeter's bent body. McNally enlarged the crack of the door and the woman turned her head.

For a moment he could see her face plainly.

There was terror in the eyes that stared fearfully back along the hall, but the face itself betrayed nothing. It was a beautiful face, satin smooth in the softly diffused light of the hall; strangely beautiful. McNally had never seen a woman's face quite like it. It was ageless, characterless; as beautiful as a face in a retouched photograph but lacking the lines and the marks of living and of having lived.

He only saw her for a fleeting few seconds, but McNally decided that he had never seen her before. She resembled none of the women whose photographs had appeared in the papers he had reviewed. He had a sense of uneasiness. Perhaps she was a plant. Skeeter might have walked into something.

He didn't care about Skeeter. The little mutt had asked for it. But a sudden break of any kind, now, might bring swift disaster upon McNally himself. Even if the woman were on the level, there was the possibility of sudden surprise for the two of them at the foot of the stairs. McNally fumbled in his pockets.

He would have to move swiftly and he would have to have luck on his side. The locked door that he had passed intrigued him. The gang had not considered it necessary to lock up the room into which they had dumped Winkler, but Skeeter had needed keys to get to the woman he had released. There was that other locked door. What lay behind that?

His fumbling fingers closed on his key ring. Borne had not considered it necessary to confiscate Needle Mike's few belongings when he made him change clothes and the keys looked innocent. McNally's lips curled. He didn't run a locksmith shop as a sideline for nothing. He separated the last key on the ring from the others and ran his nail down along the groove.

The key parted into two sections.

That was his own idea, borrowed in part from a South Broadway neighbor whose police record was longer than his pedigree. The two sections of the divided key were as efficient as most of the elaborate lock-picking kits. McNally moved swiftly to the locked door.

His nerves were drawn taut and he listened for a half-expected alarm from downstairs as he bent over the lock. It was a simple one and it clicked back in less than two seconds. He stepped into the room and pulled the door closed after him.

There was a rustling sound in the darkness.

He wasted no time now on scouting. He expected to find a cot on the far side of the room, and he did; he expected to find someone trussed up on the cot, and he did. A match flared in his fingers—and he almost dropped it with the shock of what he saw.

The trussed-up body was the body of a woman; but the face, out of which wild eyes stared, was the face of a gargoyle. Creased and furrowed and sagging and scarred, it was recognizable as human only by reason of the staring eyes and by the soft aureole of blond hair that framed it.

And as he stared nervelessly, there came a piercing scream from downstairs—

Skeeter had failed.

## CHAPTER SIX
## BLOND GARGOYLE

**THE SCREAM** from downstairs was still echoing when the match in McNally's hand went out. He was conscious of an increase in the desperate squirming of the bound woman on the cot, conscious of the fact that he didn't want to look at that hideous face again; and conscious of the fact that it was showdown time. This house would be in a mad uproar any minute now and another escape from it would be out of the question. Borne and Otero would want to know why Benita did not come down to investigate the commotion and they would find out what had happened to her.

He was striking another match as the thoughts marched double-quick through his brain. He didn't want to see what botched surgery had done to a woman's face, but he had to see. There was something that he had to know. The match flamed.

In the feeble light, he saw the woman writhing. Her eyes were almost popping from her head and in them he read a fierce desire to scream and to keep on screaming. To release the gag on her lips would be to fill this house with sound. He shuddered a little and bent down. Her hands were bound behind her and he turned her gently.

The third finger of her left hand was missing.

Ethel Dalton! It couldn't be. This woman's body, too, had deteriorated, had lost the clean lines of youth and health and vigor; but there was a solidity to it that Ethel Dalton's couldn't have had. This woman was older. Besides, there was the matter of the new tattoo and Benita's gloating tale of tattooing a woman who screamed. The cobra on Ethel Dalton's finger had been reproduced upon the finger of this deformed creature on the cot. He didn't know why, but this was not Ethel Dalton.

The scream of a woman sounded again from the stairwell and he heard the tapping steps of one who runs in high heels. It was a frantic tapping and a hoarse voice called a threat. McNally wheeled to the door.

It was a time for action. He was not willing to wait and be hunted like an animal nor was he going to cower in a room while a woman was hunted. Crouched low, but with his body delicately balanced, he hit the hallway.

The girl with the expressionless face was almost at the top of the stairs. Behind her, heavy feet pounded and a snarling voice threw a command: "I'll shoot you in the leg—"

It was a threat calculated to stop a woman more quickly than the threat of death, but the girl kept on. McNally saw her face, a face as placid as though she were serving tea—but made weird by the blazing terror in her eyes; then he was looking over the banister into the vandyke-adorned face of Felix Borne.

The surgeon, his eyes on the fleeing girl, did not see him. He was raising a pistol—and McNally plunged over the banister.

**IT WAS** a sheer, feet-first drop and McNally had time to experience the all-gone sensation of falling; then his heels bit into the shoulders of the medico and he was part of a dizzy human pinwheel that bounced crazily down the stairs.

The gun in Borne's hand went off and there was a booming roar that woke echoes through the old house. A shower of plaster cascaded down from a punctured wall. McNally was conscious of it pattering on him as he struggled to free himself from the doctor's grip. He lashed out savagely with short-arm lefts and rights and he was scarcely conscious of the return blows any more than he had been conscious of bouncing against the stairs. The doctor's lean fingers fastened to his windpipe, as he struggled to his knees, and he saw the man through a thin haze. For a second he fought for balance and then his right hand came across under Borne's rigid arm.

The vandyke tilted back and Doctor Felix Borne hit with a thud. Something crashed into McNally as he turned and he felt the blow glance off his jaw. He rolled groggily and back-pedaled desperately as he came to his feet. Otero's broad, cruel, blue-jowled face seemed to bob around unsteadily through the film over McNally's eyes. He couldn't quite locate the man, but he knew that he was there before him and that he was swinging.

Otero had always been a proud brute who liked to break a man up with his hands as long as he was running in front and it was safe to do so. Somewhere behind the fists of Otero, however, there was always a knife for emergencies. He didn't need the knife now. McNally had been battered, dazed and off balance before Otero came into the picture and Otero didn't give him a chance to get set. McNally's blows lacked steam and he could feel the iron fists smashing through his guard. His shoulders bounced against the wall and he saw Otero's right go back for the kill.

"Stop that! I'll shoot—"

The shrill, almost hysterical, voice of a woman broke on the tableau like the report of a gun. Otero hesitated and spun on his toes, his big body drawn into a crouch. McNally shook his head and drew the air into his lungs in deep gulps.

Skeeter was lying in a corner of the hallway. His face was bloody and he looked dead. Felix Borne, in another corner, was sitting up, dazedly, and holding onto his head. In the center of the hall, her back against the door, stood the girl with the mask-like, expressionless face. Her eyes were wide and, for all of her dramatic challenge and the threat of the gun in her hand, she was a grotesque figure.

Her face might have passed for that of a girl in her teens; her body was more like the body of a schoolgirl's mother. Youth and age warred in her and she was neither one thing nor the other. The gun was Doctor Borne's and she held it with a firm hand.

Otero faced it snarling and the full force of his predicament must have registered in his mind. His right hand moved with a conjurer's speed and, as a long knife flashed in his hand, he leaped.

The girl gave a choked scream and her finger tightened on the trigger. McNally launched himself from the wall in a diving tackle and the thunder of gunfire beat against his eardrums as his fingers slipped along the seams of Otero's trousers and his shoulder crashed against the man's knees.

He could feel the man folding even as he hit him; but through the echo of the shot, the girl's scream rang again, piercingly and with a new, terrifying note.

She fired again as she screamed.

**OTERO DIED** before he hit the ground. McNally felt the death-jerk in his muscles as his own grip tightened. He rolled free as the big man crashed against the boards and came up on his hands and knees, facing the girl.

She had her shoulders pressed hard against the door and her legs braced stiffly like one who sets herself against a shock. There was a bloody froth on her lips and a spreading stain on the front of her dress. Her heels were slipping in straight grooves on the floor and letting her body down slowly along the door. Her eyes were wide, startled.

McNally, leaping, caught her and her body jerked in his arms. She blinked and the startled look left her eyes. Her fingers closed tightly on McNally's arm and her voice was a broken whisper.

"Maurice..." she called softly. "Maurice! I lacked faith, Maurice. The cobra. It would keep us always together. They removed the cobra, Maurice...."

Her voice was fading out and her eyes were settling into a fixity of expression as though she were looking out beyond the bloody hallway. McNally felt a choking dryness in his throat. He was looking down on the face of a dying woman, a face he had never seen before—and it belonged to Ethel Dalton.

"Ethel!" he said. "Hold on, Ethel! I'll get you help—"

He was lowering her to the floor. Her head turned slightly as she spoke. There was an eager, hurt, pathetic note in her voice.

"Maurice...."

He had to leave her there. He was feeling again the terrible futility of a layman in the presence of death. A doctor might save her. He was afraid not, but he hoped. He looked around wildly for a telephone.

Skeeter was still lying in a corner but he had changed position slightly. Otero was a crumpled mass of flesh already in the chill grip of death from which he would never return. There had been no bulletproof vests in the way of these bullets!

There was no phone. McNally took a step toward the nearest room; then he whirled. His mind had been dazed. There had been something missing from that hallway, something that should be there. With that realization he ceased to worry about a telephone.

Doctor Borne was gone.

Scooping the gun from the floor, McNally leaped for the door. As he flung it open, he heard the whine of a starter and the choked, protesting gasp of an automobile engine that has been choked too much. The car which had brought him here was standing in front of the house.

It was twenty-five yards from the porch to the driveway where the car stood and McNally was hitting the top of his sprint when he heard the engine catch and roar into life. He pulled the gun up to hip level and blazed a snap shot at the car. His voice rode on the echo.

"Hold it, Borne! I'll lay the next one into you!"

McNally couldn't tell if his voice carried to the man in the car but he had the gun in readiness and his legs pumping like a sprinter's when the car, after a jerky, uneven start, pulled back against the curb.

Doctor Felix Borne slid from under the wheel. His eyes were blazing pools of hatred and desperation but his face was paste-white and his left arm hung limply at his side.

"I could not have driven anyway," he said hoarsely. "I have a broken arm!"

McNally's lips set in a thin line. "I don't care if you've got a broken neck!" he said grimly. "You've got a job to do! Back to the house—"

## CHAPTER SEVEN
## HORROR HOSPITAL

THE BLOODY hallway of that horror hospital was weirdly still. Doctor Felix Borne was bent above the body of Ethel Dalton. Over in a corner, Skeeter numbly sat and held his head. Slowly the surgeon straightened. His face was gray.

"She's dead," he said.

McNally had expected that but he felt a strange sense of shock. He had stumbled into the private lives of two people whom he had known all of his life and yet known scarcely at all. He had found in their weak characters the existence of a strong love. He had seen them both die within twenty-four hours. The haunting, doggerel dirge rang through his brain—

She's gone,
Let 'er go....

His shoulders twitched in protest against the shoddiness of it and his lips moved. "The Yogi didn't lie to her," he said stiffly. "Maybe the cobra had nothing to do with it, but they weren't parted."

He looked up to meet Felix Borne's burning eyes. McNally still had the gun in his hand but the fight was gone out of Borne. "What are you going to do with me?" he asked.

Skeeter groaned and struggled to his feet. McNally remembered suddenly that he was Needle Mike, that he must remain Needle Mike in the presence of Skeeter.

"I'm goin' to throw you to the cops," he said hoarsely. "Whaddye think?"

"Don't! Wait! I'll pay you—" Borne's eyes were desperate, staring. Skeeter snapped back to life with a rush.

"O.K.," he said thickly. "Lemme handle him, Mike. I know how much he's got!"

McNally's jaw hardened. "Stay where you are, Skeeter!" he growled. "You crossed me up and this roscoe means you, too. Don't get in the way of it."

He shook the gun suggestively and Skeeter pressed back against the wall, his jaw dropping. "Mike," he said, "you know better. I'd have cut you in—"

McNally ignored him. He threw a hard stare at the desperate doctor. "Spit your story about this racket!" he said. "I'll listen."

A look of hope came into Borne's eyes. He mopped at his forehead with his right hand. "It wasn't mine," he said brokenly. "I was trapped. Most of my patients weren't nerve cases at all. They were just wearing themselves out fighting the years, women who didn't dare grow old. They wanted new faces. I used to send them to plastic men, then I went to Vienna and studied the art there. I—I was very successful—"

Some of the old vanity seemed to return to the man and for a moment his eyes were alight; then he slumped. "The Gerspach case ruined me. Something went wrong. I couldn't restore her face and she was hideous. She saw herself in a mirror that I didn't know she had. She—she killed herself!"

**THERE WERE** beads of sweat on his forehead. "I had an assistant. I didn't know what to do with the body and he knew about an underworld undertaker who could get rid of it. I called him in. This fellow, Otero, and the girl came with him. They blackmailed me."

The doctor's voice dropped to a hoarse whisper. "None of my patients wanted their husbands to know that they were going to have their faces lifted. They made excuses when they left home. As soon as they were in the hospital, Otero sent letters to the husbands and said they were kidnapped. I—I was helpless—"

McNally leaned forward. "You even tried to shake down the Gerspach woman's husband after she was dead?"

"Otero did."

"Who is the woman upstairs?"

Borne shivered. "Mrs. Stone. I was nervous when I operated on her. She turned out wrong, too. She heard too much around here. She was going to make trouble."

"Why cut her up and make believe her finger belonged to somebody else?"

Skeeter cut in. "I can tell you about that, Mike. They figured a few little jolts like that would make husbands pony up quick. The racket couldn't last long. They wanted a quick stake. They was agoin' to send back the women that turned out right and they figured they'd be glad to keep their mouths shut and keep outta the publicity if they weren't hurt none."

McNally shivered. He could not picture the type of man who would keep a woman alive in order to produce ghastly souvenirs—fingers and perhaps toes or ears later—with which to threaten and scare husbands.

"There's tape in that case of his, Skeeter," McNally said. "Tie him up!"

"But—" Borne rose desperately to his feet. McNally gestured menacingly with the gun.

"As you were!" He turned hard eyes on Skeeter. "Step into it—fast!"

Skeeter had been around and he knew when a man wasn't fooling. He whipped the tape out of the case and went to work. When the surgeon was trussed up, he stepped back. Far away, on Broadway, a police siren screamed, coming closer. Someone had turned in an alarm.

Skeeter wet his lips. "You can't feed me to the cops, Mike. I'd spill you into it."

"You can't!" McNally leaned slightly forward. "I could knock you cold and leave you here. Then I'd have an alibi. Think anyone would believe you?"

Skeeter's face paled. "Aw, Mike—"

The siren was coming closer. McNally fixed his hard stare on the jade ring that had been a gift to him from a Japanese nobleman. It was on the hand of Skeeter now. McNally stretched out his hand.

"The ring, Skeeter!"

Skeeter hesitated, then hope glowed in his eyes and he passed the ring over.

McNally looked once around the hall.

There was the body of Otero, the body of Ethel Dalton and the trussed-up figure of Felix Borne. Upstairs, there was a weak sister of a man who had had a bad scare and who would spill all he knew under pressure, and there was Mrs. Stone who had been a "troublemaker" and who had ghastly evidence to present—on her own face. That was evidence enough to send the police to trial with a full case. Benita was a pretty woman and she might wiggle out, somehow; the assistant to Borne had escaped, but he was hardly necessary to cinch the case.

McNally shrugged. "Let's go," he said.

**THE DUST** storm lingered through the night and the morning was dirty gray. In the little shop on South Broadway, McNally had just completed an indigotin disulphic treatment on his finger. The snake tattoo design was unrecognizable. In time it would be gone entirely. Skeeter was sitting at the battered table with a greasy pack of cards in his hands. The door banged open and Detective Sergeant Pete Corbin stood in the doorway.

"Mike," he growled, "it's damn funny that you just showed up."

"What's funny about it?" McNally was rolling a cigarette. His eyes were freshly reddened and there was a reek of whiskey about him. Corbin squinted at him appraisingly.

"You been wanted," he said, "and you don't show till the case is cracked. Maybe you figure that lets you out?"

McNally grunted and looked toward the glaring headlines of the morning Globe that proclaimed last night's cleanup and the full confessions of Bert Winkler and Doctor Felix Borne. Corbin's grunt echoed his own.

"It don't!" Corbin said. "They tell a funny story about you bein' in the mess in a screwy way and—"

McNally had expected that. He knew that the story would be screwy to the police and that there would be nothing in it that would be a criminal linking of Needle Mike with the kidnap ring.

"Aw!" he growled. "They're trying to protect that dame, that female tattooer. I know her. She came in here one day and bought some needles. I put 'em in a jewel box on account of her being a woman and—"

Corbin's face reddened and he glared. "I was coming to that," he said. "We had your prints on that case."

McNally grinned. "Sure. Skeeter here was in the dump when I give it to her. I didn't wear gloves or nothin'."

Skeeter stiffened. A strange expression came into his eyes and he looked briefly at McNally. His face was bland as he turned to Corbin.

"That's right!" he said.

Pete Corbin rocked slowly from his toes to his heels. "Mike," he growled, "you're a damn liar and some day I'll prove it!"

He wheeled and stalked angrily out into the dust. Skeeter tilted his chair back and laid the cards down. "That'll be ten bucks, witness fees, Mike," he said softly. "Baby needs shoes."

# ABOUT THE AUTHOR

**I VENTED** my first squawk at life in the City of New York on November 16, 1900, and managed to weather the hazards of Manhattan boyhood until I was sixteen; then, while the native New Yorkers of my age were pouring in from Kansas, Missouri and Minnesota, I followed the family star of destiny to Colorado. I had prepared at Manhattan College of New York for an engineering career, but this proved to be a misdeal and I took a whirl at reporting on a Denver daily. I never progressed past the cub stage and was fervently advised by a harassed city editor that I never would. After that I became one of the young men who signed the coupon.

I went to work for a power company and studied engineering some more at night. Then a publicity job for a big electrical manufacturer took me all over the West and for a while I was national publicity director for Station KFKX at Hastings, Nebraska, the first rebroadcasting station in the world. About this time, somebody told me about the easy work and big pay of fictioneers and I decided to try my hand. By the time I found out how badly I had been deceived I was too badly bitten by the bug to ever escape.

I stayed with publicity work till February 1, 1929, but fiction was a side line for years. Since then, it has been the whole works. Now I toil not, neither do I spin—all in the world that I have to do is bite my nails and fight a type-writer and think up enough ideas to keep the wolf from having whelps on the Barrett door-step. An easy life if you like your ease to come in packages that are so hard to open.

My most interesting experience was an assignment to write an advertising campaign addressed to oil operators. This took me into all the leading oil fields in the United States and has supplied me with a wealth of story material. Another source has been aviation. I took up flying to get material and have been handling the publicity work of the Guardian Aircraft Corporation. Without taking very much time, it repaid me mightily in flying lore and experience.

Thus far, I have sold several hundred yarns and hope to sell many more. I've got to. I am married to the best little "encourager" in the world; an ink-slinger of no little skill herself. If I ever write love stories for *Argosy*, they'll be authentic, too, because—ah, well, why should you look in my lighted window. Two kiddies, boy and girl, complete the narrative—and that's all there is. Sorry if there is nothing exciting in this, but if the thing had a plot or any particular drama, I'd stick a name like Pete Jones on myself and sell the darn thing!

www.ingramcontent.com/pod-product-compliance
Lightning Source LLC
Chambersburg PA
CBHW020549020726
47494CB00006B/1987